HUNTING SNIPES

+*four*

David Martin Anderson

ConRoca Publish

This book is a work of fiction. Names, characters, places, and incidents are the product of the author's imagination or are used fictitiously. any resemblance to actual events, locales, or persons living or dead is coincidental.

If you purchase a paperback version of this book without a cover, you Should be aware that this book may have been stolen property and reported as 'unsold and destroyed' to the publisher. In such case, neither the author nor the publisher has received any payment for this 'stripped' book.

Use the above QR Code to connect to the author.
DavidMartinAnderson.com

ConRoca Publishing
132 Ridge Trail
Boerne, TX 78006
ConRocaPublishing.com

ISBN 978-1-892617-34-7 (Paperback)a
ISBN 978-1-892617-35-4 (Digital)3

Printed in the United States of America - 2021

10 9 8 7 6 5 4 3 2 1

A collection of stories….

AUTHOR'S NOTE

It was early in 2020 when I decided to write a series of short stories and novelettes as a collection for my next literary project. As a writer, I feel more comfortable with this shorter and more concise style of prose. And, unlike longer novels and novellas, and by definition, these stories deal less with weighty character development and more with brisk narrative movement; they move speedily from beginning to end focusing on plot and action. As one well known critique, Kirkus Reviews, worded, "(Anderson's) tales have plenty of energy." Hence, you will find within this collection various stories from lighthearted and humorous to earnestly serious. You will travel from West Texas in the 1860s, to modern-day southern Utah, to Iowa during the 2020 pandemic, to 1938 Brooklyn, and finally to Peru, Indiana to meet the likes of Cole Porter. Now, what facilitated this effort was a little thing called Covid-19, and while I would have gladly procrastinated in scribing this book for years, being homebound fostered a most hospitable situation to unleashing creativity.

Thank you to all my friends and lay readers for assisting me in this endeavor and, as always, providing constructive criticism. Thank you, steadfast friend, Arnie Shreffler. Thank you, Brooklyn Historical Society and NY Parks. Thank you, Bailey for resurrecting a lost manuscript. Thank you, Cole and Orson. Thank you, sweet wife, Mary, for allowing my long afternoons hibernating in front of a PC and MS WORD. And thank you, Chip-the-cat for keeping my lap warm as I typed merrily away.

Enjoy!

HUNTING SNIPES
+*four*

a collection of stories

by

David Martin Anderson

————————

ORSON WELLES AND THE
LINDSAY PARK REDEMPTION -1

RUNNER SPEAKS -47

COLETTE AND COLE -85

HUNTING SNIPES - 149

JESSICA COLLECTOR -239

ORSON WELLES AND THE LINDSAY PARK REDEMPTION

For Vander Shane

ORSON WELLES and the
LINDSAY PARK REDEMPTION

CHAPTER ONE

-A Most Fantastical Yarn-

(October 30, 1938)

"...*Ladies and gentlemen, we are interrupting this broadcast for the latest bulletin from the Intercontinental Radio News.... It is reported that at 7:50 P. M. a huge flaming object, believed to be a meteorite, fell on a farm in the neighborhood of Grover's Mill, New Jersey. The flash in the sky was visible within a radius of several hundred miles and the noise of the impact was heard as far east as Brooklyn, New York.... Ladies and gentlemen, this is Carl Phillip, your on-site news reporter, and I just arrived at the Wilmuth farm, Grover's Mill, New Jersey and I'm guessing that's the thing, directly in front of me, half buried in a vast pit. What I can see of the object doesn't look very much like a meteor, at least not the meteors I've seen in books. It looks more like a huge metallic cylinder.... Ladies and gentlemen, this is the most terrifying thing I have ever witnessed. Wait. Someone is crawling out of the hollow top. Someone or something green in appearance with two luminous disk-like eyes. It might be a <Manhattan-based announcer interrupts after 30 seconds of silence> I have just been handed a message that came in from Grover's Mill. At least forty people, including six state troopers, lie dead in a field east of the village of Grover's Mill, their bodies burned and distorted beyond all possible recognition. Of the creatures in the rocket cylinder at Grover's Mill, I can give you no authoritative information, either as to their nature or their purposes here on earth. Of their destructive instrument, I might venture some conjectural explanation based on the reports we have received. For want of a better term, I shall refer to the mysterious weapon as a heat ray. It's all too evident that these creatures have scientific knowledge* *far in advance of our own.... That is my conjecture of what appears to be a Martian invasion of earth . . ."*

Orson Welles, CBS Radio Broadcast, Mercury Theater, NYC

(October 30, 2020)

The old man struggled ascending a back staircase. He could have used an elevator but climbing six flights of stairs afforded a rare view of the projects across Leonard Street and the Brooklyn neighborhood he grew up in as a child. This apartment building, his daughter's swanky residence, has no character, he told himself—clean and efficient but definitely no character. "Not like the old days," he mumbled between strained breaths. He remembered his childhood when architects took pride in their creations and artists splashed murals on entrance foyers and people gathered in garden courtyards for conversation. He remembered when tenants boasted pridefully, "Why, yes, I do live at Two Grace Court," or Nine Prospect Park West or Ten Eyck Houses. Buildings back in those days were classy, he told himself, recalling long ago memories. Not this place, he lamented. And sadness seemed to dominate his most recent sentiments. His daughter and her second husband only called when a crisis struck, and they relied on his intervention skills to quell problems. Lately, even with their newfound wealth, crises seemed to strike with more regularity. Wealth, he surmised, might buy a fancy high-dollar loft but it could not buy your way out of family discord. Today's crisis was about the boy, his grandson.

When he reached the sixth floor, he took a deep breath and knocked on a tall mahogany door. Secretly, he wished his wife was still alive to handle these unpleasantries, but she passed on years earlier. The fact of the matter is the grandson never knew his grandmother or his father's parents. Everyone had been dead for years. Hence, the weight of holding family together fell upon his shoulders. Ironically, the timing could not have been worse. His best friend, Bert, and he were supposed to play cribbage this evening at their usual haunt, Huckleberry's Bar, around the corner on Grand. It was Bert's turn to buy. Oh, how he loved to watch Bert squirm over cribbage bets lost and Bert anteing-up on a tasty Brooklyn Brewery lager and scrumptious Grimaldi pepperoni pizza. For now, Bert would have to wait patiently at Huckleberry's. Family came first. Within a few seconds, he heard his daughter's footsteps and listened as she fumbled three sets of deadbolt locks, as the locks crisply untumbled and a safety chain brushed the other side of the door.

"Dad, thanks for coming on such short notice. I hope I didn't interrupt your plans," she said.

"Plans? *Ha.* When you're my age, Sweetie, there's only one plan. *Waking up,*" he replied, managing to cast a wink. "So, what's with Little Pete? Having a bad day, again, is he?"

Peter Grabkowitz, the II, known more affectionately as 'Little Pete,' had experienced many bad days over his eleven-year existence for he suffered from a rare genetic autoimmune deficiency. A more apropos question should have been, "Is Little Pete having a good day?" The boy's disorder had kept him confined since birth to an antiseptically clean bedroom hidden behind layers of clear plastic sheeting and purified air screened with three-deep hepa filters and noisy air pumps. For eleven years the boy had been irreparably sealed-off from the outside world. Loaded with electronic gadgets of every variety, the child lacked nothing except the one thing he craved most of all—human interaction.

Among the well-appointed electronic trappings in his drab environment centered a massive bay window, his portal to the outside world. From this lofty window perch, the boy could lean out and away from his building's facade and watch people scurry on sidewalks six floors below or he could gaze up and down Leonard Street like Zeus peering upon humans from Mount Olympus. From his roost he watched seasons come and seasons go. He watched children his age with baseball bats slung over shoulders scamper toward Sternberg Park around the corner, chattering nonstop, laughing, and soaking in banter and sunshine and memories. Yet, these same sights sustaining him over years, today left him angry. After all, his childhood had been ebbing tidally with time; he was missing out on memories. Worse, he was now old enough to understand these depressing omissions as the tide swept away. There was also newfound hope. Four weeks earlier he underwent a revolutionary bone marrow transplant to boost his immune system. Days earlier he received news the operation had succeeded. Within six months he would be healthy enough to leave his cloistered bedroom and experience life. Still, six months to an eleven-year-old loomed as endless a prison sentence as six years to an eighty-three-year-old grandfather. The boy's patience had reached a boiling point.

When the old man entered the bedroom, the boy barely noticed. "Hey, Little Pete, how are you doing today, kiddo?"

"How do you think I'm doing, Grandpa?" The boy replied curtly. "Life sucks." The boy turned to confront the old man. He moved away from the window and toward a plastic partition. "What did Mom tell you?" He asked, more of a demand than a question.

"She told me you wouldn't eat your dinner. 'Said you threw your tray on the floor, yelled at her and used the 'F' word."

The boy thought for a few seconds and exhaled a long overdue breath. His grandfather and he had always shared a special pact. When the day arrived for the boy to turn twenty-four, in the year 2033, he and his grandfather promised they would become roommates in Greenwich Village. The old man said he would become the boy's "chick magnate" at local taverns; that he would sit at bar counters and sweet talk to young women and brag about how his best-friend-grandson and he were roomies. And, most importantly, how his grandson had become the caregiver for his frail old bones. His grandfather said any young woman not falling for that line would have to possess a heart of stone. Naturally, while they had talked seriously about such matters, the boy knew it most likely would never happen. In the year 2033 his grandfather would be ninety-six years old and probably dead. Yet, the mere idea of them rooming together made for heartfelt chit chat and if the old man ever survived to that decrepit age, the boy would truly cherish his company. Recalling these things and the pact, the boy slid into a chair opposite his grandfather, two feet away, face-to-face behind the clear plastic wall, and confessed his feelings. "I shouldn't have said that, Grandpa. I was pissed," he said, staring at the floor, ashamed. "I'm sorry."

"Well, what's going on? That behavior is not typical of you. You know, six months from now you'll be out of there for the first time in your life and we begin our long journey to Greenwich. And you know what else?"

"What?"

"I get to hug and kiss you."

"That'll be nice," the boy said, "but I'm not sure about kissing. Maybe we should just plan for Greenwich Village and handshake or something."

"I believe the young ladies are already lining up," the old man teased.

The boy laughed. "Grandpa, you crack me up."

The old man laughed, too. "So, what gives? Why this outburst with your mother?"

"You wouldn't understand."

"Try me."

Returning to his window perch, the boy sat on a cushioned sill and glanced at sidewalks lit by streetlamps and filled with costumed children. "Do you know what tonight is?" He asked.

"Of course, I do. It's the day before Halloween. It's Beggar's Night. It's the night all of Brooklyn goes crazy for Trick or Treat festivities."

"That's right, Grandpa. And I'm eleven years old. Next year I'll be twelve. I'll be too old to dress up on Beggar's Night." The boy sighed. His face screwed pitifully. "I've missed out all these years and it makes me sad," he said. "Look at them down there. They're having so much fun." A few seconds passed and the boy capitulated to an angry grimace and the word "shit."

The old man capitulated, too, to an equally pitiful pout. He felt the boy's pain and for the first time in a long time struggled for words. What to do for the boy? He wondered. What can I say to help him through this gloomy mood? "I understand," he said half-heartedly. "Believe me. I do understand."

"BS, Grandpa. You've never been quarantined for eleven years. You don't know how I feel."

The old man's mouth pinched a sad smile. "You're right. And if I could change places with you, I gladly would. But I can't." He scanned the room looking for clues to the latest goings-on in the boy's life and ideas—anything to distract this deadened conversation. Then, he tactically segued the conversation. "So, where's the kitten I bought you last week?"

"He's hiding under my bed. He never comes out," the boy muttered.

"Oh, he will. Trust me. He's simply scared. This world of yours is all new to him. Give him time. Talk sweet to him. Tell him how wonderful he is, and he'll talk right back to you. Siamese love to talk." The old man thought about his earlier conversation with the boy's mother. "Say, rumor has it you still haven't named him."

"I never wanted him in the first place. Why should I give him a name?"

"Because cats deserve good names. Good American Indian names. Names that fit their persona. You know what they say?"

"No, Grandpa, what do they say?" The boy asked mockingly.

"There's nothing better for the inside of a boy than the outside of a cat."

The boy laughed out loud. "Oh, Grandpa. You are so full of beans. That's a horse you're talking about. Not a cat. I read books. That's an old one."

"Just checking your literacy. I'm glad you understand the difference. But I do know your cat needs a name. A special name. And I know he won't feel loved until you do that."

Surrendering to his grandfather's prodding, the boy fell to his knees, crawled under his bed, and retrieved the kitten, a spry red tip Siamese. He smothered it in his arms and the cat immediately began purring. He stroked its ears and kissed the top of its head.

"I've always had Siamese cats," the old man continued. "Ever since I was a tyke. They're the best breed of the cat family. They talk. They listen. They understand your deepest emotions. And, most importantly, they protect."

"Really? Protect from what?"

"From the world's unpredictable craziness." The old man paused and studied the boy's face. "Did I ever tell you the story of Marshawn the cat?"

"No, Grandpa, you have not. Is this going to be another Grandpa-full-of-beans story?"

"Maybe. Maybe not. I will tell you this much, this story is absolutely, positively, one-hundred percent—"

"*The gospel truth.* I know. I know, Grandpa. You always say that about all of your stories."

"I probably do. But this one is the real McCoy. Trust me. So, do you want to start it or shall I?"

The boy chuckled. He placed the kitten on the bed and laid the flat of his hand against the plastic partition in a familiar routine. His grandfather placed his hand against plastic, too, and they touched. The boy spoke. "Once upon a time there was a boy. His name was—"

"*Babe.* His parents named him Babe after their baseball hero Babe Ruth. The boy became known to everyone in the old neighborhood as 'the Babe' or simply 'Babe.'"

"And he was—"

"Fourteen months old."

"Grandpa, *really*? He was a baby? Come on. This story is going to be about a baby? I thought it was going to be about a cat named Marshawn and someone my age. That's what you usually do. The main character is usually some kid my age."

"I can tell you're concerned how I may be spinning a farcical tall tale, but this particular story is, indeed, all about a toddler named Babe and his amazing Siamese cat named Marshawn," the old man stated assuredly.

Striking a skeptical look, the boy reluctantly shook his head. "Okay. Go on, Grandpa. You win. I'm listening."

"Well now, the Babe was known to be an active toddler. Being somewhat hyper at fourteen months of age was not necessarily a good thing because the child had just learned to walk or, rather, stumble. Everyone said when he walked upright he resembled an inebriated orangutan—arms stretched to the sky, hips and arms swaying side to side out of sync, making strange grunting noises resembling a monkey. And not only was he active, he was also extremely curious. Oh, how he wanted to see what lay beyond his fourth-floor apartment window, but he could not venture outside because he was so young and frail and he suffered from an illness they called croup."

"He was ill?"

"That's right. Sort of like you but over time he would outgrow his illness. You, on the other hand, needed help from modern medicine." The old man drew a wry smile and looked into the boy's eyes. "Did I mention our story happened on the thirtieth of October? On Beggar's Night?"

"Honestly? Just like tonight?" The boy asked, astonished.

"Yup. That's right. And the setting was the most beautiful place on the face of the earth—"

"*Brooklyn*!"

"You better believe it, Little Pete. It all happened in Brooklyn at Lindsay Park and the Ten Eyck Houses in the year 1938. It was the same night my friend, Orson Welles, spun a most fantastical yarn…."

CHAPTER TWO

-The Cat-

"… So, Little Pete, where shall we begin our story? Should we start with Marshawn the cat, the Babe, Lindsay Park and the Ten Eyck Houses, or with our hero, Henry Ahrens? Pick one."

"I've never heard of Lindsay Park or Ten Eyck Houses. I think they're fake. And you never mentioned anything about Henry Ahrens. Who the heck is Henry Ahrens and how old was he?"

"How old?" He pondered, rubbing his chin and squinting painfully searching long ago memories. "I'm guessing in 1938 Henry was probably forty years old."

"*An-n-n-cient*," the boy mocked. "So now you're telling me that we have an old man, age forty, and a baby in this story but no kid my age. This tale of yours already sounds *bo-o-o-ring*."

"Well, forty years of age is not old. Yours truly is old. Trust me. Henry, on the other hand, was half my age and quite virile. And, once again, I must remind you that the Babe was not a baby. He was a precocious and robust toddler. As far as having a kid your age in this story?" The old man stopped himself, this time to wink at the boy as he leaned forward. "Maybe, you're the kid."

The boy puckered his mouth sucking imaginary lemons. "I don't like where this is heading, Grandpa. I think you're trying to teach me one of your crazy Grandpa life lessons. I'd rather be surfing the Internet or playing Fortnite. Do I really have to pick one?"

"Absolutely."

"Fine. Let's start with the cat."

And the old man began his story….

(1936)

Once upon a time there was a lovely lady. Her name was Margret O'Malley. She desperately wanted to have a baby but had been barren for years, so she went to see a doctor, an obstetrician, to seek help. The doctor ran a series of tests and a week later she returned to discuss the results. Now, her employer, the top banana at the White Mop factory, frowned on long lunch breaks and needed his 'Girl Friday' to 'man' the telephones. After all, she helped build his upstart business twenty years earlier as his first secretarial assistant. Who else would take sales orders? Through years of steadfast allegiance, she remained indispensable to the success of his business. And for twenty years she put off having children with longtime boyfriend-turned-husband, Tommy, however, time was now running out with her biological clock close to midnight. Fortunately, on that day, Mr. White understood her need to see an obstetrician and actually encouraged her to leave.

"Mrs. O'Malley, you're as capable as any woman half your age to birth children," her doctor stated matter-of-factly. "The test results, the gynecological exam, everything tells me you are a fully fertile human specimen ready to embark on motherhood."

"Then, why has it been so difficult? We've been trying for the past year. It doesn't make sense." She asked, completely bewildered. "Is it Tommy? Are his man-seeds not swimming like they should?"

The doctor chuckled. "His sperm count is fine. Really. No problem there." He glanced at her medical chart. "It says you'll be thirty-nine in six months. We need to rush this baby along. Time is not our ally."

"But what can I do? I feel so hopeless. Is there anything medically available?"

"There are some promising new treatments involving pregnant mare urine on the horizon. Those treatments won't be around for at least a year. Meanwhile, I suggest you refrain from relations with Tommy until fourteen days after your next menstrual cycle ceases. Concentrate on conceiving during those middle days."

Margret drew an exasperated face. "That's it. All those tests and the painful examination and that's all you can offer? Really? *Really*?"

The doctor leaned back in his chair expecting to be clobbered. "I know this is frustrating, Mrs. O'Malley. I see a great many women in your condition who may have waited too long to start a family. Some adopt children. And those who adopt miraculously conceive within months of adoption. Have you thought about it? Adoption as a way to conceive?"

"No. Tommy won't. He has too much pride. And he wants a boy to continue the O'Malley line of men. He's stubborn."

Glancing at the ceiling as if searching heaven for a solution to the dilemma, the doctor erupted into a wise all-knowing snigger. "Have any pets?" He asked slyly.

"No. We can't have a dog. We just moved into a new apartment building, the Ten Eyck. They don't allow dogs."

The doctor's eyebrows rose, impressed. "Ten Eyck? I hear it's a really swell place."

"Yes, it is. It's massive. They won't finish construction for another two years." She paused to consider the doctor's earlier question. What did having a pet have to do with the price of tea in China? She wondered. "That seems like an awfully strange question, doctor. Pets? Are you being a chump or something? Why, I oughtta—"

The doctor leaned back a second time. "Calm down, Mrs. O'Malley. I asked the question because pets can sometimes bring out nurturing instincts as much as adopted children. Pets can awaken long-dormant hormones and facilitate—"

"*Conception.*"

"Exactly."

Neither party said a word for a full minute as Margret thought about the idea. Finally, the doctor spoke, interrupting her thoughts.

"How about a cat?"

"Funny you should suggest a cat," she replied. "We have a stray kitten that keeps showing up on our fourth-floor window ledge. I think it's a Siamese. Tommy watched it one day leap from floor to floor to climb to our ledge. It paws the window like it wants in."

"Then, let it in Mrs. O'Malley. It's obvious the cat has picked you two to be its parents."

The next day, as anticipated, the stray kitten appeared on the ledge dejected, cold and hungry. When Margaret opened the window, the cat leaped inside with a December blast of arctic air chasing after it. Immediately, the poor thing began rubbing against her calves, in and out of her legs, mewing gibberish and craving human attention. She petted the top of its head and talked to it in a soft falsetto, hoping the falsetto would somehow bridge the gap between Brooklyn-styled English and cat-*ish*. "There you are, sweet kitty. Tommy and I have been waiting for you." She poured cream in a shallow bowl and placed the bowl on the floor next to a can of tuna fish. Within minutes, the cream had disappeared and the tuna half-consumed to the point where the cat's hunger pangs had been satisfied.

"Tommy, it looks like the cat we saw in the breeder's book. It's a full-blooded seal point Siamese."

Tommy seized the cat and began examining it. The little thing appeared to be remarkably healthy given the severe winter weather but a tad underweight. The enormous blue eyes, flat nose, cream-colored fur with brown socks and brown face clearly defined it as a Siamese of distinction, perhaps of pedigree lineage. He lifted its tail. "It's a Siamese, alright, and he has not been neutered."

"Well, you always wanted a boy. Now you have one with proud family jewels," Margaret teased.

Tommy laughed but became quite serious pondering the mystery behind the cat relentlessly pursuing them. "Why do you suppose he picked us? I mean, there are thousands of people around here he could have chosen but he chose you and me. Why?"

"I don't know, Tommy. Maybe he's our good luck stork?"

"Stork?"

"Maybe he'll usher in a baby for us, God willing."

Six weeks later, Margaret and Tommy discovered their 'stork' had, indeed, ushered in a miracle pregnancy—that and following the doctor's timing suggestion. The kitten, however, had remained nameless and the night Margaret announced to Tommy that she was 'with child' she also announced she had selected a name for their sweet Siamese.

"Marshawn," Margaret said. "It's an old English name. It means 'God is gracious.'"

Tommy thought the cat name totally appropriate and used the occasion to leverage a name he wanted for their unborn child. "Robert Babe O'Malley," he said. "But we'll call him Babe, as in Babe Ruth."

"And what if our child is a girl?" Margaret pressed.

The name works either way," he stated flat out.

Fortunately, their child was a boy, and no one could have been happier about it than the cat named Marshawn.

CHAPTER THREE

-The Babe-

"That's pretty cool, Grandpa. So, the cat hanging around helped the O'Malley's have a baby."

"Seems that way. I guess it brought out motherhood instincts in Margaret. And none too soon, I might add. In those days, if you didn't have a child by the time you were in your mid-thirties, the chances were slim to none you'd ever have one."

"And Marshawn, did he and the Babe get along? Did the cat like him?"

The old man guffawed, embarrassing himself. "Get along? Oh, my. They were best buddies. What do you kids call it?"

"BFF's."

"That's it. Marshawn thought Babe was the best thing since sliced bread."

The boy cast a blank stare.

"Yes. In answer to your question. Yes. Marshawn loved Babe."

The boy moved back to his bed and sat cross-legged on the side facing his grandfather. He picked up his cat and began stroking it from head to tail. The kitten hunkered into the boy's lap and purred. "Well, go on, Grandpa," the boy said without looking up. "I want to hear about Babe."

"Glad you asked. Well now, the day the O'Malley's brought Babe home from the hospital to their four-room flat at Ten Eyck the homecoming became a joyous celebration. Everyone in the building came to meet the newest and youngest tenant in the complex and what came to be known as the fourth floor 'miracle baby.' All this happened on the seventh of September, 1937…."

(1937)

When the O'Malley's arrived home, Ethel and Fred Parks and their two children, Albert, age five, and Gretchen, age 13, were first to throw open the door to an awaiting surprise party and shower the threesome with confetti and streamers. A sign prominently hung across the kitchen: WELCOME TO PLANET EARTH, BABE. A cast of other building characters emerged from hiding, also to heap congratulatory praise and toys and baby gifts upon the new arrival, the types of gifts young Babe would have to wait six months to grow into. Everyone wanted to hug and kiss the new arrival and little Babe seemed to handle the commotion in stride—cooing, smiling, all while his tiny arms excitedly flayed the air. "He's simply the cutest baby I've ever seen," Ethel Parks kept saying. Albert held the boy in his arms refusing to let go. "If I could ever have a baby brother, it would be you, Babe," he whispered. By the time the party ended, Gretchen said she counted twenty-six people who had passed Babe around the apartment without him crying one time.

Marshawn watched the welcome home party from under a bed, not sure if so many noisy humans confined in such a small space were trustworthy. But once everyone cleared out and little Babe lay asleep in his bassinet, the cat emerged confident in his new family role of god-cat first class. In the beginning, Marshawn maintained a civil distance while perched on a dresser next to the bassinet. The cat served as guardian protecting the child from monsters only a cat could fathom—a giant stuffed panda bear, baby dolls howling 'mama' when tipped over, a scary bird of prey suspended from the ceiling Tommy later explained was actually a replica of the Spirit of St. Louis (whatever that meant), and a menagerie of other frightful objects, which could, potentially, stir a newborn into endless bawling fits. These were the things commanding Marshawn's full attention as the cat took his family role quite seriously. Likewise, Marshawn was always present to supervise when

Babe's soiled cloth diapers were changed, or the boy's face needed a cat scrubbing after canned peas smeared his mouth or when Babe's golden locks needed grooming after kitchen sink baths. Sandpaper cat tongues tickled the Babe and spawned the child's first outright belly laugh, one lasting a full thirty seconds (at least that's the entry Mrs. O'Malley posted in the 'Baby's First Year' scrapbook).

Months later and in the middle of the night, Margaret and Tommy awakened to barking-like sounds emanating from the baby's room. The first time it happened, they remained fast asleep but their sentry, Marshawn, dashed into their bedroom, jumped on their chests, and screamed "HELP." Well, it was more of a bloodcurdling staccato of MEOWs awakening them and sending them sprinting to Babe's bassinet, only to discover the child choking to death. The pediatrician later diagnosed the ailment as infant croup, which explained why the coughing fits resembled a barking dog. The doctor said Babe would have died had they not responded when they did. "Next time this happens," he said, "hold Babe upright in a hot shower stall until the coughing subsides. The mist and steam will dilate his lungs." Needless to say, after the incident Marshawn became the family hero-protector and was served canned tuna every day for the rest of his life.

At eight months of age, the Babe graduated to a crib and the inseparable duo's friendship began to blossom. From that moment onward, Marshawn slept with Babe and snuggled under the boy's arm with its head tucked under a chin. Usually, the boy would chatter and coo nonstop to the cat, who must have thought all the babble a bedtime story because its eyes would cross and, inevitably, it would fall asleep.

"Don't you think those two are a little odd together," Tommy often remarked after checking the sleeping pair.

"They're best friends," Margaret replied. "Odd has no limits with love, Tommy. Leave 'em be. They're happy."

During the day Babe rolled small rubber balls on the floor for Marshawn to fetch, repeating the play over and over, giggling with each act of retrieval. The most fun, however, was 'stick-ribbon,' a game involving a short piece of ribbon tethered to an end of dowel. Babe would twirl the stick in every direction imaginable and Marshawn would chase the ribbon, ceaselessly, attempting to pounce and kill. In essence, Marshawn kept the child gainfully happy and as for the Babe, the Babe made the cat feel loved.

At age thirteen months, Babe stood for the first time but, in typical Babe fashion, was not content to move about from point A to point B, grasping furniture and human legs for support. No, the Babe danced and twirled and faltered before crashing in a tumbled heap, laughing at himself while Margaret and Tommy cringed with each disastrous fall. Even at thirteen months of age, Babe had never been content to sit still. Idleness remained as foreign to the lad as a hummingbird seeking nectar. All this infantile dancing, of course, was predicated on Margaret playing music on the record player and the only tune inciting unbridled pandemonium being Artie Shaw's *Begin the Beguine*. You see, the Babe comprehended few human words at age thirteen months and this particular tune had none; the music offered rhythm and percussion and a million dreams for toddlers who had no vocabulary. From the Babe's point of view, the only words he needed to know were Meow, Mew-Mew, and a host of other well-versed rhetoric courtesy of his cat friend. And when Artie Shaw's tune played and the boy stood and held his arms wide, Marshawn would place his paws on Babe's shoulders and the two would dance as gleefully as Fred Astaire and Ginger Rogers.

"Now, Grandpa, you don't expect me to believe Marshawn and the Babe danced together, do you? And who the heck are Fred Astaire and Ginger Rogers. Are they hip hop artists?"

The old man cast a blank stare.

"Look, Little Pete, this is my story and that's what happened. The boy and the cat liked to dance. Case closed. Now, may I continue without being interrupted?"

"Sure. My bad. But I know it didn't happen. It's all fake. Your BS-ing me."

"Well, we'll see about that...."

Now, because of the croup, the Babe's activity was mostly limited to the confines of the apartment. On a few occasions, Margret pushed him in a baby carriage around the corner to Lindsay Park but, by and large, the child remained homebound. Perhaps, this is why he so often stood for hours next to a window and watched the sights and sounds on the street below. He watched children play. He watched leaves turn colors and fall from trees. He watched a noisy, chaotic, mysterious world he wanted to be part of. For Babe, the streets and gardens and sidewalks beckoned as much as Sirens played to the senses of wanderlust sailors.

A month later Babe uttered his first human words and none too soon. His parents were concerned their son might be mentally challenged or, worse, *slow*. He had just turned fourteen months and both Tommy and Margaret vainly goaded the child into pronouncing their respective names. It became a competition of sorts for pride and family bragging rights. When Margaret would depart the room, Tommy secretly patted his chest and whispered the word Dada to Babe. "Come on sport. You can say it. I gotta be your first word. Come on. Say Dada." And, naturally, when Tommy excused himself, Margaret would ply brainwashing techniques to Babe by repeating the one word all sons treasure, the word *Mama*.   This uneasy competition lasted for weeks without either party knowing what trickery the other conspired. Babe's behavior favoring one word over the other remained uncommitted and stoic. Typically, he would sit and study his parents' faces and laugh aloud thinking this game to be so much fun. But when the time arrived for Babe to utter anything intelligible, Margaret and Tommy were both highly disappointed. The Babe stood, wobbly-legged, and mischievously eyed his parents. Meanwhile, Marshawn pawed his way in between the two adults and sat staring at his amazing buddy, the twenty-four-inch tall baby-giant.

When the child finally opened his mouth, all he did was babble nonsensical gibberish, twirling and dancing. "Abba-abba, Boo-boo-ba-ba," followed with grunts and an impression of a tiger, "Gr-r-r-r-rr".

"What's he doing?" Tommy asked, mystified.

"He wants Artie Shaw," Margaret answered, dead-pan. "Obviously, you don't speak *Babe-ish*."

She moved to their record player and selected the boy's favorite tune. Immediately, the song filled the room and Marshawn sauntered to Babe, placed its paws on the boy's bare shoulders and the two moved awkwardly around the room, the child resplendent in saggy cotton diapers leading his cat in a farcical two-step dance of sorts. When the song finished, the Babe clapped and laughed and clapped some more, much to his parents' astonishment, and that was the exact moment he spoke his first discernible human utterance, those unforgettable words, "*Marshawn a cat*."

CHAPTER FOUR

-Ten Eyck & Lindsay Park-

Little Pete chuckled. "That's hilarious, Grandpa. I guess the Babe truly loved Marshawn."

"Yes, he did. Other than young Albert, there was no one anywhere near Babe's age to play with at Ten Eyck and Albert was five years older, so their partnership would not reach fruition for years to come. Nope, it was the Babe and Marshawn all the way. Those two were true BFF's," the old man stated, proud of his new generational vernacular. As the old man continued to speak, the boy suddenly bolted to a bedroom desk and his laptop and began typing. "What are you doing?" The old man asked.

"I'm fact checking you." A minute passed before the boy found what he was Googling or, rather, what he did not find on Google. Triumphantly, he slammed his hands on the desk, turned to face his grandfather, and smugly emitted an I-told-you-so smirk. "Grandpa, there is no Ten Eyck complex in Brooklyn and there's no Lindsay Park, either. You've been BS-ing me all along, just as I thought."

The old man shook his head, expecting as much from his grandson. Truly, wherever his stories bounded, skepticism followed. "You may not find what you're looking for in there," he said, pointing to the boy's laptop, "but those landmarks I mentioned do exist. They're here," he stated, rapping his temple, "and in here," he added, patting his chest. "The Internet doesn't always get it right. Trust me. Grandparents are rarely wrong."

The boy flashed a painful grimace. While he could argue his point logically, he also knew he could never win an illogical debate with his grandfather. And, once again, the boy succumbed to the word, "shit."

"Okay. We'll have it your way, Grandpa," he said, surrendering to the notion. "Tell me all about this make-believe fantasyland you've created."

The old man laughed. "You're funny. You remind me of someone."

"Who?" The boy asked.

"Me."

(1938)

There was a time and place when the world seemed less complicated—or less problematic. Memories tend to gloss over the darker events, and we remember what we want to remember. But in those days in Brooklyn, in the old Williamsburg neighborhood of the late 1930s, memories had less to do with places, the old haunts we frequented, than people. People created memories. Places gave perspective to a bygone era.

When the idea first struck to undertake a colossal housing project, no one imagined in 1936, the year it all started, the sheer size and magnitude. 'Ten Eyck Houses' (pronounced Ike) would become the largest project of its kind in American history. The massive complex was built with Federal money under the direction of the Public Works Administration. Twenty four-story buildings, each turned at the same angle to greet morning sunlight, would scatter geometrically across twelve square blocks of Brooklyn's most impoverished neighborhood. They called it 'urban renewal' but, in reality, the 'houses' renewed human dignity.

The complex was designed by the same team of men who planned the Empire State Building; the concept stressed modern art deco utilitarianism for the 'common man.' Retail shops, a police station, a chapel, restaurants, even daycare centers tucked into first floors while people lived above. Wavy sidewalks danced between buildings with freshly planted trees providing shade to joggers and walkers and mothers pushing baby carriages. No street thoroughfare violated the twelve-block enclave, or the proud gardens carved between buildings. Ten Eyck became humankind's grandest design for twentieth century living. The project supplanted blighted tenements with refinery and class. Each building boasted a modern lobby and breathtaking murals by contemporary artists—Kelpe, Bolotowsky, Greene, Swinden—the greatest modernists of their era. Most importantly, Ten Eyck provided upward mobility for the O'Malley's of the world; the project provided safe, clean, and affordable housing, and provided future generations of New Yorkers a commodity in rare supply in the 1930s— *hope*.

Two blocks to the south and around the corner stood another unique oasis in the Williamsburg neighborhood— Lindsay Park. The idea for the park began in 1925 when less than two acres of open land were begrudgingly allocated for a raw dirt playground. It was the first park open to a poor immigrant community that flooded Brooklyn. By 1929 and with New York City awash in Roaring '20s revenue, the playground was upgraded to include swing sets, a 'girl's quarter,' open-air shelters, cyclone-styled metal fencing, a baseball backstop, and a stout brick 'comfort building' complete with modern toilets, running water, wash basins, and night lighting. The comfort building became a major attraction for the homeless and unemployable while the park, itself, served as a magnet for freethinking vagabonds, chronic substance abuse users, Marxists, and the mentally ill. During the Great Depression, dozens of tents pitched regularly around the building because the public edifice offered 24-hour access to water and bathrooms. Likewise, Lindsay Park became an ad hoc headquarters for World War I veterans still suffering from post-traumatic stress syndrome and incapable of mainstreaming into society. And unlike Ten Eyck, Lindsay Park offered little hope to its residents. If anything, the park fueled anger and despair for those journeying down the road to perdition. During the darkest days of the Depression, hundreds of (mostly) men camped at the park. Because of city policy and park underwriting with taxpayer money, vagrants could not be expelled. Fortunately, as time marched on and with jobs more plentiful, most of the tents disappeared. By October 1938, few diehards remained, and these were individuals ill-equipped to succeed in life.

CHAPTER FIVE

-Henry Ahrens-

"Have you ever studied the history of World War I?" The old man suddenly asked, stopping short his descriptions of the houses and the park.

"Some. A little. Why?"

"Because nowadays not too many people know about World War I. In 1938, with only one world conflict under America's belt, it was simply called the Great War. Nobody ever anticipated there'd be a follow-up war."

"You mean World War II?"

"That's right. After World War II most people forgot about our first war. It was too hard to see it in the rearview mirror. Back in those days, most civilians never understood how much devastation that first war wreaked on young American lives and the men who fought in France in 1918. Did you know the average age of our servicemen was only twenty-four? Other than Vietnam, that's the youngest age for American servicemen in any war."

"Why did you ask me that, Grandpa? About World War I?"

"Because earlier you asked me how old Henry Ahrens was in 1938."

"You said he was forty."

"Correct. So, how old would he have been in 1918 when he fought in the Great War?"

"That's easy. He would have been twenty."

"Exactly. A mere nine years older than you. And it was at the ripe old age of twenty he got a battlefield promotion from Sergeant to Second Lieutenant in France because of his courage under fire. He took command of thirty-five Marines at the battle of Belleau Wood and was awarded the Distinguished Service Cross for gallantry. They nicknamed his platoon the Devil Dogs, a name that has stuck with the Marine Corps to this very day. But in that fierce battle over half of his men were killed and all but he and one other soldier escaped without wounds. That disastrous escapade Henry never got over. He blamed himself for all the young men who died under his command. You could say the war and self-deprecating guilt traumatized him for life. He was unable to hold a job. He drank too much. And he harbored a compulsive need to fix his fellow man, the ones who survived battles but failed in life. To put it mildly, he had difficulty letting go of memories. Memories became his demons."

"That's really depressing but what does Henry have to do with the Babe and Marshawn?"

"Well, I am so glad you asked and are finally taking an interest in this full-of-beans story of mine." The old man teased. "You see, Henry and Orson Welles and the Babe were on a collision course at Lindsay Park on October 30, 1938, the same night our planet was attacked by little green men from Mars."

The boy struck a skeptical pose but, almost as quickly, softened his skepticism with unabashed adolescent curiosity. "Know what, Grandpa? Tell me all about Henry Ahrens. I want to know his story."

"It would be my pleasure."

(October 30, 1938)

Some men learn to let go of the past. Some men never let go. For Henry Ahrens and the men of Company B, the years following Belleau Wood would prove as costly to their sanity as the mêlée, itself. Fifteen men survived the battle but struggled to survive the anguish encapsulating their lives after the war. Six married sweethearts upon their return, raised children, lived the American dream, and somehow managed to file away catastrophic memories. Yet, within five years of returning stateside, three others had taken their own lives, two had taken the lives of noncombatants, and four were left to wander aimlessly through an American landscape as degenerate drifters afloat in a sea of indifference.

In those days, enlistees at regional recruiting offices served together throughout war campaigns. Long Island recruits served in a battalion comprised of fellow 'Islanders.' So, it made sense that when the boys of Company B returned from the Great War they kept in touch. Most of them lived within fifty miles of each other. And what started out innocently enough as fun-loving reunions eventually spiraled into a chasm of complainers incapable of helping each other rise above a horrific past. By the time the Great Depression arrived, the four veterans least capable of surviving joblessness, reunited again in the makeshift city of tents at Lindsay Park. Led by their former leader, Henry Ahrens, these men stumbled through seven years of mental fog, surviving on odd jobs, incoherent banter, soup lines, and hooch, gin being the primary benefactor of their despondency. There were over thirty other souls camped at the tent city on the grounds of Lindsay Park, too, but by October 30, 1938 only two Company B Marines remained— Henry Ahrens and his young private, Ben Sternberg.

As had been the custom, Sunday nights became radio listening nights at the park when men gathered around a 'procured' Zenith Walton radio and listened to broadcasts of *The Shadow* or whatever else struck their fancy. Ben, being a master electrician in a past life, bootlegged the radio into a park streetlamp and ran an electrical cord over a hundred feet on the ground and next to the comfort station. Sundays were the only time night beat cops didn't patrol the area and the men could get away with the illegalities that came with stealing city electricity. Hence, for three or four hours, in semi-lit darkness, thirty men (thirty-two to be exact) gathered around a radio, as much as cowboys around a campfire, and listened to tales that stoked their imaginations. On that particular Sunday night in 1938, Beggars Night, Henry Ahrens considered himself 'Irish rich.' Absent for most of the day, Henry had helped a young couple move their furnishings into a new Ten Eyck apartment around the corner from the park. The two dollars Henry earned burned a hole in his pocket, so to speak, and Henry decided to share his newfound wealth, purchasing a carton of smokes for the men and an expensive bottle of Gordon's Gin for Ben, this as darkness set in. Henry, being of somewhat sounder mind and far more sober than the others, supported his ex-private as best as any ex-lieutenant could. When he returned to the park with a new bottle of hooch, Ben's brain already clouded with dancing pink elephants. Alcohol had always been readily available in the park, usually in brown paper bags shared among men; Henry's gift of premium quality gin simply added to Ben's stash and further dumbfounded Ben's elephants.

"So, what's on the agenda tonight, fellas?" Henry asked the men circled around the radio, sitting cross-legged as twilight faded.

A man named 'Honi,' an unemployed tap dancer and a rare African American among the white faces, spoke up. "Why the usual, Mr. Ahrens, sir. We gonna listen to Edgar Bergan, then, switch it over to Mercury Theater and see what Mr. Orson Welles is up to."

Henry sat next to Ben and handed him the Gordon's. Ben's eyes lit. "You are the best friend a guy could ever have," Ben announced.

"I'm just trying to take care of you Ben. That's all. 'Trying to get you back on your feet." Henry passed out cigarettes from the carton he purchased. The men were quite pleased with the free smokes and told him he was a "swell standup guy." In reality, Henry had grown pervasively into his role of caregiver. It made no difference if these men he barely knew were remnants of Company B or not. They all needed guidance and a helping hand. They all needed fixing, according to Henry. "Say boys, I found out we can get steady work at those apartments around the corner. They need help moving in new tenants. What do you say to them apples?"

A few of the men thought the prospect of earning cash and being able to buy regular food not readily available in soup lines sounded wonderful and exclaimed as much.

Henry nudged Ben's shoulder. "How 'bout it, Ben? You up for it?"

Ben smiled sheepishly; his eyes transfixed through Henry. "Sure thing," he mumbled. "I'll look into it."

That was the best Henry could ever expect when it came to matching Ben with work—the old "I'll look into it" line.

"You know what else I discovered?" Henry asked. "I found out from that fella I helped move in how they're looking for master electricians at the dockyard. 'Seems the government is building two new Navy destroyers and there's a shortage of men with experience. They pay a hefty salary, Ben. That fella is a big shot on the project. I told him about you. He said they're hiring vets and starting pay for skilled folks is five thousand dollars."

Ben's eyes darted away. He teetered as he reached to crank the radio's volume. "I'll look into it," he mumbled again.

Henry realized a long-term overindulgence with alcohol had clearly distorted Ben's perspective on life. Recently, Ben's melancholy had taken a turn for the worse and the man now wallowed in self-pity as much as any man Henry had ever met. Ben needed positive words. Ben needed encouragement. And with a dogged determination only a close friend can provide, Henry put his arm around Ben, winked to Honi, and began to sing:

"Nothing's impossible I have found,
For when my chin is on the ground,
I pick myself up,
Dust myself off,
And start all over again.

Don't lose your confidence if you slip,
Be grateful for a pleasant trip,
And pick yourself up,
Dust yourself off,
Start all over again...."

The other men began to harmonize with their familiar 'boom-boom' background vocals. This was not the first time Henry had serenaded his friend nor the first time they had participated in song. Meanwhile, Honi began slapping his thighs and making a syncopated percussion sound; he tap danced around the radio, hoofing to everyone's delight with a performance as grand as anything Broadway had to offer. And as for the thirty men that Beggar's Night and their sentiments? The men loved Henry Ahrens for trying to save them from themselves.

"...Work like a soul inspired,
Until the battle of the day is won.
You may be sick and tired,
But you'll be a man, my son!

Will you remember the famous men,
Who had to fall to rise again?
So take a deep breath,
Pick yourself up,
Dust yourself off,
And start all over again...."

CHAPTER SIX

-The Great Beggar's Night Adventure-

"Wait a minute, Grandpa. Are you saying Henry sang to his friend the same song you sing to me?"

"That's right. It's a great song and it's been around— *for a long, long time.* Since 1936. I didn't invent it."

The boy nodded his head, understanding the deeper meaning of the words. He thought the song "pretty cool" and never realized it was so "ancient." "This park where Henry Ahrens lived," he continued, "it was around the corner from where the Babe lived. Right?"

"Yup. About two blocks."

Curiosity drove the boy to the next question. "What was the big deal listening to the radio back and that man? What's his name?"

"Orson Welles?"

"Ya, him. Who was he?"

"He was a great performer. An actor with a fantastic imagination. You see, on Beggar's Night in 1938 he broadcast a show over the radio airwaves the likes of which no one had ever experienced. He faked a real-time invasion from Mars and of little green men who wanted to take over our planet. It was called 'The War of the Worlds.' Of course, he was pretending but the news broadcast seemed so realistic people thought an invasion was actually taking place. When that happened, panic set in. People got frightened and did crazy things."

"And those men in Lindsay Park, did they believe people from Mars were attacking? Did they go crazy and panic?"

The old man made a belly laugh. "My, oh, my. I believe I have your full attention now," he said, pleased with the boy's re-enthused interest. "Slow your horses, Little Pete. Let me tell you what happened next and, then, I think you'll understand. Okay?"

"Okay."

"Well, do you remember what I said about Babe longing to see what lay beyond his bedroom window? About him being sickly and his parents confining him to their fourth-floor apartment except for a few excursions in a carriage to the park?"

"Of course. He was kind of like me. He wanted out."

"That's right. And on Beggar's Night, 1938, he watched those children below his bedroom window scurrying about and dressed in full costume and, unlike you, he had no earthly idea what was going on. All he knew was that he was missing out on something wonderful and his instincts told him to join the revelers."

"But how, Grandpa? He was only fourteen months old. How?"

The old man smiled all-knowingly. "Let's just say he had some help...."

(October 30, 1938; 8:30 PM)

Watching from his crib parked across from a bedroom window, the revelers four floors below mesmerized the Babe to the brink of baby-hysterics. Unbridled excitement heightened the child's emotions and, reactively, he began rocking his crib back and forth. What the Babe discovered was akin to Newton's third law of motion—when one body exerts a force on a second body, the second body simultaneously exerts a force equal in magnitude and opposite in direction on the first body. Simply put, the casters on the crib legs facilitated the crib's inertia, moving it in spurts across the floor and scooting it directly to the open window. At that point, the child hoisted himself onto the sill and outside on the ledge where scaffolding had been erected to finish the building project next door. From there, he crawled on all fours on dangerously narrow planking wearing nothing but a soiled cloth diaper and an ecstatically happy face.

Marshawn witnessed this great escape and (if cats can think such thoughts) reasoned it knew all about Ten Eyck ledges and windowsills far, far better than the Babe. Thus, Marshawn followed the child out the window, leaped over the boy, and turned as if to say, "Ain't this grand? Follow me, Babe. Follow me." With its tail flagpole vertical and its pink behind aglow from nearby streetlights, the Babe had no problem chasing after Marshawn's iridescent buttock.

A half an hour earlier, Margaret and Tommy O'Malley and their best friends, Ethel and Fred Parks, had decided to walk Brooklyn's streets and take in the sights of Halloween festivities and indulge a nightcap at Rossini's Tavern. Gretchen Parks and little brother, Albert, were tonight's babysitters. Upon arrival, Albert asked if he could play with Babe and Margaret told him how the little man had already been put to bed and, when last she checked, lay fast asleep with Marshawn. Now, thirty minutes later and with his older teen sister ignoring him and no one to entertain his slightest whims, seven-year-old Albert decided to play one of the O'Malley's records. Naturally, the one record already cued-up on the turntable was none other than Artie Shaw's *Begin the Beguine*. And the moment the tune erupted, and the melody filled the four-room apartment, the Babe stirred as did Marshawn. The child stood in his crib, wiped sleep from his eyes, and stretched to stare out a window to view children dressed in strange costumes. Babe O'Malley was now fully awake and poised to begin his beguine.

Scaffolding for bricklayers in those days was nothing more than thick planks of wood twelve inches wide and quite dangerous, even for adult bricklayers. How the Babe managed to crawl on all fours the sixty-foot distance to reach the debris chute that plummeted to the first floor is anyone's guess but, following Marshawn's lead, the child did exactly that, sliding head first on his stomach with a perfect 10.0 belly flop to the parquet floor of what would become the lobby of 'house' 24C. Unscathed and laughing hysterically, Babe stood and stumbled to Marshawn minus his dirty diaper—*naked*. Somewhere along the plummet the diaper disappeared and now Marshawn was not the only one with an exposed pink buttock. In his excitement, the Babe began dancing and twirling for he had succeeded where no fourteen-month-old had ever succeeded before at Ten Eyck: *he had flown the coop*. With exuberant gusto, the orangutan took possession of the child. As his arms rose jubilantly skyward in celebration, they accidentally knocked over a board balanced on a sawhorse. When the board fell, the sawhorse collided against a table saw, the table saw's legs collapsed forward and tipped into a bucket full of nails, the bucket swung wildly tethered to a pulley and crashed against wall scaffolding supporting an overhead can of green paint for the half-finished mural by Paul Kelpe. Watching all of this unfold, the Babe's last words were "Uh-oh."

When the paint can fell over, the color green drenched the child's entire body. And as much as the Babe wanted to cry, he simply could not. After all, green was his favorite color and, given the semi-lit recess of the 24C lobby, he knew he wore the color well. With an earsplitting joyous shriek, "Abba-abba, Abba-abba, Gr-r-r-r," he did an about face and chased after Marshawn who, by now, had literally hightailed across Leonard Street, frightened by the paint-covered creature in pursuit. Babe failed to keep pace with his four-legged friend fleeing for the safer confines of an abandoned and condemned building. By the time Marshawn dashed through an open doorway to hide, the Babe stood in the middle of the sidewalk confused as to his best friend's whereabouts and ignored by oblivious costumed children swarming around him.

CHAPTER SEVEN

-Mars Invades Brooklyn-

"Grandpa, are you telling me the Babe was covered in green paint and running around naked and nobody noticed?"

"That's right. Why would anyone notice? First, he was only two-feet tall. Adults rarely look below their waists. Why would they pay any attention to someone so short? Second, all the children were wearing costumes. To them, Babe was simply another reveler out celebrating Beggar's Night as some sort of green monster. Why would he stand out in the crowd?"

The boy thought through the explanation and bought the answer hook, line, and sinker. "Fine. So, the Babe watched Marshawn run into an abandoned building and disappear. Why didn't he go after his cat?"

"I don't know. Maybe it was too dark. Maybe the building spooked him. Maybe the sights outside his apartment overwhelmed him. And, let's not forget he was only fourteen months old. Who's to say any cognitive thinking was going on in his little toddler brain? 'Guess we'll never know. All we know for sure is that he felt a need to waddle and stumble to Lindsay Park two blocks away and seek help. Maybe he had seen the men in their tent city on a previous outing and thought they'd come to his aid. Maybe he heard the radio blaring and followed the noise. In any case he was in a state of panic and needed help."

(October 30, 1938; 8:45 PM)

By 8:45 PM Henry Ahrens had abandoned all thirty-one men at the Lindsay Park tent city for free nourishment at the local soup kitchen next door. While the food at the kitchen was considered only slightly better than Marine Corps hash, Henry decided surviving on gin and cigarettes alone was an impossible feat—at six-foot and a hundred forty-five pounds, even scarecrow Marines needed an occasional meal. His departure left the men temporarily without their leader. It meant no one with a clear head remained to explain how the Mercury Theater broadcast they were listening to and the fake news of an invasion from Mars was a publicity stunt.

Suddenly, little Babe stumbles orangutan-style upon the men at Lindsay Park and straight to the radio. He turns to Ben and excitedly screeches, "Abba-abba. Gr-r-r-rr."

Pickled from the effects of gin, none of the men had sense to recognize the interloper as a toddler covered with paint. What they thought they were seeing was one of the little green men described in the radio broadcast.

"Don't hurt us," Honi cried out. "Please, don't hurt us."

The Babe, of course, had no idea what the man was saying or why thirty-one faces were paralyzed in fright.

Ben added to Honi's pleas for mercy and understanding. "Do you come in peace or to destroy us?"

"*Peas*," the Babe mimicked, nodding his head up and down, smiling. "Peas." For the lad absolutely loved peas.

Ben plied the strange looking creature with a second formidable question. "Are you a Martian," he yelled, hoping a louder voice might somehow bridge the communication gap between earthling and extraterrestrial.

Upon hearing Ben's words, the Babe cocked his head for he thought he understood a smidgen of what the man had just spouted. "Marshawn?" He asked.

"Yes," Ben said, pointing to the Babe. "You a Martian?"

And, then, with all of the verb and pluck the Babe could muster, he burst forth with the only words he knew, "No. Marshawn a cat." And he pointed in the direction of the dilapidated building where his cat had disappeared.

Honi blinked. He stood and turned to the men. "Did he say what I thought he said?"

One of the men shouted, "Hell, yes. He said, 'Martians attack.'"

All the men jumped to their feet in a panic. Ben, being the ranking second-in-command and a formidable ex-

Marine, took charge. "To hell with these green bastards and
their heat ray. Let's take the fight to 'em. Are you with me
boys?"

"Hell, yes," they shouted.

Honi seized the Babe's hand. "Show us little Martian
man where your buddies are holed up."

One of the men yelled, "Grab anything you can get your
hands on to fight 'em." Less than twenty seconds later every
man was armed with a makeshift weapon—baseball bats,
two-by-fours, glass bottles, chains, and the weapon to end
the war of all wars, kerosene in a Coca-Cola bottle, Malakoff
cocktail style—everyone knew Martians hate fire.

Tired of dragging the Babe by the hand, Honi hoisted
the boy on his shoulders, draping the child around his neck.
The Babe held onto Honi's hair with one hand and pointed
out their heading with the other, resembling Julius Caesar
conquering Gauls. Boisterous and angry, the mob moved
with haste along the two-block distance parting Beggar's
Night revelers en route. "We're the Brooklyn people's
liberation army. Out of our way, maggots," they threatened.

When they reached the abandoned building, Babe
thought he saw Marshawn perched on a third-floor window.
"Marshawn," he squealed, pointing to the cat.

Naturally, no one saw a cat. They were looking for
larger versions of Babe. Ben marched to the front and to
what remained of the building's dilapidated wood facade. He
stood in an open doorway and turned to face his troops.
"Alright boys, you know what we gotta do. Right?"

The man holding the kerosene bottle stuffed it with a rag
and lit the wick. "Burn 'em out. That's what we gotta do,"
he answered, throwing the bottle against the building.
Flames ignited with an explosion, shot vertically, and
consumed the first two floors in less than a minute. Babe
watched in horror.

By the time Henry Ahrens returned to the park and
realized his company of men were nowhere to be found, a
passerby costumed child motioned toward the Ten Eyck

complex and the fire across the street. Without forethought, he sprinted to the location and found the mob gazing in wonderment at the building ablaze. He seized Ben by the arm and shook him. "My God, what have you done?"

"We found the enemy, Lieutenant," he slurred. "And we captured one of the little Martians, too," he stated proudly, thumbing the air toward the child.

Henry gazed at the Babe astraddle Honi's shoulders. He reached up and wiped paint from the boy's eyes and immediately recognized the creature underneath as a human toddler. "For Pete's sake, he's just a little boy. Look," he said to the mob, displaying green paint on the palms of his hands. He lifted the Babe off Honi's shoulders and knelt next to the child, gazing into the boy's eyes. "Are you okay?" He asked softly.

The Babe began to bawl hysterically, pointing to the flames. "Cat," he said. "Cat." And with a sense of utmost urgency, he added a new word to his vocabulary. "Babe *love* Marshawn. Marshawn a cat." And he cried some more.

Henry looked toward the third floor where Babe pointed and saw Marshawn in the window, frightened and frantic. He glanced at Babe one last time and said, "Don't cry, little boy. I'll fix this."

Maybe, that became the moment Henry Ahrens had been waiting for since 1918, the moment to fix the past and reunite with all those souls he left behind in France. Maybe, it was his way of satisfying karma and balancing a world that had forgotten about his kind. In any case, he never hesitated to do what needed to be done and he dashed inside the burning building to rescue a little boy's cat. By the time he reached the third floor, he was besieged by the inferno and in severe agony, but he still pressed onward, ever onward, exactly as he did on that fateful day in Belleau Wood so many years before. And, somehow, he managed to grab hold of Marshawn, lean out the window, and toss the cat to awaiting hands below. Overcome with smoke and flames, he staggered backward and perished with the building, winning this last battle in a forgotten war.

Albert and Gretchen heard fire trucks and rushed into Babe's bedroom for a better view. When they discovered the Babe missing and a window open, Gretchen assumed the worst and began scouring the building and the grounds below. Albert, however, was drawn by the spectacle of fire and scrambled down four flights of stairs and across Leonard Street to the scene. He pushed through the mob's legs to the front, looked skyward and saw a cat tumbling from heaven. In knee-jerk fashion, he reached out and snagged Marshawn in his arms before it hit ground. As he turned to retreat from the pack of adults, there stood Babe wiping away tears.

"Babe. Where have you been?" He asked, quite pleased he found his little friend. Obviously, the Babe still drenched head to toe in paint and seven-year-old Albert recognized something horribly amiss. "Let's go home and clean you up," he said, seizing Babe's hand and leading him back across the street.

Gretchen and Albert washed Babe and put the child back in his crib with Marshawn, this time making sure the window was shut and locked. They promised to keep the incident a secret for fear of the trouble they might get into for botching their first baby sitting opportunity and, for the next eighty years, they never told anyone about what happened that Beggar's Night in 1938.

CHAPTER EIGHT

"...So, for over eighty years, no one ever knew what happened until today," the boy's grandfather stated. "Now, you know the true story of Marshawn the cat."

The boy fell back in his chair, still holding his kitten. "That is so amazing, Grandpa. It all happened because the Babe ventured out—"

"*Before the time was right,*" the old man interrupted. "Listen to me, Little Pete—to everything there is a season and a time to every purpose under heaven. All things in our lives happen for a reason. Trust me. The good Lord has not forgotten you. He has blessed you with a miracle. I think you can wait six more months before you head out there," he said, nudging his nose toward the bay window. "Your season will come."

"Yes. I suppose it will."

"And next year you will not be too old to go Trick or Treating with me. Will you?"

The boy exhaled and shook his head 'No.'

"I mean, if you're wearing a costume mask, who will know how old you are, anyway. Right?"

The boy nodded his head, agreeing with his grandfather.

After a few seconds of silence, the boy spoke. He was clenching his cat for fear of ever letting it go. "Grandpa, what happened to Ben and all of those men who set the fire?"

"As far as the men, it seems they disbanded and went their separate ways. 'Far as Ben Sternberg, I heard the death of his best friend, Henry Ahrens, weighed heavy on his conscience. He sobered up. Took a job on the docks building navy ships. Married a woman who became a community activist. And, years later, the city renamed Lindsay Park after her."

The boy's eyes widened. "So, our park, Sternberg Park, was once actually called Lindsay Park?"

"Yup."

The boy turned and looked out the window at the housing complex across the street. "That means the Williamsburg Apartments were once named—"

"Ten Eyck Houses."

The boy pondered these new revelations and the story and became quite serious. All of this meant one thing: *his grandfather had not been BS-ing him.* "Grandpa," he finally said, "I think I have a name for my cat."

"That's good news. And what name have you come up with?"

"Henry."

The old man paused before saying anything. He swallowed hard and responded with, "I think Henry Ahrens would like that and I would, too." He wanted to say more but his phone began vibrating in his pocket and interrupted his thoughts. He checked the text message. It was from Bert. "*Are you ever coming?*" Yes, he told himself. I'm coming Bert. Hold your horses.

The boy understood his grandfather's long friendship with Bert. He stood and moved to the plastic partition knowing time was up. He placed the flat of his hand against plastic and his grandfather reciprocated the gesture in what had become their customary parting routine. And the old man sang their song:

"Nothing's impossible I have found,
For when my chin is on the ground,
I pick myself up,
Dust myself off,
And start all over again.

Don't lose your confidence if you slip,
Be grateful for a pleasant trip,
And pick yourself up,
Dust yourself off,
Start all over again...."

When the old man finished singing, he winked at his grandson. "I love you, *Peter*," he said. "I guess this means we're still on for Greenwich Village in 2033. Right?"

The boy grinned. "Hell, yes, Grandpa."

Before the old man saw himself out of the building, his daughter intercepted him in a hallway. "I heard you singing to Pete. I guess everything is alright?"

"Yup. The boy is happy once again. He's a good boy. The best."

His daughter did not say anything in return. There was no need. She leaned forward, kissed him on the cheek and whispered, "I love you, Dad."

"I love you, too, Sweetie," he said.

Huckleberry's Bar sprawled void of patrons except for an old codger propped in a corner booth nursing a warm beer. "Glad you could finally make it," the voice boomed, hinting of cantankerous sarcasm. "Everything go smoothly with the grandson?"

"Yes, Albert," the old man replied, exasperated with his friend's impatience. "I told him our story. About Marshawn the cat and how you caught it midair as it fell from a burning building. And I told him about that poor man, Henry Ahrens, who died in the fire." He hesitated and capitulated to a soft whistle. "I guess I broke our promise. Sorry. Now, Little Pete knows the story. I hope that's okay with you."

"Of course, it is. We can't get in trouble now. Look at us. We're old." Bert laughed. "Shoot, Babe, you wouldn't have remembered anything had I not kept the story alive all these years and retold it a hundred times as you grew up. You were only fourteen months old back then and quite green, as I recall." He chuckled on his play of words. "Say, did you use your old name, Babe?"

"Yes. You're the only one who calls me Babe, anymore. And I changed the last name of the child, too. I didn't want Little Pete getting hung up on the connection between me and the lesson of the story. Besides, he'll figure it out soon enough. He's as sharp as they come."

The two men smiled at each other and said nothing more about the incident. For Robert *Babe* O'Hara, telling the story to his grandson was as much a relief as attending confessional. He was finally absolved. Now, someone else could pass it along.

Thirsty and famished, the old man ordered a Brooklyn Brewery lager and asked Bert about their missing Grimaldi pepperoni pizza. "It's coming, Babe. Like we agreed, it's my turn to buy. It's coming."

When Babe's beer was served, Bert suggested they toast the night. The Babe thought the gesture a splendid idea. "Here's to Beggar's Night, my friend," Bert said, clanking his glass stein against Babe's.

"And to eighty-three years of non-stop friendship," the Babe replied with one-upmanship grace.

"To the Henry Ahrens of this world. May God always grant them redemption," Bert stated.

"And to Orson Welles and Lindsay Park."

With their final toast, the two friends began swapping stories about the old days in Brooklyn and savoring sweet memories from an era a long, long time ago.

Pick Yourself Up

Words and Music by Dorothy Fields
and Jerome Kern

RUNNER SPEAKS

For Tyler

RUNNER SPEAKS

CHAPTER ONE

(December 26, 1867 – 4:00 PM – West Texas)

Two horses gallop through a parched winter landscape in a frenzied race against time. Their slobbered bits drip rabid wet between strained wails. Blood cascades down both horses' necks where angry quirts demanded speed. One mount bears up under the weight of a seasoned white soldier. The other struggles to keep pace. The second rider, a black soldier, raises a gloved hand requesting permission for water but the white officer ignores his signal and points to danger ahead. Yanking back hard on reins, both horses skid inches from a cliff's drop-off. Dust explodes skyward only to avalanche into a two-hundred-foot chasm. Riders hurriedly dismount and mooch rubber-legged to an unforgiving precipice to stare into a never-ending veil. Before them spreads a Pecos River Gorge wide and comatose. Their destination lurks out there, somewhere, in this bleak wilderness. The two men take note of an old rutted and rock-strewn Butterfield Mail Route meandering to the basin. The trail provides the safest means to descend this caprock abyss but doing so will take time. As they gaze beyond river flats and plot a next move, a brisk norther slaps their backs. No doubt, winter is serving notice this late December day—*the U.S. Cavalry is losing a forsaken race and with it all hope to save innocent lives.*

Captain William Frohock and his yellow-legged consort, Sergeant Benjamin Sharpe, have been riding without water for eighty miles. Their hastened departure came late that morning when news arrived of renegade hostiles migrating south out of the Concho valley. Both

captain and his commander assumed Kickapoo and
Comanchero intent is to raid a lightly garrisoned Fort
Lancaster and steal horse and mule herds. A surprise attack
puts forty-odd defenders in harm's way. Both officers wisely
suspect stubborn Lancaster soldiers will never surrender
homegrown livestock without a fight. Hence, the isolated
outpost needed to be warned and the experienced captain
volunteered. Sergeant Sharpe accompanied his officer, and
they rode off together from headquarters at Fort Stockton.

Now, after four straight hours tackling an unforgiving
land on horseback, they pose anxious atop a strategic
lookout. Captain Frohock scans terrain with a spyglass. He
casts an eye north of the confluence where Live Oak Creek
and the Pecos River merge and locates their fort. Smoke
bellows from a handful of chimneys. Soldiers dot parade
grounds in gnat-sized swarms as shadows stretch eastward
and threaten to overtake humanity. Frohock has never laid
eyes on Fort Lancaster and has no idea of its capability to
withstand an assault. Poorly designed pre-Civil War, the
grounds sprawl gangly and without forethought and seem
more a ghost town than a US Cavalry stronghold. Had it not
been for a Stars and Stripes towering over the dregs, any
passerby might assume as much. Indeed, after years of
abandonment, the rubble fort lies thirstier and more parched
than the land the cavalry has sworn to protect. Over half the
encampment pummels in ruins. Moreover, like forts of its
day in Texas, there are no defensive walls or parapets or
strategic berms; there has never been an attack on any Texas
fort and, as ill-thought-out thinking goes, no need for such
embellishments. Only a handful of dilapidated buildings
serve as protection from nature's elements or anything cruel
crawling out of shadows.

Clearly, what once housed over one hundred fifty
cavalry soldiers this day supports less than one-third that
number. The small company only recently reoccupied the
once-proud battlement. Their mission is to provide escort
protection for mail stages and a small re-supply station
situated on the banks of the creek. This reincarnation of the

fort comes courtesy of a new type of soldier-adventurer. This
time all volunteers guarding West Texas' most bleak outpost
are of African American heritage carrying a proud moniker
'Buffalo Soldier.' Only Captain Frohock and Lieutenant
Frederic Smith, the fort's lone commissioned officer, bear
white faces.

As Frohock continues to scan terrain, he notices
movement a mile upstream along the creek. He watches a
teamster lead twenty horses from the station to a pooled
watering hole. As he observes this sight, one of the horses
stirs spooked and jerk-raises its head. The teamster, likewise,
glances toward a distant commotion and draws his handgun.
Seconds later, wisps of arrows rain upon the man and he
collapses by water's edge. Immediately, ten hostiles swarm
and lasso the teamster and drag his lifeless body into bushes.
The captain watches what appears to be a chieftain
hammering the man's head with a stone mallet with such
force blood explodes into gray shadows with raw crimson
vengeance.

"What you see, suh?" The sergeant asks.

"Death," the Captain answers as wind slaps his neck. He
continues watching a frenzy of hacking but knows better
than to allow emotions to hold sway over tactical rational.
He has seen death by the thousands a few years earlier at
Antietam. One more death viewed through a spyglass means
little. He scans an area farther out for a better assessment,
this time taking a silent headcount of enemy. On a whim, he
checks flatland south for what seems like minutes until his
sergeant reluctantly interrupts.

"What you got now, suh?"

"Four hundred north. Equal amount south. Seven to
eight hundred, total," he replies impassively.

The sergeant shakes his head. "No way our brunettes
gonna survive this."

"They'll survive," Frohock replies, spitting chaw on the
ground and wiping his mouth dry with the back of a glove.
"You didn't fight alongside of 'em at Fort Wagner. I did."
Stirred by the memory, Frohock remounts his horse and

spurs its shallow flanks. The horse leaps down the precipice and skids vertical on hindquarters with caliche and limestone spraying air. Sergeant Sharpe follows. When both men reach the basin the captain un-holsters his revolver and fires off shots in the air. Cursing, he swats his horse with reins and charges in the direction of an unaware fort while shooting on the run. "Maybe they'll heed our warning," he yells over a shoulder to Sergeant Sharpe. "God help 'em if they don't."

Their hope is to reach the encampment before hostiles and find their small detachment of 9th US Cavalry fully deployed for the inevitable onslaught. Sergeant Sharpe unsheathes his Spencer repeating carbine and takes shots at clouds while beseeching a prayer. "Dear Lord, please protect our brave boys," he pleads.

Ten minutes later, the two men ride past an empty parade ground and draw-up to a U-shaped facility presumed to be a livery. The rock and adobe building stretches with twenty or more stalls and over a hundred and fifty mules and horses corralled in its center. Six or seven men have scaled the roof and lay prostrate firing Spencers as arrows whiz by. A few more men fire rounds from behind shutter-styled stall windows. Outside, Frohock twirls his horse three-sixty in tight circles to assess fortifications. Across the grounds, more defensive positions stir. The warning shots have worked, and the men appear fully prepared for an attack. The captain spurs his horse a second time and jumps railing into the corral. Again, Sergeant Sharpe follows. Feverishly, they dismount and run for cover as an arrow strikes Sharpe's horse in the neck.

"Where the hell is Lieutenant Smith?" Frohock barks at a sharpshooter readying a one-eyed aim at a target two hundred yards away. The kneeling blue coat corporal squeezes the trigger and curses after a miss.

"Why do white men always give us shit for weapons?" The corporal replies turning around, not realizing the man standing behind is a captain. "Sorry, suh. I had no idea, suh." He jumps up stiff-legged, shoulders back with chest puffed to formal attention.

Frohock understands the corporal's frustration. Spencer rifles are old hand-me-downs from white troopers refusing to accept black men as equals. Two years earlier, most Buffalo Soldiers were slaves with no station in life. Even well-trained Civil War coloreds were never afforded the army's best equipment, freedmen or not. Inaccurate and of poor quality, a broadside of a barn parked one hundred yards away is poor target practice for a Spencer.

"Corporal, at ease. Cursing is not helping. Now, show me our defensive lines and where the lieutenant is located."

The corporal slides out a Bowie knife. He carves a layout of the encampment in dirt and highlights three locations where he presumes thirty-four men and two women hole-up.

"*Women*? What women?" Frohock presses.

"Why, the Lieutenant's wife and her sister-in-law. They arrived by coach last week. They been helping out. Sewing. Baking. Doin' things women folk do. And we sure glad—"

"Enough, corporal," Captain Frohock interrupts. He dashes to his horse and yanks off a saddlebag. He pulls out his spyglass and returns to the open window to scan buildings, one-by-one, first spotting soldiers and, ultimately, locating two women. He watches the women move from sidewall to sidewall with aprons weighed heavy by cartridges; they are unafraid assisting men reload their weapons. He turns slightly and locates a hostile hoard sweeping in human waves from the north toward the building the women occupy.

"Turn the horses loose," he blurts.

"What's that, suh?"

"You heard me. We need a diversion. Release the damn horses."

The corporal eyes Sergeant Sharpe.

"Do as he say," Sharpe restates.

The corporal inches to the corral gate under cover of roof overhang and throws open railing while waving his hat to shoo mules and pintos and yearlings. Within a minute, all animals have reverted to ancestral instincts and race south toward the Pecos River. A band of savages breaks off on horseback chasing after the released livestock. No doubt, the hostiles approaching from the south will also participate in this scattered roundup. However, the ones to the north and on foot stay. Arrows continue flying.

"Why are they still out there?" The corporal asks.

Frohock knows exactly why. "The Kickapoos want the livestock but the Comancheros want what's over there," he says, eyeing the mess hall where he last spotted women.

Silently, he re-glasses the horizon and movement in the bush toward the creek. Warriors are slowly falling back to regroup. Again, his field of vision sweeps closer in toward the mess hall and the two women scurrying about. As he absorbs these sights, a specter broaches his field of vision and passes between his vantage and the mess hall. He refocuses the spyglass aperture on the thing causing the blur. A young man sprints barefoot along the perimeter of the parade ground oblivious to the siege taking place. The expression on the boy's face is bland and out of touch with the turmoil swirling around him. Watching the lad run, it strikes the captain odd how the hostiles seem indifferent to what should be an easy target. No arrows land within fifty feet of the boy. And the boy moves blithely without care, miraculously unscathed as though invisible.

"Who the hell is that?" Frohock asks, pointing to the distant figure.

"Him?" The corporal responds, peering out the window and shielding his eyes for a better focus. "Good question, suh. None of us really knows. He came with the fort when we arrived in the summer. Well, actually, with the stagecoach station. The teamster man, he say he found the boy when he gots here 'bout a year ago. Just wandering around the place. Living off the land. Barefoot. Crazy as a loon. Half human. Half animal. When he not hunting, he runs. That what he do. Runs."

The captain re-scopes the boy and focuses on the child's appearance. The boy dresses in rags and animal pelts. His hair is un-brushed with matted locks hanging to his shoulders. The lad's face hides dark behind a mask of hair and filth.

"Why haven't they killed him?"

"My guess, suh, is they scouted us days ago. The savages, they probably took note of the boy. Probably saw the women, too. Crazy to us sometimes means sacred to them. They probably think killing a sacred human being brings bad juju."

"Does he have a name?"

"None he plan on sharing. You see, he don't talk. Don't talk at all. Does some work with horses for our teamster but pretty much keeps away from our kind." The corporal sniggered over a recollection. "Like I say, he runs all the time. So, we calls him *Runner*. Teamster man, he say once the boy say something to him in broken English. He say the boy gots some sorta accent like he be German. I can check around. See if we can get the teamster here. He's more familiar than—"

"He's dead. The hostiles killed him out by the creek."

The corporal suddenly becomes less chatty. No words pass for what seems like minutes. He mulls over the teamster, a man he barely knew, then crosses himself and says three Hail Mary's recalling a few meager memories.

All hostility ceases with nightfall's approach. The captain expects the attack to resume in the morning. He knows attempting to put down over eight hundred hostiles will exhaust their supply of ammunition. Worse, he knows what Comancheros do to captives. This battle will be fought to the death and, now, with horses sprung loose, there is no way of relaying a message back to Fort Stockton of their dire predicament. "Sequester the lad, corporal. Sergeant Sharpe, you go with him. Bring him back here and if he doesn't cooperate, use force."

Minutes later, they return with the boy holstered in arms. The boy struggles but proves no match for two able-bodied men. Up close, he appears gaunter and frailer than from a distance. Post-pubescent blonde facial hair drapes chaotically around his smooth adolescent cheeks and the captain guesses the youth's age at no more than sixteen. Worse, the boy's body reeks of adult-sized odor and of improperly tanned pelts and festered cuts and years without a good old-fashioned scrubbing. "Throw him in the horse trough. Clean him up and get that godawful stench off him."

With the cessation of fighting, the fort's survivors slowly congregate outside their buildings and begin shuffling dazed and exhausted towards the livery. Lieutenant Smith leads the contingent of wounded and women, a total of twenty-nine souls, across parade grounds and south to the U-shaped stronghold. Captain Frohock greets them inside the empty corral.

A first assessment of battlefield casualties appears bleak: seven dead or missing and seven more wounded, not counting the teamster and his subordinate. Of the seven wounded, three remain severely hurt and cannot take up arms for tomorrow's fight. The lieutenant's wife, Mary Ann, states she can shoot anything moving within fifty yards and, if the situation arises, she will do her part. The lieutenant vouches for her riflery skill. The other woman, Martha, says she will gladly continue to rearm men. They all agree consolidating their position and limited provisions, especially ammunition, will be the best tactical defense against an inevitable morning onslaught. Besides, the corral's well and new hand pump provide unlimited access to water. If ammunition lasts, they can hang on. One by one, they disband into empty stalls with few words exchanged. Some men overturn wagons along the open side of the U-shaped facility and fortify gaps with boxes and barrels and anything else stopping an arrow. Four men climb rooftop and serve as spotters for movement. The one trained medical corpsman and Martha begin attending to wounded. Nevertheless, the mood, while glum, is also calm and professional. Everyone has a part in defending the fort's remaining citadel and prove both capable and up to task. More importantly, even without words exchanged, even after releasing horses and mules to hostiles, they begin to understand why this fight will not simply go away—*the women.*

Lieutenant Smith and Captain Frohock establish a center stall as their makeshift officer's headquarters. Mary Ann joins them about the time the boy is dragged in wet and naked. Night air already is turning cold and thick and promises to dip into the lower forties. Mary Ann covers the lad with a horse blanket while the corporal outfits him in stable muck overalls and a pair of boots. As horrendous as his overalls appear, the sweet odor of day's old manure-encrusted dungarees smells far better than rancid pelts. The lull allows Mary Ann to sheer the boy's hair while he squirms under the strong arms of Smith and the corporal. A horse brush and comb provide strategic weapons redefining the boy's appearance from that of full animal to half-human. All the while, the boy casts frightened glances at Captain Frohock and the other men like a caged animal about to be devoured by wolves. He has never trusted soldiers and when the 9th invaded his fort six months earlier, he avoided direct contact. This is why he stayed close to the stagecoach station outside the confines of military encampment. In his mind, the only good thing about Fort Lancaster has been the wide-open parade ground and a place to run free without cat's claw and cholla shredding his feet. His only friend, the teamster named Frederick, he heard them say Comancheros killed. Still, friends of my friend do not necessarily make soldiers of the 9th his friend. Soldiers remind him of a past and of men's evil ways. Better to be an animal on the run than human prey to cruel soldiers, he tells himself. It is this sort of cognitive thinking that has kept the lad's mind preoccupied for years and, of course, those fond memories of family and friends and a long-ago home near Comfort on the banks of the Guadalupe.

Pondering these things, the boy watches the captain move closer and lean against stall railing for a better look-see at his appearance. The man lifts his chin, peers into his eyes and smiles. No one has smiled at him in years.

"Son, you look a shit load better," Frohock pipes. "And, frankly, I don't know what you've gone through living out here by yourself or why. But it is quite obvious to me you've been to hell and back. Awful sorry for whatever caused you to be stuck in this cesspool, but I need your help. Hell, we all need your help."

The boy pushes weighted hands off his shoulders. He stands and draws closer.

"You have a name, lad?" The Captain inquires.

There is no response. Everyone can plainly see the boy wants to say something but his mouth freezes attempting to find words.

"It's okay, son. I heard you don't speak. All I need you to do for now is nod your head if you understand what I'm saying. OK?"

The boy responds in the affirmative.

"Good. They say you are called Runner. They say you never tire and have uncanny endurance. Is it true?"

This time the boy hesitates before responding in any fashion. He dislikes being questioned by anyone in authority and grunts with displeasure. The woman, Mary Ann, gently takes his hand and squeezes it encouraging him to respond, once again, in the affirmative. "We need your help," Mary Ann pleads.

The boy has not stood this close to a woman in five years. Yes, he had seen plenty of women, elegant and refined city-bred ladies, but only from a distance when they pause at the station and never in such close quarters and never a woman with such grace. He loses himself in her eyes. He guesses she is no more than five years older and far more experienced in the ways of the world.

"Tell him what we need him to do," Mary Ann says, turning to the captain.

"Son, I know words do not come easily to you. That is not a problem. I have written a letter to my commander. I need you to take it to him. It says we're in trouble and if he doesn't bring a full detachment within two days, we may all be dead. You don't want that on your conscience, do you?"

The lad shakes his head 'No.'

"Good. I take it you know the road to Fort Stockton. That is where I need you to go. I need you to fly like the wind tonight. Can you do that? Take this envelope to Commander James B. Harris at Fort Stockton?"

The boy glances around the room to study everyone's face. He feels uneasy being in close proximity with so many strangers. Worse, he still seethes over their abducting him by brute force and insulting his body with soap and water and clothes and boots. God, how he hates boots. Nevertheless, he is not unsympathetic to their circumstance. While running through the parade ground during the attack, he saw arrows fly and sensed death, yet, at that moment he did not care about these people or about his own demise, for that matter. He had forsaken life years earlier. If one does not value one's own life, how can one empathize with others' plight? For years, he has drawn a protective wall around his emotions to survive in the wilds, alone. Then, these strangers invaded his safe haven with their stagecoach station and reoccupation of the fort. He tried ignoring them. He tried pretending they did not exist. Running kept his mind free of this wayward mob of humanity and with them all the painful memories. Nevertheless, despite his incessant running and attempts to block feelings of empathy, he senses their dread.

When the woman touches him a second time, this time on a shoulder, he turns completely around to face her from only a few inches. He feels her heavy breath and smells her warm body drenched moist with sweat and worry. Her eyes begin to well with tears and he realizes he cannot allow hostiles to defile her.

Unexpectedly, he stabs the envelope and stashes it in a pocket. He turns and makes an about-face canter out of the stall. Captain Frohock chases after him. "Follow the trail to Fort Stockton, son, but don't set foot on it," he warns. "They'll have scouts looking everywhere for a messenger. Keep a hundred yards away. Keep to the bush. Understand?"

The boy nods his head 'Yes.' Of course, he understands. None of this is new to him.

"The trail is long. Over eighty miles long. And treacherous. Be careful. Stay low. Avoid contact."

The boy knows all these things, too. He knows of the route and has seen a map but has never ventured more than a few miles west from the station. For years, he has spied on hostiles moving through his river gorge and knows their habits and mannerisms. He is not about to allow them to turn this adopted home of his into a valley of death. Meekly, he glances at night sky and searches for heaven, God, or anything to guide his way. The western skyline splashes foreboding in pale indigo with daylight all but extinguished. The eastern sky pitches black with a scattering of fresh stars. A three-quarters moon peaks reluctantly from behind the eastern horizon. The weather, while cold, promises to forgive him of his past and provide a clear firmament for his journey. Yes, he tells himself. He can do this thing and this time he will not fail. After all, he has been preparing himself for this day for five years. Life has come full circle and tonight provides hope for redemption. Yanking off his boots, his leathered feet expose cracked and hardened. He tosses the boots at the captain, pounds his chest at the moon, and defies any man to stop him. A few seconds later, he bolts toward the creek and the river and the trail he knows far better than hostiles. Into the night he vanishes, never hearing Captain Frohock's parting words, "God speed, Runner. God speed."

CHAPTER TWO

(August 9, 1862 – 5 years earlier)

They fled the Hill Country of Texas heading west, all sixty-one of them, seeking sanctuary in Mexico. Eventually they would turn east for the Union controlled port of New Orleans. Six days into their beleaguered flight, a wagon train of German refugees closed in on the Nueces River deciding to pitch camp in a prairie next to a dead thicket of live oaks. Two days more and they would reach the Rio Grande and begin life anew; they would be free of threats from men clad in gray uniforms; free to never bear arms in a cause for which they did not believe and forced to swear allegiance to evil. Most free thinkers in Comfort had grown accustomed to Confederates meddling in their affairs. They had grown indifferent to issues of slavery and the growing prospect their young men might become conscripted into a losing war. But not Fritz Tegener's family and his closest friends. The Lutheran Church for years instilled how all people were equal under God regardless of ethnicity. This included black men and those unfortunate among them locked in chains by white masters. These were the very reasons why they left Germany—the oppression, tyranny, inequality. Now, they were confronted, again, with these same indignities in Texas and found themselves fleeing a belief system as foreign to their nature as the shores of Germany had been ten years earlier.

When the rebel detachment rode into their town demanding allegiance to the Confederacy, they stated hell would "freeze over" before they would deny their beliefs. The most adamant ones decided to seek greener pastures where they could raise children without duress and follow their own consciences. Clandestinely, they stole out of town under cover of darkness. Then, word came as they approached the Nueces River. A rebel detachment had tracked them and encircled their position preparing to do battle. Fritz Tegener knew they were outnumbered three-to-one. He knew they could not defend themselves against so many well-trained soldiers. A slaughter would ensue unless they held on until help arrived from the one remaining Union detachment stationed at Fort Lancaster one hundred miles away. As night approached, Fritz turned to his eleven-year-old son, Karl, and explained their circumstances. He told Karl to follow the Nueces and head north to the spot where an abandoned Butterfield Mail Route fords the river and where the trail runs due west to the fort.

And, thus, the boy began his journey in darkness running boot-high through the stream, never suspecting his father's true motivation was not to be rescued but, rather, to see his son spared inevitable carnage. At best, young Karl would not reach the fort for four days. Yet, Fritz knew his son possessed the mettle to accomplish the impossible. The boy was a natural frontiersman who could set traps and fish and hunt game better than any adult. The boy was a survivor. When night arrived, Karl made a sacred promise he would see the task through or die trying.

As Karl sloshed through the river, his boots weighed heavy from knee-high seepage. When daylight arrived, he no longer needed the Nueces for reckoning and climbed an embankment and scaled a nearby hill to view the land north and what appeared to be endless tree covered tors. Skeptically, he wondered how he could ever reach Fort Lancaster in time to save his family and, soon, succumbed to a sinking feeling his task might have been doomed from start. Peering south, he heard crisp cackles of gunfire and knew battle had commenced. Smoke bawled his direction. He glanced north, again, and then at his battered boots. All-night wading in the Nueces ruined his only shoes with August sunshine now threatening to distort leather shrinking about his feet. He yanked off the boots and stood barefoot on limestone with white heals and toes exposed mushed and soggy. With over ninety-five miles to go, he knew his delicate feet could not withstand an excruciating descent barefoot through a vitriol wilderness. He also knew the boots festered worthless.

Few white men, let alone eleven-year-olds, had ever trekked the land north. Comanche and Apache raiders used the untamed wilderness to hide their forays, but his kind never dared venture into what Karl's Mexican friends called "la tierra de nadie (no man's land)." Clearly, no one sane would pursue this journey, this unfathomable task. Moreover, at some defining moment on the hill the lad must have realized his father had sent him on a fool's errand with no possible motivation other than to save him despair. Still, he refused to dishonor his pledge, regardless of intent. "Verdammte Stiefel (Damned Boots)," he muttered, staring at his feet and shaking his fist. Then, he did what anyone his age would have done to solve an impossible dilemma: he took off his shirt, ripped it into strips, and wrapped tatters around his feet. He checked pant pockets. A folding knife and two fishhooks with string neatly tucked away with jerky grabbed before his departure. He took a deep breath and charged down the hill to the north and began running for a fort he had never heard of with an uncompromising hope Union soldiers would come to his aid.

Forty-five miles and two days later Karl located the trail and followed it west for another fifty miles and two days until he stumbled upon Fort Lancaster. By now his feet mangled in a bloody mass and his burnt shoulders and parched mouth cracked from exposure to a relentless sun and heat and thirst. And much to the boy's chagrin, the post lay strewn in shambles and void of life. A weathered Confederate flag masted above the parade ground. Angry at the sight of the flag, he fell to his knees and buried his face in his hands and cried, exhausted by the four-day ordeal. He had failed to save his family from certain death and an inevitable massacre. "What should I do, Dear Lord, what should I do?" He muttered in German.

Minutes later, a lone traveler ambled by in a horse drawn wagon laden with supplies and heading west. An old man stopped long enough to check out the empty fort and the shirtless, barefoot boy who appeared abandonded and forgotten. The traveler dressed in white and the white of his hat and of the horses glistened from a harsh midday sun. The boy pivoted his hand to block the light but had difficulty discerning the figure behind the voice.

"Need a ride?" The man asked, when, in fact, the man should have emphatically stated, "Get in, child. You're much too young to be here by yourself. Come with me."

"No," Karl answered. "Ver are der men? Das Union soldiers?" He asked in broken English.

The old man chuckled. "Hell, son. They all left to go fight a war." He rose from his seat and stood in the wagon and peered around the desolate landscape. "Ironic, ain't it?"

"Vat?"

"This fort. It's supposed to protect people like ye. Now it don't protect shit."

Young Karl slowly deciphered the man's words and, once again, grew angry. He moved to the flagpole and hoisted down the flag, throwing it on the ground. "Hast you matches?" He asked.

The old man reached in a pocket and tossed the boy a tin. "Inside that. There's enough in there to last you a year. Keep 'em." The stranger paused to study the boy's face. "Say, what you reckon on doing?"

At first, Karl did not respond. He pondered the question, not sure if the man meant what he planned to do with the matches or do with his life given his predicament. "Ich be here," he finally uttered, pointing to the ground. "Dist ist my fort now," he said angrily, pounding his chest. He opened the tin and struck a matchhead against a thumbnail, tossing the match on the flag and igniting a tarnished cloth. He watched Stars and Bars disintegrate into ashes with the ashes blown away by a northern breeze. Satisfied he scorched everything Confederate from his life, he turned to ask the traveler a question but by then the old man had vanished.

CHAPTER THREE

(December 26, 1867 – 7:30 PM)

Crawling belly-low to the river, Karl knows Kickapoo warriors will be soaking horses where a freshwater spring slogs into a brackish bight in the Pecos. He also knows better than to cross a spot upstream where scouts sentry for shadows lit by moonlight. Instead, he fords downstream under cover of mesquite scrub and an errant sycamore with octopus limbs collapsing over water. He wades the stream and hikes its bank to a caliche bench, and slides between limestone boulders sheared from a looming cliff towering overhead. He disrobes, tying his muck overalls around his belly, and uses the white of his bare back and torso to camouflage body parts against like-colored stone. Hastily, he scales the cliff's wall until he reaches its crest. He redresses himself as cold air sets in and his body revolts and shivers uncontrollably. He peers over the same ledge Captain Frohock and Sergeant Sharpe stood upon less than four hours earlier and, like those two soldiers, marvels at a bird's eye view of desolation at its best. Even at night under an insipid moon, what makes the land bleak is not the overwhelming absence of humanity as much as the absence of civility. Colorless and barely discernable, he spies his fort's shadow in the distance. To the south, he can make out captured horses and mules corralled haphazardly in a wickiup-styled shelter. Below, he spots three young warriors peering up at him; they easily sight him standing atop the cliff, alone. The three whoop and catcall jeers taunting his manhood. Rather than run, he flashes a two-fisted 'up-yours' gesture he learned as a child, a gesture they surely understand and despise. He loathes savages who devour his wild berries, hunt his jackrabbits and squirrels, and defile his land, and he has tormented them whenever they pass through his valley. Hiding among them, he has tossed rattlesnakes in their midst while they slept. Defiantly, he would defecate upstream as they drank from his river, simply to watch human excrement float by their startled faces. Now, gazing down upon them, he cannot turn and flee but, instead, decides to insult them one more time by raining urine from two hundred feet. When an arrow scorches his head, he spins and hightails west into scrub.

Like all thoughts crossing Karl's mind, rational behavior wavers between lucidity and flights of fancy. Five years of self-imposed isolation have worsened his fragile mental state as does the peyote he has consumed with too much frequency and eagerness. Early on, he watched hostiles set small deliberate fires, drop cacti into embers, and inhale toxic fumes to glimpse visions and demons. Likewise, he mimicked their behavior—stomach flat to the ground, head inches from fire, smoke fanned into his tarnished face to absorb hallucinogenic as though the fumes gave breath to his very life.

Peyote helped him dream of family dancing among stars and moon. It helped him recall their faces. Peyote calmed his troubled soul and left him content. This night, however, adds a new chapter to his vision quest and forces him to face his demons head-on. It forces him to stay focused long enough to see innocent lives saved. No more failures. No more death. No more peyote.

And so, convinced of the righteousness of this mission, he begins running toward Fort Stockton. He adroitly slides between withered winter brush and cactus; he leaps over prickly pear and cat's claw and rocks and anything potentially besmirching his experienced weathered feet. Guided by moonlight and a clear night sky, he runs serpentine along a worn Butterfield trail that resembles an unfurled gray ribbon ever shrinking westward into darkness.

Run Karl, run, his mind spins. Do not look back. Forget the savages and keep your word to the captain. A person's word is all a person has in the wilderness. A person's word is everything. Do not fail. Run, Karl, run.

In a way, he finds nightfall exhilarating. He has experienced the same feelings whenever he runs for extended lengths of time—euphoria, happiness, contentment. Running is more than a diversion. It is catharsis. Running clears his mind and stifles bad memories. Sometimes when he runs, he thinks about what he might do if he ever should leave his valley and the fort that has so faithfully guarded his emotions. Years earlier, his father wanted him to learn the craft of stonemason. "German masons are the best," his father told him, "but you can do anything you want, Karl. This is America where even a poor German Schweinebauer (pig farmer) can own his own land. America is a bountiful country where no one bows to a king. Where all men are equal under God. This place is a land of milk and honey."

He believed most everything his father extolled in those days. And why not? When his mother died giving birth to his sister, his father became the only adult to provide nurturing. His father taught him the craft of survival, of building fires and hunting small game by simply setting traps. They fished together. They played together. His father taught him chess and not merely the mechanics of the game but also skills that accompany well-thought-out strategy. "You must always think at least two moves ahead, Karl," his father lectured. "Without fore-thinking two moves, you will lose in life." Why would he not believe the man's words?

Thus, running at night through withered Texas bush and leaping over obstacles, Karl plans two moves ahead of what he might do if he should ever leave his Pecos valley. Maybe I will become a soldier, he tells himself. I will guard innocents and protect people from evil men and vermin and savages who take pleasure in torture and death. Maybe this Commander Harris will hire me in Fort Stockton. Maybe I can be their scout and teach them what I have learned. Preoccupied on these cursory thoughts, he fails to see three Comancheros ahead and a stone mallet swinging wildly into his chest and knocking him unconscious.

CHAPTER FOUR

(December 27, 1867 – 4:00 AM)

His name is No-ko-aht. He is chief of the Kickapoo band
plundering Texas. His ultimate destination is Mexico,
southwest of Piedras Negras. To journey there, his people
need horses to carry warriors and mules to transport food,
materials, and women with children. This is his third foray
through the Pecos wilderness from Kansas. His previous two
passed by an abandoned Fort Lancaster. Not this time. This
time the fort breathes life, much to his liking. His braves
have bragged how they can steal livestock from ill-equipped
and outnumbered Buffalo Soldiers no one respects, not even
white soldiers. For days, they have scouted a poorly
defended fort. They believed Buffalo Soldiers could be
overwhelmed with a surprise attack. That is, until the
yellow-leg captain rode out of the west and warned the fort.
Now, faced with over twenty Kickapoo warrior dead on the
first day's attack, he second-guesses this strategy.

The chief has collaborated with a Comanchero leader, a
mugwump known by the name Mecina. The Comanchero
people he does not care for. They are crude half-breeds with
inferior Mestizo and Anglo bloodlines and practice barbaric
Comanche ways. The Comanche have never shown respect
for his god nor the good Kickapoo human beings, his
ancestors, who once roamed earth. Worse, they do not speak
the noble Algonquian tongue. His own tribe has wandered
farther and farther south to avoid Americans and, most
recently, ruthless hordes of Comanche. Two weeks earlier, a
ragtag band of Comancheros began accompanying his
people, and living off Kickapoo exploits. He would prefer to
be rid of them before reaching Mexico.

No-ko-aht's true destination is still over one hundred
miles south. This infertile land they are passing through in
Texas is filled with scat and cacti and inferior Comancheros,
he tells himself. He hates this land. He hates yellow-leg

cavalry soldiers and white men and, today, black men posing as yellow-leg white men. The chieftain, Mecina, he barely tolerates but does so to maintain an uneasy alliance. His great Kickapoo tribe has provided nearly seven hundred warriors on this costly ill-informed raid. By comparison, Mecina's warriors number less than twenty—barely enough to earn respect, and they have lost no men. These two tribes have different objectives: the Kickapoos require livestock to survive; the Comancheros crave white woman for trade as barter.

It is when No-ko-aht hears of the capture of the boy-spirit, he and Mecina and Mecina's informant ride west, alone, out of the Pecos Gorge and follow a trail for five miles until two Comanchero braves are located celebrating their capture of the crazed animal-boy whom they spotted standing on the cliff. For three days, the Kickapoo chief has been watching this same lad from afar and believes the white waif possesses special powers. Upon inspection of the boy's lifeless body, No-ko-aht states someone has cleaned the lad, but it is, nevertheless, the same spirit who dwells inside the mortal and the spirit is strong with this one. In a sense, he reveres the boy and tells Mecina's young warriors how powerful ghosts guard the lad's soul. Anyone who harms the boy will infuriate He-That-Hears-All and destruction will rain upon all evildoers.

Mecina disagrees and believes the lad is nothing more than a crazed human, a lunatic messenger, sent to summon cavalry stationed at Fort Stockton. The two chieftains argue. While the boy remains unconscious on the ground, Mecina rifles the boy's muck overalls and discovers an envelope stashed in a pocket. He tears it open and reads English words his Mormon teacher taught him on the reservation he grew up on as a child. He translates English into illiterate sounding Algonquian but No-ko-aht refuses to listen, grabs the letter, and shreds it, throwing it in Mecina's face.

The boy stirs awake by this heated exchange. Earlier, when his abductors drug his lifeless body out of the bush, they tossed him untied in a tumbled heap on the trail. Rather than kill him outright, they thought better of it and one of the three raced back to camp to inform Mecina of their prize. Now, as the boy regains his wits, he lies limp and contorted on his back slowly regaining composure. Without drawing attention to himself, he pats his bruised chest where a mallet landed, and he guesses at least one broken rib is causing the severe pain he is experiencing. The blow must have knocked wind out of him and rendered him unconscious. Taking slow measured breaths, he moans softly gazing at night sky and a three-quarters moon and wonders why he is still alive. He fears he has lost precious time, perhaps hours, on his westward flight. Blinking and re-blinking to clear his vision, he glances right and in the direction of Fort Stockton. Standing below, three young Comanchero warriors are preoccupied laughing and chattering while urinating on his feet. Unbeknownst to them, the boy is plotting an escape. These savages are not much older than me, he rationalizes— a year at most. They appear to be the same three sighted earlier at the cliff's base. Insulted by his show of disrespect, they must have chased after him on horseback and swung around blindsiding him. Infuriated with their antics, the boy jumps to his feet and shoves one of them to the ground. Startled by his sudden reanimation, one of the standing braves draws a knife; the other threatens a familiar stone mallet. The brave on the ground slinks toward Mecina. Before the two threatening harm can do damage, No-ko-aht steps in between them all. Eyes draw to the noble leader. How dare they defile this sacred spirit? He asks angrily, pointing to the boy. With everyone distracted by the chief, the boy takes off running west on the trail.

No-ko-aht ignores the boy's flight and admonishes the Comanchero warriors and their leader, Mecina. He explains the boy is the same child he has seen in his vision-dreams— the boy is the spirit who fled demons in gray coats many years before but stumbled in his journey. Anyone who survives this desolate scat-land, isolated and alone, deserves their respect, he proclaims. More importantly, he adds, the boy has great power. To harm the boy will bring misfortune

to all. Besides, he argues, by the time the boy reaches Fort
Stockton they will have already taken the Buffalo Soldiers'
fort. "Calle sune kata il pasha (Let him run for no reason),"
he says.

Mecina, again, disagrees. The Comanchero chieftain
does not believe in Kickapoo superstitions let alone peyote
visions-quests. "If this boy is protected by a powerful spirit,"
he argues, "let us hunt him like a dog. He is already loose
and running fast as chupacabra. Let us see if your vision is
greater than mighty Comanchero hunters."

No-ka-aht is outnumbered four to one and realizes to
keep the alliance together he must appease Mecina.

"Net inenia ut malewi ke Kisseowa hahbii (No man can
undo what God plans)," he sneers. "If you are true hunters,"
he taunts, "go ahead. Hunt the boy but only on foot. Any fool
can catch a child on a horse. Prove your manhood. Go. Run
after him. See if you can catch him," he baits. He warns the
Comancheros if they do pursue the runner, the runner will
defeat them. He has seen the boy with his own eyes, and no
one can stop him—not white men in gray uniforms or
tagalong Comanchero warriors. "Vaya ala muchacho," he
says, using what few Spanish words he knows. "If you catch
him, bring me his scalp and my people will honor you with
this last raid on the fort. If you fail, my tribe will move on
without you. You will have to take white women on your
own."

The young braves pound their chests and whoop and
shout. They accept the challenge. "We will see which of us
are real men," they say. "Old women Kickapoo or brave
Comancheros." That said, they turn and chase after the boy.

Mecina watches his warriors vanish into darkness on
foot. It occurs to him the old chief has outfoxed him.
Certainly, the boy cannot survive this night, he tries assuring
himself. But the more he thinks on the possibility, the more
he realizes how the slimmest of chances to fail means the
white women and bounty they could fetch is put at great risk.
His band of warriors needs these women not only for their
pleasure but also for rifles they can barter. He turns to face

No-ko-aht and scoffs. "I will make sure your boy-spirit dies a painful death," he states. "When I do, all your visions will cease, old man, and your Kickapoo men will help us take the fort." He turns west and takes off on foot running, yelping and chasing after his young warriors.

When Karl reaches high ground above a dry estuary, he turns around at loss as to why no one is following him. Where are they? He wonders. For now, he has a one-hundred-yard head start with no pursuers, at least pursuers on horseback. He dreads horse-warriors knowing they will swiftly outmaneuver him; they will cover far more ground than he can on foot. As he peers through a dim moonlit landscape, he discerns an old chief arguing with another man, presumably another chieftain, as his three young assailants listen to the exchange of words. He hears the chief's angry voice echo off a nearby hill. As he watches, the three young warriors begin to holler and whoop with exaggerated bravado. Their shadows abruptly take off on foot moving his direction. They spread fifty or more feet apart in a V-formation, meticulously forging rocks and a thicket of cactus to retrace his tracks, but they are not on a full out-and-out run. The three are attempting to flush him out slowly and methodically and move clumsily and noisily with taunts. It is the moment Karl realizes his capture and anticipated execution have turned into a cat and mouse game—they are hunters and he the hunted. He takes solace horses are not involved and in the fact his skill at this game, in all likelihood, exceeds theirs but he must stay two moves ahead of the hunters—always two moves ahead to survive three cats against one mouse. They know his ultimate endgame, Fort Stockton. Therefore, it serves no purpose to crisscross the trail and serpentine in and out of scrub brush as Captain Frohock asked. Tracking him is moot given his obvious destination. Besides, snaking back and forth around the trail will only cause him to lose valuable time. His best hope is to stick to the route and, where it takes wide exaggerated turns, improvise with shortcuts in direct beelines through brush. I will use speed and cover of night to my advantage, Karl tells himself. With sunrise he will surely become easier to spot and a far more visible prey. His best strategy is to distance himself from the hunters as much as possible before darkness dissipates.

There is also an angry side to Karl. If he runs without putting up a fight, it shows cowardice. He ran once before, and it served no purpose—no lives were saved. These warriors chasing after him he already loathes. They are no more adroit at this game of survival than he. Certainly, they will expect him to flee like a frightened jackrabbit and when that happens, they will pounce, pulverizing him first with arrows, then knives and, ultimately, an executioner's stone mallet. His counterintuitive nature tells him to do the opposite of what they expect: go on the attack. Maybe slowing them down, having them worry he may cause as much physical carnage as they might cause him will slow their arrogant hunter's pursuit. Yes. That is exactly what I will do, he rationalizes. I will hurt them one-by-one as I retreat to Fort Stockton.

Turning for any source of weaponry, he spies a cholla spine. Its barbs are winter hard and two inches long and the spine is nearly three feet in length. He rips a cloth leg off his muck overalls below the knee and layers stiff denim around and around the cactus. He snaps the plant at its base and brandishes it two-handed. He slides behind a boulder as a warrior approaches on foot and when his adversary speeds by, he whistles. Startled, the Comanchero turns and drops his mallet. The boy swings and bats his adversary in the face. A scream pierces a still night air. The two other warriors dash to their friend's aid only to find a massive tree cholla embedded in bloodied eyes. Their comrade withers in pain, blinded. Meanwhile, Karl sprints west following the trail and brandishes a new stone mallet. He grins quite pleased with himself. There is one less savage to slow him down.

This is not the first time Karl has run with his friend, the moon, over a shoulder. When he first arrived at an abandoned Fort Lancaster, he discovered night provided the best time to set traps and catch game. Typically, he hunted rock squirrels and soon discovered coyotes appreciated his creative efforts, destroying his wooden Fallenkäfig (caged traps) and eating his captive squirrels while he slept. That mistake only happened one time. After that incident, he began guarding cages from coyotes by sleeping in the wilderness. Now, running at night under a three-quarters moon, he spots a lone coyote chasing after him. It is as though the creature is taunting him by reversing the food chain pecking order. Or is the animal sensing captured game awaiting wherever the boy bounds? Keep running, Karl tells himself. Don't look back. Don't look at the coyote. Keep running. Keep running. Keep running.

CHAPTER FIVE

(December 27, 1867 – 7:10 AM)

Sunrise arrives in West Texas early—*perhaps, too early*. Watching terrain transform from moonscape to sunlit landscape, Karl guesses he has run for over two hours, meaning he has covered at least twenty miles or one-fourth the distance to Fort Stockton. He continually glances over a shoulder and spots none of his pursuers. Could it be he has outpaced them this early in the game? He questions. His feet have not buckled under despite the fact he has never run for this length of time or so far and so blindly in darkness. The adrenalin high he is experiencing is waning and he knows whatever delusional feelings of invincibility he is sensing will soon implode. It has been nearly twelve hours since he last drank water, and his mouth is dry and spiraling dryer by the minute. Ahead he spies a rare watering hole. He has heard stagecoach drivers refer to the spring as "the devil's tank." It may well be his last opportunity to soak his feet and rest before Comancheros appear over the horizon. While he hopes they have given up this game of cat and mouse, he knows from their behavior they are too stubborn to forego this twisted rite of passage. He is confident he can keep both warriors at bay simply by running a fast pace but is unaware their leader, Mecina, has joined them in the hunt— unknowingly, once again the odds are three against one with the new member an experienced killer.

Oddly, the same coyote has followed him the entire distance and skirts around him sprinting to water's edge. By the time he settles to his side of the pool, the coyote has set up camp on the other side. Karl ignores the animal and falls to his knees gulping handfuls of water until his stomach brims and his thirst satisfied. He pivots to dip his burning feet in the pool and immediately emits a deep sigh from the relief water provides. A minute gives way to five, then ten. He realizes if he stays any longer, he might fall asleep or, worse, be captured. Having almost forgotten the coyote, he decides to study it out of curiosity. Sitting passively, the coyote stares back seemingly content in this farcical faceoff. The boy notices for the first time the animal's coat is both winter thick and pure white. White is a rare color for a coyote in Texas. White coats on animals usually accompany snowfalls but this corner of Texas rarely experiences snow. The boy guesses his coyote friend is either a rarity or an albino or something incredibly special. Looking back on his summer trapping exploits, he feels somewhat guilty, now, for not sharing squirrel meat with the lonesome fellow. Then again, he muses, maybe his new friend sees him as one giant tasty squirrel. Suddenly, the coyote's head pivots to glimpse past the boy and toward the trail. Karl's uninvited guests, the Comancheros, must be arriving. The boy stands and bends down to grab his new mallet. An arrow whizzes overhead. His pursuers are close. Too close. He spins and takes off west in a full sprint, this time aiming for a distant hill and cover. The coyote follows.

Run, Karl, run, he coaxes himself. You are faster than these Comanchero savages. You are smarter. You know this land better than they do. Run, Karl, run.

High ground has many tactical advantages. It can provide a commanding view of one's approaching enemy. It can force an opponent to expend energy on difficult terrain with a steep ascent; it can weaken battle readiness and hinder hand-to-hand combat capability. Equally important, high ground can offer a defender shelter against arrows, lances, and bullets. In this case, Karl's high ground provides a perfect roost to locate Comancheros on the attack and to plan a defense. He knows moccasin-clad warriors' feet can easily outlast his own on the remaining sixty-mile run to Fort Stockton. His feet have endured amazingly well, all things considered, but the ability to continue running at the pace set earlier simply cannot be sustained. With this stark revelation, Karl decides it best to hold his high ground and defend himself with his only weapon, the mallet.

His hill sweeps skyward, rising to a wide mesa-like peak. Atop the peak, huge granite boulders scatter in two rows; the trail passes in between. The boy scales the first boulder closest to the hill's eastern front and peers down from fifteen feet. Anyone following the trail must funnel past his vantage before descending the other side. The only option for a passerby is to circumvent the hill altogether and the boy suspects his pursuers will never do that—too much time could be lost. No, he assures himself. They will surely move through this gap and when they do, I will kill them.

Watching from this vantage, Karl locates both braves run clumsily to the left of the weathered trail meandering topside Their eyes hover down, not up, for fear of slipping on caliche; they stumble circumventing clumps of prickly pears but continue running and climbing the trail. Both appear to be leerier of snakes than young German boys who are far more venomous. The second warrior, a bowman, carries a quiver over a shoulder and a readied arrow in his bow; the one leading the charge brandishes a knife.

As the bowman passes underneath, Karl leaps crashing on top of the Comanchero and hammers a crushing blow to the lad's head. The second warrior turns and lunges at the boy and comes up short with the knife. Swinging wildly upward, Karl retaliates and makes contact with the warrior's chin and drives teeth with jawbone through the skull. Both young braves sprawl convulsing next to each other, dead, in pools of blood. The battle has ended as quickly as it began. Given the consequences of failure, the boy feels no remorse whatsoever and emits a sigh of satisfaction. The game is over. Finally, over.

Eyeing moccasins, Karl kneels beside the bowman and steals shoes. He slides soft leather around his own feet and admires the feel. Suddenly, a hand seizes the boy by the back of the neck, lifts him and throws him hard against a boulder. The boy crumples. His mallet flies and lodges in a crevice. Mecina jumps on top and pins Karl underneath with a chokehold. The chieftain glances back at his two young warriors mangled beyond recognition and rages for revenge.

He threatens to disembowel the boy but thinks of a more eternal solution. "Tomare' sus ojos para que no puedes ver en el cielo (I will take your eyes, so you are blind in heaven)," he says in Spanish while wielding a pointy steel blade inches from the boy's face. "Entones, te martare' (Then, I will kill you)." Karl squirms under Mecina's weight and screams.

No one knows for certain why at that precise moment a feral white coyote sprung from shadows and went on a rampage. When the animal heard cries of help, perhaps, it was a parental instinct to protect a child causing the creature to come to the boy's aid. In any case, the coyote charged Mecina from behind and ripped the man's throat. After a second lunge, Mecina falls backward on ground in shock with blood gushing from an artery. The second effort provides the boy enough time to dislodge the knife from Mecina's hand and thrust it into the chieftain's heart.

Karl stands and surveys three lifeless bodies and realizes there will be no more impediments slowing his quest to reach Fort Stockton. Only his own faltering endurance can doom this mission. Once again, he takes off running but this time at a slower, steadier pace, donning new moccasins and without a weighty mallet. Coming off the hill to flatter land, he repeatedly calls out to the white coyote, but the creature has disappeared.

When the sun reaches its midday zenith and Mecina has not returned with the boy's scalp, No-ko-aht instructs his tribe to gather stolen livestock and begin the march south. A handful of Comanchero warriors want the Kickapoo to help them attack the fort and take women but the wise chief refuses. "Come with us," he tells them. "Forget the white women. Death will haunt you seeking battle by yourselves. You can live off the glory of the great Kickapoo nation and feed you bellies." With only fifteen warriors remaining, their new chieftain acquiesces to the offer and within an hour all hostiles have moved south following the Pecos River on their way to Mexico. The survivors at Fort Lancaster are, at last, safe.

By sundown, Karl stumbles dehydrated and disoriented along the Butterfield trail. He is fatigued and losing hope with Fort Stockton nowhere in sight. Exhausted, he falls to his knees parched from thirst and fears he has failed. His stolen moccasins are shredded and, once again, his battered feet expose bloodied. He can barely walk. He collapses, slamming hard into dirt, only to roll over on his back and stare at sky wondering why God has forsaken him on this second lifesaving mission. He shakes his fist at a passing cloud, unable to find solace in today's tortuous ordeal. Up ahead and from over the next hill a rumbling sound perks his attention. The noise grows louder moving his direction. He turns to see what is causing the stir and spies a wagon pulled by a team of white horses trotting in-line with the setting sun. The sun's glare pales insignificant compared to the white of the horses and the old man driving them east. Karl shields his eyes.

"Howdy," the voice calls out. "You lost, again?"

The boy nods his head 'Yes.'

"Well, if it's Fort Stockton ye seek, it's just over the hill. Can't miss it."

Karl stands and stretches on tiptoes, turning away from the wagon master to peer over the crest.

"That's right, son. You can't miss it," the old man adds. "Why, this old trail will always lead ye home. Trust me."

Then something happened that, years later, Karl could never explain. After the old man shouts a giddy-up, the team of horses and the wagon rumble by the boy in a ghostly blur. "You know," the voice calls out, "everyone back home is sure proud of ye."

By the time Karl turns to thank the wagon master for the kind words, the man and his horses have vanished.

Twenty minutes later Karl hobbles past a sentry at Fort Stockton. The sight of the boy tattered and limping with bloodied feet causes uproar and everyone bivouacked rushes outside their living quarters curious about their visitor. Commander Harris is dispatched and rushes with the fort's doctor to talk with a person he assumes to be a lone survivor of an Indian raid. Recognizing the commander as the lead officer, the boy reaches in a pocket to present the letter written by Captain Frohock. Of course, no one knows the Kickapoo are no longer a threat to Fort Lancaster, including young Karl, but the boy frets, anyway, because the letter entrusted to him is nowhere to be found.

"What is it, lad?" Commander Harris asks, baffled. "Talk to me."

The boy's face contorts attempting to say something, anything. He knows that if he does not disclose the dire situation at Fort Lancaster, an impending second wave attack by hostiles will wipe out remaining survivors. His face twists painfully searching for words. You must tell this man what is happening, he mulls. You must express yourself or everyone will die. As frustration peaks, so does Karl's anger until anger gives sway to words. "Der savages attack Fort Lancaster," he bursts. "Captain Frohock needs help."

Commander Harris turns to his second-in-command and orders troops saddle-up and prepare to ride all night. They will depart within thirty minutes. The second-in-command salutes and twirls an about-face; a bugler blows to arms and the entire detachment scatters to a drill they know all-to-well.

Harris wraps an arm around Karl's shoulder and helps the boy limp to his officer's residence. "Come, lad. Mrs. Harris will make you a fine supper. You deserve it. Looks like you haven't eaten in days."

When they reach the front porch, Karl's exhaustion overwhelms his emotions, and he erupts bawling and buries his head in the commander's shoulder. Harris lifts the boy's chin. "There, there, lad. You've done well today. You've saved a great many souls." Then, as an afterthought, the commander asks an inevitable question. "Do you have any kin we can notify?"

"Nein. All dead."

The commander expresses his regrets and realizes Karl is an orphan with no home. "And what name do you go by, lad?"

Wiping away tears, the boy steps back to look Commander Harris in the eyes. He stands tall throwing back his shoulders. "Mein name ist *Runner*," he states proudly.

"Well, Runner, we could use someone like you here. Would you like to stay? You can put up quarters with Mrs. Harris and me. We have no children. How does that sound?"

The boy smiles. He likes the sound of it. He likes it a great deal.

CHAPTER SIX

(July 1, 1898 – 31 years later – San Juan Heights, Cuba)

Six hundred men of the 10th Cavalry spread wide in a shallow trench at the base of a hill with bayonets readied. Their mission is to assault the left flank of San Juan Hill and support white counterparts attempting to take high ground from Spanish infantry slowly shredding American troops with gunfire and shrapnel. Like most well-intentioned strategies, this one fell apart earlier in the day with word their horses failed to be unloaded on Cuban docks. Undaunted, the Buffalo Soldiers said they could attack on foot, anyway, and were far better fighters than regular infantry battalions, or so they bragged. Their commander is a seasoned cavalry officer, a West Point graduate named Runner. He served with distinction during the Indian Wars and he is credited with rounding up renegade Apache tribes in Arizona ten years earlier. His exploits have not only won him national distinction but also medals and commendations. At age forty-seven, he is considered young for a full bird Colonel. When this war ends, his next promotion is within sight. His soldiers revere him because he takes pride in leading men of color and says he will gladly lay down his life for any one of them.

As the time approaches to charge the hill, Colonel Karl 'Runner' Tegener senses apprehension in his troops' faces and, now, paces in front of them in an open field. Posing as an easy enemy target, Colonel Tegener cannot deny his men one last rallying cry. Without their horses, the cavalry soldiers have been second-guessing their ability to win this fight. As he speaks, bullets streak by his head; shells explode less than one hundred feet behind his back. He ignores these ominous rites of wartime and struts in front of his men and shouts words of encouragement. He tells them he is proud of them all—how there are no better soldiers than the fighting men of the 10th. "Good soldiers", he says, "may need horses to seek greatness. But you are the men of the 10th. You are already great." He also tells his soldiers he would never ask them to do anything he, himself, would never do. Then, with an air of confidence, he draws his saber, points it skyward and thrusts it at a passing cloud. With the other hand, he brandishes a revolver and aims it at the enemy. He calls out to his color-bearer, a young private, to stand next to him with the flag and the two of them, together, challenge six hundred men to stay up with them as they run and take the hill. "Follow me, men," he yells, waving them forward.

One of the soldiers hollers, "But, sir, you have no boots. You're barefoot."

Runner smiles at the man and casts a wink. "It is quite all right, son," he hollers back. "Barefoot is the way I came into this world and it shall also be the way I go out." He pounds his chest, bellies an Indian whoop call, and yells the word *charge*. Six hundred Buffalo Soldiers mimic his whoop and follow him up the hill.

<u>COLETTE AND COLE</u>

For Candy

COLETTE and COLE

CHAPTER ONE

Wasn't it Frederick Nietzsche who once said, "One cannot fully appreciate life until one contemplates suicide"? Those words never rang truer than a month past my high school graduation. I had just been accepted into Yale. My eighteenth birthday loomed four weeks away. And it was a glorious time to be alive in Peru, Indiana. So much promise stood before me and, yet, if anything could have gone wrong, then it surely happened during that fateful summer of 2015. It all began to unravel a few months earlier, in February, when my parents perished in a horrific airplane accident. Like most unexpected tragedies, their deaths caught me completely off guard. Overwhelmed might me a more apropos way of describing my emotions at the time.

As had been the custom, my father's company provided private charters whenever he visited any number of corporate factories scattered around the world and, like most of those international business trips, my mother accompanied him. Years earlier, Father volunteered to take on the family enterprise after my grandfather passed away. No one else in the extended trust fund family wanted to work for a living let alone manage a demanding business. That left Father to contend with a faltering company in the hope of turning it around. Fortunately, for all my family ne'er-do-wells, he came highly qualified and ambitious and our struggling family empire soon reversed course. Within five years of assuming the helm, Father had quadrupled sales of a stodgy shoe line into the hottest athletic clothier in the world. Profits skyrocketed and our publicly traded stock ventured into record territory. Father built factories in Mexico and Vietnam and, yes, Indiana, and never thought twice about leaving the business. Naturally, with so much success, he pictured himself running the business forever and ever. And it was this sort of cavalier invincibility, which left his estate so ill-prepared to handle his and my mother's abrupt departure. It left me, my parents' only child, lonely and dangling precipitously close to a complete nervous breakdown.

Please call me Colette. I suppose you're thinking my French name is a tad eccentric for a Midwestern girl born into a Generation Z era. I mean, who nowadays names their American child Colette? Father said the name seemed fitting since I was conceived in the village of Corbie in France while he and Mother motored around the countryside honeymooning. Corbie, you see, is the birthplace of Saint Colette. Trust me. I am no saint, but my parents said the town and the iconic woman cast a spell on them and they thought it only fitting to name me after her.

Shortly after my parent's death and not being especially close to any of my parents' family, I declared myself legally emancipated. This was fairly easy to do because I was of age, seventeen, and had amassed a personal wealth eclipsing three hundred fifty thousand dollars, most of it invested in college savings. Money, as I discovered, can buy a great many things quickly including our local district judge's ruling in a record thirty-minute hearing. This left me financially independent to await the arrival of my eighteenth birthday on July 1, and the planned reading of my parent's Last Will and Testament. I presumed the full inheritance of over one hundred fifty million dollars, including company preferred stock, would be turned over to me on my eighteenth birthday. I also assumed I would take over the company once I completed studies at Yale. Given my situation, there was no way I was going to leave Peru (pronounced Pee-roo) in the middle of my last high school semester to live with relatives I neither knew nor cared about. No, I remained a PHS fighting Tiger through and through. Case closed. And, more importantly, I had a serious boyfriend—Conrad.

Most people who knew Conrad and me said it would never work. "He's a dumb jock," they said. "You're the brilliant nerdy heiress to the Thomas family fortune. You two have nothing in common. Absolutely nothing." Of course, *they* were right. It was during our prom dance when Conrad announced he was romantically involved with a precocious junior cheerleader. I remember my heart sinking to a new low and asking Conrad, "Why?" to which he shrugged his shoulders and coldly stated, "You're not fun anymore. All you do is mope." No kidding, Conrad. As if this wasn't enough of a blow, shortly thereafter, my father's attorney and company CFO, Arthur Metcalf, telephoned me. "We have a problem," he said. "I need to speak privately with you."

Apparently, I wasn't the only heir to the family fortune. According to my parent's will, a will written seventeen years earlier and never updated, when I turned eighteen and upon their deaths, I would inherit all their assets and share the wealth equally with siblings. But I had no siblings. After a third miscarriage, my parents gave up on the idea. Bottom line, I thought I would be the sole beneficiary. As it turned out, however, years before Mother, Father had unwittingly sired a child while attending Notre Dame. I use the word 'unwittingly' because Father never knew about the 'love child.' The woman, on the other hand, must have known Father did not love her and their encounter merely a one-night stand. So, she abruptly vanished in the night and returned to her hometown of Keokuk, Iowa. My understanding is the woman never divulged the sperm donor's identity until she discovered news of Father's untimely demise and the size of his estate. I can only guess it was the same moment when she revealed her long-kept secret to their daughter, Jennifer, who by age twenty-six had become a clever lawyer with a specialty in (wait for it) *estate planning*. Indeed, Jennifer possessed all the earmarks of an unscrupulous attorney—shrewd, shifty, deceitful, and bawdy. Did I mention Jennifer financed her way through Drake Law School as a topless dancer working for tips? Discovering all of this, I seethed angry over a situation for which I had no control. Who was this opportunistic stranger worming her way into the family business and competing with me, the legitimate child, for corporate leadership? Worse, this long-lost half-sister parlayed older, wiser, and far better equipped to fight for the Thomas estate. Bottom line: *I was doomed.*

Weighed heavily by these revelations and being seventeen and hormonally unhinged, my emotions sank to a new low: deceased parents, no family support, no boyfriend, and a long-lost sibling destined to consume my inheritance. Understandably, I was unable to cope with so many disastrous events occurring simultaneously, and I quickly spiraled into a dark abyss. Under the spell of this deep depression, I resolved to throw myself into the Wabash River and end my life. I remember writing a parting letter to Conrad and sealing it in a Ziploc bag, stashing it inside my Dolce & Gabbana jeans pocket, and hoping when they found my body floating downstream to the Ohio River the letter would survive. I hoped Conrad and his little girl cheerleader made each other miserable until death due them part. And in the midst of this turmoil, I recalled an abandoned trestle bridge five miles upstream from Peru; the bridge made the perfect lair for my dramatic swan song.

That afternoon as I straddled rotted railroad ties to the bridge's center span, rain began pouring in sheets with thunder rattling one-hundred-year-old iron girders. I thought the bridge might collapse before I could fling myself over railing. Inching my way to a guard rail, I remember throwing a leg over a rusted pipe and preparing for a leap into churning water. As I readied to take the plunge, a loud crack and blinding flash threw me back and onto splintered railroad ties. I remember sensing death but not really caring because for the first time in months I no longer felt sad or alone. And, as I drifted away, unconscious, a strange mix of bells and music and boisterous revelry awaited me in a dreamland filled with debaucherously happy people dressed in eighteenth century garb and quaffing endless gin martinis. *Gin martinis?* Who drinks gin martinis anymore?

"So, we finally meet," the voice eked, awakening me from my stupor. "I've been waiting for you, Collette Thomas, *Sweetie.*"

I remember being totally confused and at loss for words. This was not Indiana anymore. Everything felt like one of those old-time black and white movies. "Who, who are you?" I stammered.

"What? You don't recognize me?" He countered, spinning around and around to provide a better glimpse of his elegant costume.

Are you George Washington? I thought.

"Washington? Heavens no. I prefer the look of the Marques de Lafayette, if it's alright with you," he replied disappointedly.

"Can you read my mind?" I asked, baffled by his spontaneity.

"Of course, I can. Where we are, Sweetie, mouths only serve one purpose—*to sing.*"

At this point I wasn't quite sure what to say and was afraid to vocalize the most basic of questions, especially since he clearly read thoughts. It was all very disturbing.

"You're thinking, 'Where am I?'" He smiled, preempting my next question. "We're exactly where we're supposed to be. Well, technically, we're at my little palace, Ca' Rezonnico, in Venice. And if everything worked out the way I hoped, it's the year 1927 and Linda and I are throwing the most marvelous party of all time, a French eighteenth century extravaganza. So, how old do I look? Divinely young and handsome? Come on, guess my age." He asked seeking my flattery.

I remember starring at his saucer-puppy eyes and handsome face and well-coiffured hair. His smile put me at ease, and I responded as though we had known each other for a lifetime. "Thirty. Thirty-two at most," I responded.

He smiled vainly. "Now, ain't that swell. It means I still have both legs and I'm once more healthy, wealthy, and wise." He one-eye winked. "So, Sweetie, how are things in old Pee-roo?"

"Things could be better. A whole lot better." I answered. And just who is this man? I wondered. He looks familiar. Am I dead? Is he like my hero, Ciri, in Witcher 3? Is he my guardian?

"Obviously, you have a million questions," he stated, no doubt reading all of my unexpressed feelings. "Here. Have a virgin martini. I made this one especially for you. My non-alcoholic versions are quite heavenly, don't ye know."

As I one-handed the drink, he seized my free hand and dragged me to a baby grand piano. He patted the bench and asked me to sit next to him.

"My name is Cole. You wanted to know if you are dead and the answer is—*beats me.*" He giggled. "Time will tell. Time always is the determining factor when it comes to death. For now, let's just say you're in a special place between heaven and hell—"

"Purgatory?"

"Why, yes. Very perceptive. You see, I'm stuck here. I became a non-believer and have nowhere else to go. You, on the other hand, are here because your Catholic upbringing says it's a sin to take your own life. The good news for you, however, is the Great Maestro upstairs," he said pointing to a passing cloud, "stopped you in the nick of time. I guess the jury is still out what happens next. Too bad you're not a Buddhist. Buddhists choose their own destiny. But, like me, your childhood was too engrained in, you know," he lowered his voice, "*the Institution.*"

"Church?"

"Yowza."

Cole began to strum the piano. "You know," he stated, "wasn't it Nietzsche who said, 'Without music life would be a mistake'?"

"Music a mistake? I really don't know anything about music. I mean, I can't sing or carry a note. I barely remember lyrics. I'm a mess musically."

"Ah-h-h-h. I'm beginning to understand. That may be the root of your problem, Sweetie. A person needs music to fill one's heart. You, my dear girl, need to sing and rejoice.

You need to forget your troubles and get happy. When I was alive, wealth was a wonderful thing but toward the end it never made me happy. What made me happy was having the entire world sing my songs."

"Singing? You're saying singing songs will make me happy?"

"Yowza. Yowza. Yowza, Missy Colette." He paused to consider my situation and appeared sidetracked in deep conjecture. He glanced at another passing cloud and began conversing with an invisible specter. "Why, yes. Yours is a grand idea. I do like it, Maestro. By golly, I like it a lot," he proclaimed, only to turn back and face me eye-to-eye with a wry twisted smile. "Congratulations, Sweetie. You get to go back to earth. You get a redo. You're going to sing yourself happy, after all. And here's the best part," he whispered. "You're only going to sing my songs." He sniggered announcing the revelation.

"Your songs?" I pressed. "Who are you?"

"Why, I'm Cole, of course. Cole Porter in the flesh. Ta-da," he bellowed chording the piano for dramatic affect.

"You're Cole Porter? *The* Cole Porter? You grew up in my Peru. I've read about you. You're like the most famous person to ever come out of my hometown."

"At your service, Sweetie. And you and me, why, we're Pee-roo kindred souls. Know what else?"

"What?"

"I predict you'll survive all this turmoil in your life and come out stronger for it. You're really quite a capable and intelligent young lady. You just need to regain confidence. You need to believe in yourself. I do. I believe in you. I believe you're absolutely wonderful. Know what else?"

"No. What, Cole?"

"You're the top." His piano suddenly ignited with a familiar old melody. "♫ You're the Coliseum. You're the top. You're the Louve Museum. You're a melody from a symphony by Strauss. You're a Bendel bonnet, a Shakespeare sonnet, you're Mickey Mouse—"

"♫ Mickey Mouse? ♫" I sang.

"Absolutely. ♪ You're the Nile. You're the Tower of Pisa. You're the smile on the Mona Lisa—"

"♫ I'm a worthless check. A total wreck. A flop ♫," I replied crooning words to lyrics I never knew but, now, somehow miraculously recalled—*and on key.* I instantly covered my mouth having no idea where all this was coming from. Clearly, I had lost control of my facilities.

"♫ But if, Sweetie, I'm the bottom, you're the top ♫," he finished.

Cole grabbed my virgin martini, delicately laid it on the piano and unexpectedly gave me a shove. I remember falling forever downward and back to earth. I remember him hollering as I fell, "Sing my name three times and I'll come a-running. Anything for you, Sweetie-e-e-e...."

CHAPTER TWO

Arthur Metcalf stormed into the Riverside MHMR Center. Two weeks after Colette Thomas's disappearance no one knew her whereabouts. In fact, no one reported her missing or seemed to care. It was by pure happenstance that when he dropped by the Thomas estate to discuss Colette's legal options concerning her estranged half-sister, the maid nonchalantly stated the child's bed had not been slept in for days. The maid assumed "Missy Thomas" and her boyfriend were secretly rendezvousing elsewhere for the summer. Fortunately, Arthur knew the details about the couple's breakup, as did everyone else in town, and rightfully suspected foul play or worse. When the A.P.B. finally issued a day later, staff at Riverside Mental Health heeded the bulletin and contacted Peru police who, in turn, called Arthur. Hence, an angry lawyer seeking restitution.

Located in neighboring Wabash, Riverside had become the default county mental shelter. Anyone without proper I.D. automatically ended up dumped on the doorsteps of the facility. And like most underfunded state mental institutions, Riverside was best known for overcrowding, sloppy patient reconciliations, and a turnstile approach to hired staff. Out-of-the-box and unemployed psychiatric doctors fresh from medical school reluctantly hired on, met their residency requirements, and moved onto higher paying private practices. This meant the facility populated with young, brainy but inexperienced M.D.s. It meant few employees had worked at Riverside for more than five years, including janitorial staff, or cared about their jobs knowing their commitment was short lived. Riverside had become a waystation for the chronic underachiever with the lone exception of young Dr. Meriwether Rubottom or "Rube" to those who knew him best.

Unlike his cohorts, thirty-year-old Rube found the variety of patients with their copious maladies both fascinating and challenging. He especially found the relaxed atmosphere and lack of procedural supervision liberating. It allowed him to dabble in new types of therapy, experiment with unheard of field trial medications, and prescribe unorthodox rehabilitation treatments without following established medical protocols. This rare professional freedom facilitated the young doctor's exuberance because at Riverside, as a front billboard broadcast, "Anything Goes."

When Rube heard how a haughty legal counselor was raising a ruckus at the front desk and demanding to see his patient, Jane Doe, rather than recoil on what would have appeared to be an inevitably contentious head-to-head confrontation, he embraced the challenge and straightaway proceeded to make the visitor's acquaintance. From a far corner of the rambling Riverside psych ward, Rube cheerfully pranced along the hallway and sang aloud, in the manner he always did, and much to everyone's chagrin. Full of spontaneous gaiety and mirth, he tap danced his way down the corridor, serenaded aged nurse Hagan and twirled sweet intern Roggensack in an impromptu dance of sorts as his booming vibrato bounced off walls to the awaiting, fuming ears of Arthur Metcalf. Nothing could have been more ill-timed than Rube's frivolous song in a gloomy mental hospital. "…♪ In olden days, a glimpse of stocking was looked on as something shocking but, now, God knows. Anything goes. Good authors, too, who once knew better words, now, only use four-letter words writing prose. Anything goes…. ♫," he sang merrily.

By the time Rube rounded the corner to the front desk station, Arthur found himself tapping his foot in rhythm to the song's familiar cadence. Any earlier anger adversely weighing his temperament had by now evaporated into a feeling of unbridled contentment singing in unison with the young doctor. "♫ If driving fast cars you like, if low bars you like, if old hymns you like, if bare limbs you like, if Mae West you like, or me undressed you like, why, nobody will oppose. Anything goes ♫," he chortled.

When the duo finished, they eyed each other speechless and somewhat embarrassed by the commotion they wreaked. Rube broke the silence and asked an inevitable question, "I'm sorry but have we ever met?"

"No, son, we have not. But we do have something in common."

"Knowing words to old standards?" Rube pressed with an innocent grin.

"Not exactly. It appears your Jane Doe patient is my ward. Her real name is Colette Thomas. I'm her legal counselor and I need you to tell me how she came to be confined here and how I can get her the hell out."

With Arthur's simple introduction, Rube explained how a hiker found Colette passed out and slightly fried by a bolt of lightning. He told of an emergency vehicle called to the scene and how paramedics discovered the girl had turned blue but still breathing and in remarkably good health. Once fully revived, they determined she lacked any memory of who she was or why she was on an abandoned bridge in the middle of a thunderstorm.

"Then, why did they bring her to Riverside?" Arthur pressed, appearing agitated.

"Because of this," Rube replied, handing Colette's suicide note to him. "Anyone attempting suicide in the four-county region is brought here for analysis. That's what I do. That's my specialty. Suicide prevention. Getting people back on track with their lives." Arthur silently read with his lips moving in sync with the words scribed on the note. When his lips stopped moving, Rube continued. "It appeared to the paramedics the girl had been preparing to plunge off the bridge when lightning struck her. The bolt entered her right orbital cortex and exited her right foot. Remarkably, there was no physical damage she can't recover from in a few days."

"And her memory? She can regain her memory, right?"

"More than likely. My guess is she was highly distraught before the accident, which is why she was there. To end it all. But, now, she's developed transcortical mixed aphasia with her amnesia. She has an elated mood with hyper-prosody and repetitive singing."

"Repetitive singing?"

"She doesn't talk. All she does is sing. *Constantly.*" Rube paused to take a deep breath. "Her condition isn't all that unusual. We see it occasionally in oxygen deprived patients. It's called Musical Hallucinations or, simply, M.H. From patients' perspectives, it's sort of like having a nonstop radio in their head playing music. Some people describe it as a musical jukebox. Given her unique situation, the condition should go away in time as her memories return. We also have a drug called Valproate. It can cure the symptoms within a few minutes, but I recommend only using it as a last resort. Her brain needs to heal holistically without stimulants. Plus, there are too many risks with a sudden jolt back to reality."

Arthur turned away, upset, and abruptly reversed course muttering the word "Crap." "You don't understand," he said. "Colette turns eighteen in two weeks. If she's not of sound mind by her eighteenth birthday, she can't inherit her parents' estate." He went on to explain the girl's family history including a mysterious opportunistic half-sister laying claim to the Thomas fortune and awaiting DNA test results. "If Colette isn't coherent, soon, she may lose it all including control of the company. And if that happens, I wouldn't be surprised to see her half-sister sell their controlling interest to the highest bidder. Jobs could be lost. The business moved overseas. And that, doctor, would be a real tragedy."

Rube mulled the image, cringed, and sympathetically shook his head. "I agree. It's certainly not a pretty picture you paint but we have to look at it as to what's best for Colette. She's quite happy right now. Far from the depressed state she must have wallowed in when all of this started. And I've found a way to communicate with her." He explained how to keep Colette from singing an epiphany of songs, he plastered duct tape over her mouth, forcing her to communicate by writing on tablet paper. "I realize it may sound crude, but she doesn't seem to mind my Draconian measure at all. In fact, she called it 'so-o-o-o twentieth century' and insisted we move into the twenty-first century by texting each other." He chuckled on the recollection. "She's remarkable, you know. I bought her a prepaid cell phone and, now, we text constantly. Communication is a good sign, wouldn't you agree, Arthur?" Rube shared the cell number and asked Arthur not to give it out to anyone else. "I think hearing from you will be a good thing. It can spark memories."

"Why not give her the Valproate?"

"Because her brain will never heal properly. She'll drift back to her previous depressed state and not understand why. Is that worth it, Arthur? To be a miserably depressed rich kid or a happy person without a care in the world? She's joyously happy right now. Infectiously happy. And quite a good singer, too, I might add."

Arthur scratched his head. "Are we talking about the same person? The Colette Thomas I know has the worst off-key voice in the state of Indiana. No pitch. No rhythm whatsoever and no appreciation for music. She's a nerd-kid."

Rube laughed. "Oh? Try explaining that to her imaginary mentor, Cole Porter. His songs are all she sings."

"Cole Porter? How in the world would she know Cole Porter songs? I don't even think she's heard of the man let alone recognizes any of those old tunes."

"Rube laughed, again. "God only knows, Arthur. For now, it's as big a mystery to me as it is to you. She claims she speaks to the man's ghost."

Taken aback with the revelation, Arthur insisted on seeing his client before he left the facility. Rube led him along the same long corridor he had earlier scampered down before veering into a large mess hall styled room. Inside, twenty or more patients with various psychoses were clapping and swaying back and forth with the most euphoric ecstatic leers and listening to a magnetic songstress. From Arthur's perspective, the scene resembled a Cuckoo's Nest-like setting; catatonic patients awakened by a musical blast from the past. Atop one of the tables, Colette was dancing and entertaining the throng as professionally as any USO performer.

"Like I said," Rube uttered from the corner of his mouth, "she's quite infectious."

Meanwhile, unmoved by two sane visitors looking on, Colette belted out show tunes as prodigiously as Ethan Merman. "…♫ Oh, give me land, lots of land under starry skies above. Don't fence me in. Let me ride through the wide-open country that I love. Don't fence me in. Let me be by myself in the evenin' breeze and listen to the murmur of the cottonwood trees, send me off forever but I ask you please. Don't fence me in…. ♫"

"Did I mention she wants out of here? 'Doesn't enjoy being cooped up. Other than that one minor complaint, she is an incredibly happy young lady," Rube added.

Arthur watched the spectacle, mesmerized by a Colette he barely recognized. "All I can say is we need her sane within two weeks, doctor. I can't hold off the vulture much longer."

Rube exhaled and stared beyond Colette and past a picture window. "And those who were seen dancing were thought to be insane by those who could not hear the music."

"What's that you say?" Arthur asked.

Rube's eyes re-fixed on Colette. "Oh, just a little something Nietzsche once said." His mouth puckered wondering what a true definition of sanity could possibly be. "I'll do my best to coax her back to reality," he stated dryly. "I'll do my best."

CHAPTER THREE

"You're back, Sweetie. What took you so long?" Cole asked.

I remember looking around my surroundings and not sure if I was dreaming or if I was back in the place he called purgatory. "How'd I get here?" I asked.

"Easy-peasy. You sang my name three times. Don't you remember? Your doctor friend had just sedated you and, before you passed out, you felt you were losing control and desperately needed me. Please tell me you needed me. I so want to be needed."

I thought about his explanation. I supposed he was right. I was singing strapped in bed when Doctor Rubottom came into my room. It was close to midnight and he calmly said it was time for me to sleep. "You can't sing all night long, Colette," he said. "We need to face tomorrow with a new voice." When he administered the sedative, I remember falling and falling and falling and not liking the feeling of losing control. In desperation I belted out "Cole Porter" three times. I wanted to be anyplace but freefalling. And, then, I landed safely in a soft Victorian couch. "Yes. I did call you, Cole. I did need you. So, where are we?" I finally asked.

"Well, this time it appears we're at my rue Monsieur home in Paris. You picked an ideal place and setting. It must be 1930. It's spring. And it's oh so beautiful here." He moved to what appeared to be the same piano I saw in Venice and sat and turned to face me. At first, I couldn't tell if he was talking directly to me or to an audience of his admirers behind me. "You know," he said, "Every time I look down on this timeless town, whether blue or gray be her skies, whether loud be her cheers or soft be her tears, more and more do I realize—"

"*What?*" I asked running out of patience.

"That I love Paris," he said unremarkably. And he began a long musical introduction on the piano only to burst aloud as only he could burst so easily, "♫ I love Paris in the springtime. I love Paris in the fall. I love Paris in the winter when it drizzles. I love Paris in the summer when it sizzles. I love Paris every moment, every moment of the year. I love Paris. Why, oh why do I love Paris? Because my love is near. ♫" He stopped and smiled a most contented pleased-with-himself smile. "That would be you, my love. Because you are back with me. Oh, how I missed you."

"But Cole, you barely know me."

"Ha. You may think so but it's not true. The truth of the matter is I've known you your entire life, Colette Thomas. I know everything about you. I was there when you were conceived in Corbie, when you were born in Peru, when you got your first tooth and when you lost your first tooth, when you put on your first training bra, when you became a woman, when—"

"I get it, Cole. You've been like a guardian angel to me."

He smiled coyly. "Now, that's a nice thought. A genuinely nice thought. In my lifetime a great many people would have called me a guardian devil. But no one is perfect. Are we?" He glanced skyward and cringed. "Well, except for the Grand Maestro, of course."

"Why did you pick me to watch over?"

"Actually, He did." Again, he craned his neck skyward. "And, I suppose, some of it has to do with our Peru commonality and moneyed backgrounds and your parents' love of France and Paris. I think they would want me to watch over you. After all, we are Pee-roo—"

"*Kindred souls*," I interrupted.

"Exactly. So, do you want to tell me why you did it? Or, rather, why you tried to do it? Tried to fling yourself off the bridge?"

"You should already know why. I mean, if you were there when I received my first training bra, you must certainly know how I was feeling horrible and lonely these past few months."

"Yes. Of course, I know. But sometimes it's good to talk about these things. Or, perhaps, sing about them," he added with a wink. "Life, sweet Colette, is about moments. It's about how we process the good times and bad times and raw human emotions into positive learning experiences. Trust me when I say I know about bad times and was able to survive life to the bitter end. I can't tell you how many times I wanted to end it all, but you know what saved me from doing one of those things? Just one of those things?"

"No. Please tell me."

"Songs. Singing. Rejoicing in the Maestro's music and gifts He so graciously granted me." He glanced at his watch. "Oh, drat, Sweetie. It's time for you to go back."

"But I just arrived, Cole. And I want to meet your friends."

"Next time. They will all be here for you when you return. I promise. Now, let's exit this joint with a positive thought. With a song. A solo by you."

And like all of his songs running amuck in my head, this one came almost preordained and spontaneously. His hands magically lit up the piano and I began to sing as though I had known the words to the melody my entire life. "♫It was just one of those things. Just one of those crazy flings. One of those bells that now and then rings. Just one of those things.... ♫"

CHAPTER FOUR

Her name was Jennifer or Jenny or Sweet Baby Jen-Jen—so many adorable monikers and all rooted from the innocence one hopes to find reflected in a child's eyes. Indeed, an abundance of virtuousness abounded in those early years but that was, after all, a lifetime ago—twenty years to be exact. So, let's rewind the hands of time to gain a better appreciation of how Sweet Baby Jen-Jen evolved into an aggressive cutthroat lawyer without scruples or moral compass. You see, all those monikers applied aptly to a six-year-old. After all, children are by definition blameless until corrupted by fate or life's hard knocks and it is, then, as adults the inner child must choose his or her path. Clearly, human beings do not start off rotten to the core. *Or do they?*

For Jennifer Garfield life began in small town Keokuk; it began resplendent in wonderment, joy, and youthful exuberance. However, her life also commenced with a freeloading mother of questionable character and doting but seemingly well-intentioned grandparents. Sadly, life for the young sprite spiraled hellishly when the grandparents passed away and left her mother buried under a mountain of debt, only to be pursued by relentless debt collectors. How does one survive in the gulags of rural Iowa on a river town prosperity forgot sometime in the 1960s? You might ask. How does one achieve success in life raised by a single mother with no vocational skills whatsoever and possessing no self-esteem or ambition? Answer: *Not easily*. Given this unsavory combination, Jen-Jen's mother felt compelled to use what few ribald talents she possessed to attract men of means to assist in paying mounting bills. Her mother's discreet relationships in small town Keokuk enabled the child to eat with a roof overhead but always with one eye propped open at night as drunken suitors wandered into her bedroom seeking pay-for-play favors. With a combination of beauty, charm and pedophile admirers, Jen-Jen learned at a young age what kept a jaded world a-spinnin'. *Cha-ching.*

From these encounters the child grew into a hardened teen beset by anger with anger driving her to seek a better life in the nearby metropolis of Des Moines. Unlike the mother, Jennifer became determined to better her sad lot, free of men for props. Perhaps, it was the unknown inner-Thomas ambition in Jennifer propelling her from the muddy waters of the mighty Mississippi and into a muck-free future. Whatever the innate incentive, she fled a debaucherous lifestyle with the sort of bright-eyed verb and pluck one would expect of a young Horatio Alger. To seek an education at that station in life meant traversing a long, lonely road working as a night janitor, studying, and working some more. Education became the child's way out. When money fell short for law school tuition, an opportunity presented itself to earn extra cash waitressing at a local men's cabaret establishment, and when a marquee pole dancer failed to appear one evening, on a whim and slightly tipsy, Jennifer filled the vacancy. Surprisingly, she earned more money in one night than during an entire week as a waitress and, not surprisingly, decided to pursue the 'profession' to finish her schooling debt-free. *Cha-ching.*

What soon distinguished Jennifer from other performers, however, was not her subtle firm physique but, rather, her creative approach to an old trade. Almost from the get-go, her act evolved into singing show tunes while teasingly shedding clothes from behind feathered hand-fans, a-la' Gypsy Rose Lee. This throwback style to a yesteryear burlesque came courtesy of an old documentary watched one night on the queen of striptease. Naturally, all the naïve men loved the corny shtick. A few fat cats enjoyed it so much they paid hefty sums for private parties including none other than the principle partner at Knudsen & Evans, Des Moines' most prominent attorneys-at-law. With money now abundantly plentiful, sweet Jennifer transformed herself into the stage presence of *Jenny-Baby* and one of the hottest attractions in the city. This newfound wealth ushered in unquenchable material cravings—fast cars, drugs, and smarmy suitors. Cocaine became Jenny-Baby's drug of choice and her favorite stage song espoused her predilection to this adverse stimulant. And, of course, the song of choice, an old Cole Porter standard, fit her as snugly as the long satin gloves discarded on stage one finger at a time. Saturday nights at 10:00 PM farm boys and legal scholars alike lined up to hear her erotic femme fatale rendition:

"♪ My story is much too sad to be told. But practically everything leaves me totally cold. The only exception I know is the case is when I'm out on a quiet spree, fighting vainly the old ennui, and I suddenly turn and see you boys' fabulous face. I get no kick from champagne. Mere alcohol doesn't thrill me at all. So, tell me why it should be true, that I get a kick out of you. Some get a kick from cocaine. I'm sure that if I took even one sniff that it would bore me terif-f-f-f-fickly, too. Yet, I get a kick out of you…. ♪"

With the old 'bump and grind' working to her advantage, men happily stuffed twenty- and ten-dollar bills behind tawdry feathers and into in her brimming G-string; this money helped pay off school debt and finance a new red Porsche Targa. *Cha-ching.*

By the conclusion of her 3L-year, Jenny-Baby had procured a prestigious job at Knudsen & Evans, and by the age of twenty-six, a mere two years out of law school, became the youngest partner in the firm's one-hundred-year history.

Much to no one's surprise, Jennifer attracted a slew of highbrow clients to the firm. And much to everyone's surprise, Jennifer's legal talents were even more provocative then her fan dances. She proved quite capable and assertive and manipulated favorable rulings for her clients in the courtroom of Judge Joseph S. Kelly, an old friend. Given this upstart success in the material world and with Keokuk no longer visible in the rearview mirror, one would have guessed Jennifer to be quite pleased with her accomplishments, but the truth of the matter is she was not. In fact, material needs had not eclipsed her emotional need to erase scarred memories and fill a void in her life. That void, simply put, was to be loved. Men, certainly, were never going to fill the need nor were a nonexistent Iowa family. From Jennifer's perspective, other than a debaucherous mother-pimp, she had no family. That is until one day in late May when she received a much-delayed word Milton Thomas, the wealthy Indiana tycoon and sports apparel king, had perished in a freak airplane accident and that Milton had finally been fingered by her mother as her true biological father. *Cha-ching.*

Within a matter of hours, Jennifer had located the Thomas estate trustee, Arthur Metcalf, who also happened to be the chief executor of the family will. That first phone call Jennifer placed to Arthur did not go well. Being highly skeptical of any claim to the Thomas inheritance months after Milton's death, Arthur, naturally, insisted upon a DNA test. Any comparison to Jennifer's DNA would take thirty-two days. "Why so long?" Jennifer asked. "Modern DNA matching tests take less seventy-two hours." Arthur insisted he would need to find multiple sources for Milton's DNA—combs, hairbrushes, unwashed clothes—and how this could become a prolonged task given the fact it had been over four months since Milton's demise. "The house and all of his belongings have been thoroughly cleaned since then. I'll have to send in experts to find anything," he replied. The truth of the matter is Arthur had already extracted Milton's DNA months earlier in the event such a preposterous claim came forward. Arthur was simply stalling for time and needed Colette to achieve her eighteenth birthday, which loomed, coincidentally, thirty-three days away.

But Jenifer, being ever dutiful and assertive, found it difficult to sit on her hands and telephoned Arthur a second time, two weeks later, this time pressing with questions posed more as demands. "Do I have any siblings?" she probed.

And this is where Arthur should have remained coy by refusing to answer the question altogether until the DNA test date. "Yes. You would have one sister and no brothers," he said.

"And what is her name and age?"

"Her name is Colette. She is seventeen. You can meet her in fifteen days, the day after we verify your DNA test."

Of course, Jennifer already had the answers to these questions, having run Internet searches on every Tom, Dick, and Harry named Thomas residing in Peru. She simply wanted to size up Arthur's candor. Immediately, her mind began churning. She knew inheritance in Indiana cannot be obtained until one achieves an eighteenth birthday. Waiting fifteen days played to her advantage. Fifteen days gave her more time to plot and scheme on legal procedures to tie up the inheritance, overthrow a minor half-sister, and assume the helm of Thomas Enterprises.

"I'd absolutely love to meet Colette. In fact, I insist on meeting her."

"Simply not possible," Arthur stated. "She's out of town and will be indisposed for the next two weeks." Clearly, this was a factual statement.

"Where is she?"

Arthur leaned back in his chair and stared at a painting of Saint Colette that Milton had gifted him years earlier. Milton had asked his good friend to always watch out for his daughter if some unfortunate event was to beset the Thomas family. Arthur pledged he would. Now, this exquisite painting of Colette's namesake hung prominently on an office wall and stared Arthur smack-dab in the face. The saintess appeared to evoke feverous piety Arthur found disturbingly challenging. He vacillated between revealing the truth or fabricating an out-and-out lie. "She's with her choir, the Riverside troubadours, on tour," he finally blurted. "The last time I saw her, she was singing her crazy head off." Clearly, this was a stretch.

"Oh? I'm glad someone else in the family likes to sing. It must be in our family DNA."

"Perhaps it is," Arthur responded eyeing the painting. Saint Colette seemed to stir to life with a one-eye sly-devil wink at Arthur. Arthur winked back.

CHAPTER FIVE

Colette sat opposite Rube in his aged sterile office resplendent in tarnished 1970-vintage chrome chairs and mauve painted walls and a crack in a puckered ceiling threatening to collapse. One of Rube's legs draped nonchalantly over an arm on his chair. He was leaning back sideways looking down and engaged with his cell phone. A lone framed 5 X 7 photo sat awkwardly in a corner on top of his desk. Centered in the photo sat Rube and his Golden Labrador, Elvis. The pair posed for what appeared to be a professionally taken camera still. Rube's arm wrapped around the dog's neck; the dog was leaning into Rube's shoulder. Both were smiling gleefully. Studying the photo, Colette wanted to smile, too, but duct tape covered most of her face from below her nose to her chin. By now, two weeks since being admitted into Riverside, she better understood the reason for the tape. She knew tape had become a stopgap solution to her compulsion to sing and, once peeled away, she would belt out Cole Porter show tunes to hospital staff or anyone within earshot. Oddly, a taped mouth fostered an inner dialogue with coherent thoughts and facilitated an ability to think rationally. Memories, however, were still hard to come by. Nevertheless, with or without tape she felt at peace and happy, not euphorically happy but content. She gazed at Rube and his expressive blue eyes and his dreamy smile. Secretly, she wished these two-a-day thirty-minute sessions would never end. She wished she could get to know her psychiatrist better as a person, maybe go on a date or something. She guessed he was only ten or so years older. What's ten years? She asked herself. Why, when he's ninety, I'll be eighty. That would make me a trophy wife, even by retirement home standards. She smiled on the thought. He glanced up and saw her eyes expressively pinch tiny crow's feet wrinkles where none had existed a moment before. He texted her.

> You're smiling, aren't you?

Yes. I was wondering how old you are.

I'm 30. Old enough to be you're big brother.

I'd like that. I've never had a brother or sister. Or cousin. Or anyone near my age in my family.

Colette, are you remembering you have a family??? This could be a breakthrough!

I guess I am. Last night I had a dream about two people. In my dream I called them Mother and Father. We seemed happy. But there was no one else, so I assumed I was an only child. Do I have parents, Dr. Rubottom? Brothers and sisters? And if I do, where are they?

Of course you have parents. Don't we all? As to why they're not here? I think that's one of the things we need to work on—your memories. Sometimes memories can be painful. It's normal to suppress painful events but, most often, we learn to grow and learn from that pain. Pain can make us stronger and better human beings. It's nice to have the support of family to weather the pain but, in the end, it's really our own pain to weather. You know, it was Nietzsche who said, 'In pain there is as much wisdom as there is pleasure. Pain is one of the best preservatives of the human species. In suffering we find greatness.' My job is to help you through your pain and remember events that you subconsciously want to suppress. But I also want you to be happy. You can be happy, even with painful memories. The two can coexist. Do you understand all of this?

Yes. I think so. Do you think my singing has something to do with not being able to remember any of these things? That it's my way of suppressing pain?

Most likely, that is the case. Tell me more about your dreams. The other day, you told me you can summon Cole Porter by silently singing his name three times. When I asked you to demonstrate that ability, you repeated his name and fell into a self-imposed hypnotic state. I listened to you talk to someone but I never heard his voice. Why do you suppose that's the case? That only you can hear his voice and not me?

I wish I knew. It's all a mystery to me. I do wish you could see him and talk with him. He's a lot of fun and he throws the best parties. He's taught me all of his songs. He told me I'm going to meet his friends soon, too, and that he thinks of me night and day and how much he misses me when we're not together. He's your age, you know. And very handsome. Are you jealous?

Ha! Should I be? You know, the man was gay. He preferred men over women.

I don't believe that. He's married. Her name is Linda. He flirts with me and I think he wants to leave her. We're only ten years apart, you know.

> I've got news for you, Colette. He never leaves his wife. I've done my research on the man. He sticks with his wife to the end. It was a marriage of convenience to hide the fact he was a homosexual. Back then, that sort of a lifestyle was taboo. Look, I don't want you to get hurt in an impossible relationship.

> Oh, really? I thought you just told me that we can grow as human beings through experienced pain?

Exasperated, Rube threw his hands in the air and decided to speak as opposed to text. He deftly laid his phone on the desk and made eye contact with Colette. "You're absolutely correct. Here's the deal. I want you to think about a couple of things between now and tomorrow morning. Why is it you can visualize and talk to a man who has been dead for nearly sixty years? Do you have a special gift to talk with the dead? And why is it only you can see and talk with him and no one else? I would love to talk with him. Tell him that. Tell him to include me in his little séance circle. Would you, please?" Rube spouted sarcastically.

> I'll be more than happy to. Anything else, Dr. Rubottom?

"Yes. Let's see if we're making any progress on your singing compulsion. Please remove your tape. Let's see what happens."

Colette slowly peeled away duct tape and wiped glue shards from the corners of her mouth. She smiled demurely with Rube looking on but said nothing.

"Are you happy, Collette?" He asked.

With a healthy teenage infatuation motivating her response, she wanted to say 'Yes. I'm happy anytime I'm with you, Dr. Rubottom,' but as her lips parted to express those sentiments, she erupted uncontrollably into song.

"♫ Night and Day, you are the one. Only you beneath the moon and under the sun—" She threw her hands over her mouth to stop the sounds erupting from out of nowhere; her eyes crossed staring at the hands struggling to keep her lips from parting. Sadly, predictably, her hands and arms flung wide as though an invisible force yanked them away and threw them to her sides. She attempted to cover her mouth, again, but ultimately ceded to an uncontrollable urge, and continued singing, this time with her eyes meeting his as if in a lover's rhapsody.   "—♫Whether near to me or far, it's no matter darling where you are. I think of you night and day. Night and day, why is it so? That this longing for you follows me wherever I go. In the roaring traffic's boom, in the silence of this lonely room, I think of you night and day.... ♫"

When she finished, Rube wanted to hop over his desk and sweep his beautiful young patient in his arms. He had never been serenaded by anyone and her voice sounded so lovely singing acapella. Yet, he knew that, technically, she was still a minor; professional decorum forbids such unprofessional behavior. Doctors and patients should never cross the line. Maintain your composure, man, he told himself. Don't fall in love with the girl.

CHAPTER SIX

By the time Conrad Witty caught word of Colette Thomas' admittance into Riverside, her stay had already been extended into a third week. For days, rumors had circulated in Peru how his ex-girlfriend had attempted to end her life by jumping off an old railroad trestle bridge spanning the Wabash River. They said severe despair had driven the girl into suicidal depression and, empathetically, Conrad felt guilty over his role in Colette's sad initiative. Less than a week earlier, his latest girlfriend had dumped him for someone her own age, none other than next fall's PHS's first string quarterback and presumptive valedictorian, Trevor Brumbach. Conrad knew his brawn could never compete against Trevor's brain, so he never bothered to put up a fight. The only place Conrad ever put up a fight was on the gridiron as a hulking 6'– 4" defensive end and, in another month, he would begin the first of many two-a-days at Hocking Junior College at Nelsonville, the only school offering him an athletic scholarship. With a mediocre 'C+' average, the more prestigious Indiana state universities rejected his applications; Colette's Yale would never consider him, not for their football program or even as a part-time dormitory busboy. Dwelling on these thoughts and in deep introspection, he began to appreciate Colette's anguish. He never felt good about the way he unloaded his betrayal on Colette's frail shoulders. And, truth be told, he would not miss the hyperactive cheerleader he once lusted after; her kisses were sloppy and wet. Colette kissed him with eyes closed while pressed tight against his body; sometimes, she didn't come up for air for two whole minutes. God, how he missed Colette's passionate kisses. More than once he drove by her magnificent mansion and wanted to apologize but he knew Colette would burst into one of her bawling fits and, frankly, he no longer possessed the emotional strength to help her in that department. It had been five months since they last smooched and, well, by late May the cheerleader came in handy. He had needs, too. Now, contemplating how he might have contributed to Colette's attempt at suicide, he cringed despising himself for being too insensitive and lacking the maturity to be a port in her storm. Maybe he truly was, as a mutual friend described, a complete asshole.

When Arthur Metcalf called Conrad out of the blue, Arthur asked him to drop by Riverside and visit Colette. Arthur explained how Colette had been struck by lightning and lost all memory. He explained how she communicated by texting because whenever she opened her mouth a compulsive singing disorder kept her in a state of "musical flairs." "I think it'll be good for you to speak with her one-on-one," Arthur said. "Of course, she'll have no idea who you are, but it might trigger memories. And we need her to regain all of her memories within ten days, by her eighteenth birthday, or it could ruin her inheritance and any chance she has to attend Yale."

Conrad understood. He understood how important attending Yale had been to Colette and her father. The Yale business school was to prepare her for taking over the family business. He and she had talked about being apart, she in Connecticut and he in Ohio, and how distance might affect their relationship. Colette said she would gladly enroll at Hocking, but Conrad insisted she make her parents proud and go to the best Ivy League school possible. After all, she had worked nonstop for years to achieve both magna cum laude status and a SAT national merit score—long before he entered the picture. She definitely needed to do the right thing by her family and go to Yale. While they skirted the subject of marriage, both sensed how after four years of college their relationship would continue right where it left off. Four years could be tamed with Christmas and spring breaks and ten weeks together during the summers in between classes. As a couple, they had plans and hopes and dreams, all without ever saying, "I love you." Now, Conrad wished he had said those three words. Now, Colette had no memory of who he was or those plans they made or the bonehead mistake with the junior cheerleader.

At Riverside, Conrad checked in at the front desk and self-escorted to a back patio where Colette had been ushered for their reunion. Rube observed from a distance but he neither wanted to mediate nor interfere with what he hoped would become a catalyst reunion igniting Colette's memory. Conrad approached her from behind. Colette appeared engrossed in a book on the history of American music standards and attempting to learn everything possible about Cole Porter and his friends. When Conrad tapped her on the shoulder, she spun to greet him with a most exuberant smile. Her mouth covered in duct tape, but it was not hard to recognize Colette's smile as her eyes alit joyously. He had not seen this unbridled expression of joy beam from her face in months. She stood and instantly gave him a hug as though she recognized him. Startled, Conrad stepped back.

"You know me?" He asked, bewildered. "They said you wouldn't know me."

Colette reached for her phone and gave it to Conrad. Using hand signals, she asked him to call himself with her phone so they could communicate. He did, and when his phone began to twitter, he hung up and returned the phone. She retrieved his number and immediately began to send him text messages. He glanced at his phone's screen to read what she wrote.

> No. I have no idea who you are. They told me your name is Conrad and that we are friends. Best friends. Friendship is so important. I am glad you're my good friend, Conrad, and that you came to visit me.
>
>

Conrad read the text and swallowed hard. "Yes. We are best friends," he replied. He thought carefully about what to say next. As Colette's eyes searched his for answers, he remembered how much he adored her. Her expressive eyes told him everything. Her eyes could hide neither sadness nor giddiness. The Colette he once knew may have lost her memory, but she had not forgotten how to smile. "We, we were a couple," he eked. "And I really liked you. I mean, I really, really liked you. No, I mean I like you right now. I really like you now. And a lot. And, and—"

She placed her finger over his mouth and began typing on her phone.

> I can tell that in my previous life I must have been blessed to have someone as wonderful as you call me a friend. I must have been your girlfriend. Right?

"Yes, you were, and I was darned lucky to have you. But I was an idiot. And, and—"

Once again, Colette stopped Conrad from finishing words she knew could only make him uncomfortable and, perhaps, guilty over something she might never recall.

> Fresh start, Conrad. You and I have a fresh start.

"You want to start over with me? No kidding?"

> Of course. Look at you. You're tall and handsome and so muscular and very sweet. How could I not have fallen for you?

She reached for his arm and felt a bicep.

> And you're so strong! I'll bet you can bench press 200 pounds. I'm told you were a Fighting Tiger football player. I'll bet you were really good!

"First team All-District and I can bench press 250," Conrad gushed." I'll be starting for Hocking Junior College in the fall. Do you remember that? And you're going to Yale. Remember that?"

Colette shook her head 'No.'

> Why wouldn't we be going to school together if we're best friends???

Conrad shrugged his shoulders. He was afraid by dumping too much history, too quickly, on Colette might make for information overload and he quickly changed the subject. "They tell me that you sing and have a wonderful voice. You may not remember this, but I love to sing, too. I was the captain of the PHS boy's glee club. How about if I peel away the tape on your mouth and you sing to me? I've never heard you sing, and I'd like—"

Before Conrad finished his sentence, Colette had peeled back tape on her own volition and hastily sent him another text message.

> Here's one I bet you know. My friend, Cole Porter wrote it. Let's sing it together. I'll start—

"♫ If you're ever in a jam, here I am— ♫" She signaled for Conrad to sing the next line.

"♫ If you're ever in a mess, S.O.S— ♫" He belted, grinning ear-to-ear over a song his glee club sang the year before at the PHS Spring Folly.

"♫ If you're ever so happy but land in jail, I'm your bail—♫"

Together, they sang the next lines in perfect harmony.
"♫ It's friendship, friendship. Boom-Boom. Just the perfect blend-ship. When other friendships have been forgot, Boom-Boom, ours will still be hot. La da la da la da dig dig dig. ♫"

When they finished singing, Conrad threw his arms around Colette. "I love you. I should have said those words months ago. I'm such an idiot."

Colette leaned into Conrad and whispered, "I love you, too."

No one heard her say those words except Conrad. Colette slapped tape back over her mouth before another song burst forth. While she hesitated to tell the boy that she loved him, a boy she did not recognize, she sensed he was special and truly loved her, and for those very reasons she could not break his heart.

From fifty feet away, Rube scribbled his observation in a paper journal: Colette responds to male teen stimulus and has shown a first spark of recovery. Love appears to be the answer. Halleluiah.

CHAPTER SEVEN

"♫ Cole Porter. Cole Porter. Cole Porter ♫," I sang.

"At your service, Sweetie," he replied. "So, you decided to come to the party to meet my dearest friends. I knew you would. I knew you'd come back. What's up sweet girl?"

"My shrink, I mean, my psychiatrist wants to meet you. Can I bring him next time I visit?"

"Of course, you can. The more the merrier, I always say. Is he my type?"

"Your type? I think he's more my type. I will tell you this, he doesn't believe me when I tell him about us. He's skeptical. I guess it's part of his job."

"Ha. 'Guess we'll show him. Won't we?"

"Say, what on earth are you wearing?" I asked, eying his odd ensemble.

"This old thing?" He smiled, admiring his sports jacket creation patched together with gaudy mismatched cloth samples tailored to fit his slight physique. "I call it my 'David's coat.' It's a reminder of my Baptist roots." He giggled. "'Just can't shed those old Bible school stories," he added with a wink.

And exactly where was I? I wondered. I remember glancing around the room and spying a tall set of glass doors opening to a palatial backyard with swaying palm trees and hibiscus in full bloom and a host of exotic flowers bending to a slight breeze. A whiff of salty ocean air filled the room. "You never cease to amaze me, Cole. Where am I this time?"

"Hollywood. It's January 1936. You're at my home on Sunset Boulevard. I tell people this place is like living on the moon. By the way, Linda has fled to Paris. She can't stand California or my boyfriends, so I fill the void with grand parties and sparkling champagne and, naturally, my latest music scores. Care for champagne?"

"Sure thing," I answered. "How can I refuse champagne from my favorite guardian angel, Cole Porter?" As he handed me an elegant, gold rimmed fluted glass, it suddenly occurred to me he and I were not the only ones attached to his piano. "Are you composing a song with all this commotion and these noisy souls hovering around you? How can you do that? How do you concentrate?"

"Oh, Sweetie, it's not hard. Truth of the matter, I'd rather compose on a horse than on a piano. Noisy house guests just make composing on a piano more tolerable."

"Did you say a horse?"

"Absolutely. I am quite the accomplished horseman. Not too many people know that personal tidbit. Now, you know. I learned to ride at the age of six back in Indiana. Besides, pianos are stifling anchors. Horses are fun. I'm quite happy on a horse. How about you? Where are you happiest?"

His question caught me off guard and my response not the least bit spontaneous. "I guess…. I guess, right now, I'm happiest when I sing your songs."

"Well, I do appreciate you singing my songs," he said, "but someday they'll fade away, like me. So, what happens then, Colette Thomas?"

"Hm-m-m. I've learned to love singing, Cole. You can take credit for that but if you fade way, I'll just switch over to other composers—Dylan, McCartney, Simon."

Cole drew a blank stare. "Who?" He asked

"Look, I adore your songs, Cole. They're the best. But you did say you enjoy riding horses. Right?"

"Absolutely"

"And do you always ride the same horse?"

He smiled. "Not sure how you mean that but 'No,' I do not."

"Maybe someday I'll ride another horse and branch out. 'Learn to appreciate other great composers like—"

"Those three you mentioned whom I have never heard of?"

"Fine. How about Irving Berlin and George Gershwin? Heard of them?" I asked.

He laughed. Well, it was more of a closed-eye snigger. "Irving Berlin, is it? George Gershwin? Now, those two numbskulls I know all too well." He whistled and waved two souls passing by to his piano. "Hey, boys, look who's here. It's sweet Colette from Pee-roo. The one I told you about." The two flew straight to me as if they had known me for years.

"George Gershwin at your service. We've heard so much about you from Cole."

"Ignore this pompous brute. I'm the one who writes America's songs," the other man interrupted. "Irving Berlin at your disposal. And if I must speak out of turn, it's only to praise your gorgeous mug, honey. As I always say, 'A pretty girl is like a melody.' Colette with you by my side, I could write a million melodies."

George pushed past Irving. "My. My. My. Colette. Cole never told us how beautiful you are. All he told us is you sing like a nightingale."

"And only his songs," Irving muttered.

"Have you ever considered jumping ship?" George pressed. "Step up the syncopation. Cole ain't the only game in town. I've got rhythm. I've got music. Who could ask for anything more? Besides, you need someone to watch over you."

"That's right. Forget Cole. He's a master of delusion. Why, neither George nor I would ever squander your talent on just our songs. Spread your wings little nightingale. Sing. Dance. Let's face the music and dance."

For no apparent reason Irving snapped his fingers. Instantaneously, my scrungy sweats materialized into an elegant full-length silk gown with puffed shoulders. I glanced in a mirror. My brown ponytail had turned blond and my hair bobbed short and tight as a Brillo pad. "It's 1936, Colette, let's cut a rug," he said. With another snap of his fingers, little Irving Berlin's attire transformed into formal black tails with a top hat and white gloves. He glanced skyward. "Hit it Maestro." The room went dark for a few seconds, only to re-ignite with a full-scale orchestra and band members radiating white and floating airborne with wings.

"Whoa. Is Tommy Dorsey our conductor?" I asked.

"You better believe it, honey."

I looked at my Birkenstocks. "What? No high heels, Irving? How am I going to dance without pumps?" I asked, towering over him.

"You're already tall enough, Colette. No need to press our luck."

Within seconds, the band's music filled the room with Irving tiptoe-leading me while singing dreadfully in my ear. "♫ Heaven. I'm in heaven. And my heart beats so that I can hardly speak. And I seem to find the happiness I seek, when we're out together dancing, cheek to cheek. Heaven. I'm in heaven. And the cares that hang around me through the week, seem to vanish like a gambler's lucky streak, when we're out together dancing, cheek to cheek.... ♫"

And in the same fashion as the voice I never knew I possessed, my feet began to follow my friend's elegant lead across a billowy dance floor as though I had known the moves to this wistful fox-trot all along. Before he could finish his charming song, George tapped him on the shoulder. "My turn," he said abruptly. He snapped his fingers and the music stopped to morph into one of his tunes.

"Colette, I want you to sing this song to me as we dance," he said. "It's my best one." He turned to look at Cole who nodded his head in approval.

"But, George, I'm not sure I know the words to this melody."

"You know the words, alright. Trust your instincts. Like all of your lost memories, this one is there waiting for you to open the door."

By the end of the first refrain, something happened. It was as though someone had thrown a light switch. I began to remember lyrics to a melancholy old song Mother used to sing to me as a child. George pressed against me slow dancing one-two, one-two. "Sing it, Colette. Sing it for me."

"♫ There's a somebody I'm longing to see. I hope that he turns out to be, someone who'll watch over me. I'm a little lamb who's lost in the wood. I know I could always be good, with someone who'll watch over me…. ♪"

When I finished, I found my head lying on George's shoulder. I was crying.

"You're not alone or lost, Colette, my little lamb. You never were. You'll never be. We're all here for you. Me. Irving. Cole. Sing the rest of your life, sweet girl. Be happy. Love. Be happy. Dance. Be happy. The world is waiting for you."

Little Irving drew closer and together he and George hugged me. Naturally, Cole refused to be outdone and the four of us group-hugged until Cole ruined the moment. "Time for you to return, Sweetie," he said. "See you and that psychiatrist friend of yours in the funny papers." He gave me a shove and I fell back to reality.

CHAPTER EIGHT

When the disturbance outside his office reached a shrill, Arthur Metcalf arose from his chair, bolted to the door, and stormed into his secretary's cubical. "What the hell is going on, Freddie?" He bellowed.

The burly secretary continued wagging his finger at the comely female visitor, inadvertently ignoring his boss. Freddie's exasperation had reached the point of no return. "I've told this woman ten times you're not available," Freddie screeched. "I've told her to make an appointment, but she insists—"

"It's fine, Freddie. Truly it is. Thank you. I'll take things from here," Arthur interjected.

Still incensed, Freddie re-collapsed into an office chair but starred daggers at the visitor. In a twisted sort of way, he enjoyed putting annoying people in their place, especially those named Jennifer Garfield. Freddie knew all the juicy gossip associated with sweet Colette's opportunistic half-sister. Any barrier to slowing down the Keokuk juggernaut, as he so colorfully quipped, played to his liking as prodigiously as tire spikes at an Indiana roadblock. Meanwhile, Arthur found himself gawking at Jennifer and thinking how attractive the woman appeared in person; far more attractive than the scads of humdrum Facebook photo shots with her distorted puckered-lip selfies. Based on those older posts, she also appeared to have had recent breast augmentation. Now, savoring Jennifer's tight-fitting summer ensemble, Arthur secretly stirred a raging bull. Freddie, by comparison, sat immune to Jennifer's wiles. Of course, not to cast an appearance of rudeness, Arthur smiled disingenuously and waved the uninvited guest into his office. Jennifer strutted past both men while sneering at Freddie. Arthur's neck craned eyeing her provocative saunter.

"I take it you're the Jennifer Garfield I've been conversing with over the phone," he called out after her. "To be honest, I had no idea you were arriving today. I presumed you would arrive tomorrow for the reading of—"

"And the name is Jennifer Garfield-Thomas," she replied curtly. "Please address me as such. The DNA test results came in last night. I'm sure you saw the affidavit. This morning, before I flew out of Des Moines, my friend, Judge Kelly, approved the name change. Now, there shouldn't be any confusion regarding my status with Thomas Enterprises or my inheritance. Do you understand, Arthur?" She asked the question with an egregious cold arrogance one would expect of royal bloodlines querying servants over the tardiness of tea.

"Yes, I do Ms. Thomas." Arthur circled past her and straight to his desk. He hunkered into a cushy executive chair, oblivious to her newfound haughtiness and more consumed by her beauty. Not-so-subtly, his eyes glued to her long legs exposed by an oh-so-short summer skirt with a semi-sheer halter top.

"Arthur, I hired an investigator last week to do discovery on Colette. It seems my sister is nowhere to be found. Rumor has it she may be locked up at one of the local mental rehabilitation facilities but, naturally, none of the centers would disclose private information to my man. So, tell me Arthur, is Colette currently institutionalized? Did you lie to me about her whereabouts? And is she mentally sound enough to inherit her half of Milton Thomas' fortune or is she as batshit crazy as rumor suggests?"

Arthur peeled his eyes away from Jennifer's legs and suddenly struck a serious pose, refocusing on her smug face. "The girl is my ward, Jennifer, and she is none of your damn business. I don't care if your DNA matches hers. You're not her real family and, as far as I'm concerned, you're not a part of Thomas Enterprises' family, either. You're not cut from the same cloth as Colette. Not by a longshot."

Jennifer's arrogant half-smile soured into a tacit profanity-laced tirade enunciated with the utmost linguistic clarity. She proceeded to rant about Arthur eating dog feces, how he fornicated his mother, and how she wished he would shove his Yale law degree up his anus "where the sun don't shine"—well, with fewer words and more vulgarity. She also informed Arthur how the "queer" secretary and he would be the first to lose their jobs when she took over the company and how her mentally incompetent teenage half-sister would remain under lock and key "until hell freezes over." "You may be her ward," she said, "but I'm her only family and I'll fight you in court for her power of attorney. Blood trumps Daddy's CFO." She abruptly stood and stormed out of the office but dramatically posed in the doorway for one final parting shot. "Your loyalties are to the wrong person, Arthur. Too bad. I heard you're a smart man. Apparently, you're not smart enough. I'll be back here at 1:00 PM tomorrow for the reading of the will. If Colette isn't sane tomorrow, we'll both know it. I'm bringing in my own psychiatrist to evaluate her."

"Oh? Anyone I know?"

"His name is Rubottom. Dr. Meriwether Rubottom. He works nearby in Wabash. He came highly referred by the Indiana ABPN. They selected him as an impartial observer for me. So, don't think for a minute you can pull the wool over this woman's eyes. Got it?"

Arthur threw his hands in an 'I surrender' pose and struck a sarcastic tone. "I gotta hand it to you, Jennifer. You have clearly out maneuvered me on this one. Didn't see it coming. By all means, bring in your expert."

After Jennifer left the building, Freddie ran into Arthur's office. "Did Jennifer Garfield just hire our man, Rube?"

"No worries, Freddie. I don't think she realizes the connection. Besides, Rube loves Colette as much as we do. He's on our side. He would never betray her." Arthur pondered the situation a bit longer, rubbing his chin as a thought occurred. "You know, Freddie, I believe Nietzsche was wrong."

"About what, boss?"

"He said 'Man is the cruelest animal.' However, I believe that self-serving woman is."

CHAPTER NINE

Good afternoon, Colette. This is Arthur Metcalf. We met a few weeks ago when I came to visit you. I was with Dr. Rubottom. Remember me?

Of course, I do, Arthur. You're the older gentleman who was wearing the wire rim glasses. You also were wearing a pair of cool Tony-Z Harden basketball high-tops with your pinstripe suite. You're quite a spiffy dresser, Arthur.

Why thank you, Colette. I appreciate the compliment. Those shoes are actually a big seller for Thomas Sports Apparel Enterprises. I consider my wearing Tony's shoes as free advertising for the company:)

LOL Do you work for them?

I do. Ever heard of the company?

THOMAS ENTERPRISES. Inc.

The name rings a bell. Is this one of the memories I need to work on?

Yes. Eventually. But it does bring me to why I'm texting you. It turns out Dr. Rubottom thought it might be a good idea for me to reach out to you. He felt encouraged by some recent progress you've made and thought that communicating directly with you would help keep us moving in the right direction.

I'd like that, Arthur. Other than Dr. Rubottom and my friend, Conrad, I don't really have anyone to text with. So, how do we know each other?

Well, I have to be somewhat coy, here, because your doctor wants your brain to trigger the memories on its own without outside interference. Let's just say we have a mutual friend who binds the two of us.

Mutual friend? Oh, Arthur, that's easy. You're probably talking about my father but, it is true, I have no recollection of him. I assume that he is no longer alive?

Correct. He is not.

Is my mother alive?

No

Do I have any siblings or am I alone in this world?

Actually, that's part of the reason I'm reaching out to you. Let me digress. Have you ever heard of the legal term, 'Contested Will'?

I think so. Isn't it when a person disputes or challenges a will's instructions?

That's pretty close. You are a smart young lady. As a matter of conjecture, let's just say I'm the executor of a will. My client has recently passed away and the will instructs me to assign an entire estate's assets evenly to all living children. In our example there is only one child. Let's call this child Party A. However, out of nowhere, Party B shows up and claims he/she is also family. DNA tests prove a blood connection. So, in theory, Party B gets to split the estate 50/50 with Party A.

OK. That's seems fair, I guess. Family is family.

Yes. I suppose it is fair as long as it doesn't conflict with the deceased person's intent or the explicit wording of the will. But what if there also is a technical clause in the will that can disqualify Party A? In that event, this new and unknown Party B inherits everything and Party 'A' gets nothing. Is that fair?

I guess it depends if Party A violated some stipulations to qualify for the estate or is a felon or is not mentally—

Competent?

I think you better understand the awkward position the executor in my example has found himself. And here's the rub…. *I'm that executor*, Colette, and I've got a problem that is not going to go away. I can't solve it without Party A remembering who she is. The will I'm referring to is being read tomorrow on Party A's 18th birthday. Party A is required to be there for the reading. That's the law. I'm sorry if this makes you feel sad but I felt that I needed to tell you.

I wish I could help.

Actually, you might be able to solve our problem once and for all. As it turns out, Dr. Rubottom has a drug he can administer to you. He says it's 100% effective at restoring memories in patients with your condition. It works almost instantaneously.

How come he hasn't told me about it?

I think that's something you and he need to discuss. Can you do that? Talk to him? It's important. If our Party B gets ahold of Party A's assets, good people could lose their jobs. *A lot of people will be sad.*

Of course, I'll talk to him. Thank you so much for telling me this, Arthur. I'll see you tomorrow.

CHAPTER TEN

"Good afternoon, Colette. Are you ready to begin our experiment?" Rube had already positioned himself in a chair on the patient side of his desk before she entered the office. With overhead lights turned off and blinds drawn, the only light in the room washed filtered gray between loose blind slats. Scattered sunlight cast an eerie curtain call for his proposed transcendental romp.

Colette fumbled her way inside the room and sat less than a foot to his side. During their earlier morning session, she told him how Cole Porter gave the go-ahead for him to accompany her on the next visit. Obviously skeptical, he told her the timing could not have been better; in less than twenty-four hours they were scheduled to attend the reading of Milton Thomas' will at Arthur Metcalf's office. He alluded to Milton being a relative but purposely left off details. All she knew for certain was how for the first time in weeks she would be leaving the Riverside campus and how he, Rube, would be escorting her. Perhaps she was the "Party A" Arthur had mentioned. She reached for her cell phone.

> OMG. Speaking of Arthur Metcalf, he texted me a few hours ago. He said you have a drug that you can give me that will restore my memory and stop this singing obsession. Is it true?

"Yes. There is a drug, but I don't believe you're ready for it. There are too many adverse side effects in patients with your syndrome. We still have nearly twenty-four hours until the reading of Milton's will. The drug will always be there if we need it. A lot can happen between now and then, like the experiment we're getting ready to conduct. Are you ready?"

> Yes, I'm ready.

"Then, let's do this." Rube was eager to dispel "these flights of fancy," as he called her delusions, and holistically entice Colette back to reality to face her suppressed memories and, hopefully, end the musical hallucinations without the use of Valproate. He knew the drug would force her brain to 'crash land' in the same state it had been in four weeks earlier. It meant a return to the old manic Colette. "Let's face the music and dance," he added cavalierly.

> ??? Cole didn't write that line. His friend, Irving Berlin, did. That's Irving's song. ☹

"Sorry. 'Didn't know. I thought it was an expression. A timely expression," Rube countered sheepishly. He leaned forward and swiped the pendulum on a hypnosis metronome propped on his desk. Clock-like ticking beat at a spellbinding 70 bpm cadence.

Colette reached for his hand fearing this journey might never materialize and possibly dispel everything she recounted as a hoax or, worse, prove her insanity. He squeezed her hand for assurance and for the next thirty seconds they watched the faint silhouette of the metronome hand sweep back and forth, back and forth, back and forth. He listened to the distinct ticking meld into a one long melodious indistinguishable timbre. About the time he was ready to give up on the notion of self-hypnosis, Colette yanked off her duct tape and burst into song, "♫ Cole. Cole. Cole. ♫" Instantly, in sync, their bodies jerked backward as though a truck rear-ended their chairs. Whiplashed, Rube glanced to his right. She was smiling a relieved I-told-you-so smile at him and still holding his hand.

Oh my God. What's happening? Are we falling? He wondered.

"Yes, we are," Colette replied calmly.

He turned to look away and drew a most bewildered look. Can you read my thoughts? How is it possible? And you're talking?

"Yes, I can read your thoughts and, yes, I can talk where we're going. Where we're going, mouths are only needed for singing," she answered. "But, if you find it all too strange or uncomfortable, feel free to talk out loud. I will, too. Either way, I can hear you. I always hear you Rube, darling."

As she spoke, air whooshed by their freefalling bodies. Resembling a wind tunnel, the sound grew louder until it stopped altogether, and they crashed into a chaise lounge. On the second bounce he smacked face-down onto hard parquet.

"Are you okay, Rube?" Colette called out.

Dazed, Rube stood and felt his legs and arms and face. Miraculously, nothing hurt or seemed the worse from the sudden landing. He helped Colette off the couch and looked around their surroundings. The room they fell into huddled dark, void of life, and mysterious. It appeared to be a small but elegant studio with a baby grand at its center.

Where are we, Colette? How did we get here? Am I dreaming? He wondered.

"I don't know where we are, Rube. Every time I drop in on Cole it's a different place. A different setting. I do recognize his piano. As far as this being a dream, you tell me. A dream would explain everything except you and me experiencing the same illusion. So, can it really be a dream?"

At a loss for a rational explanation, Rube said nothing in reply. He waited for his eyes to adjust to a dark netherworld veiled in a mysterious fog with a dim glow from a moon breaking the still. His inner-psychiatrist and analytical nature convinced him he was experiencing something akin to mass hysteria with a delusional mal-episode. The power of suggestion is so strong that I must be experiencing what Colette described in our sessions, he assured himself.

"The only delusion is your delusion you're delusional. I'd say your experience here is more de-lovely than de-lusional."

"Who's speaking? Who's saying these things?" Rube spouted, spinning around and around, attempting to catch a glimpse of the face behind the voice.

"Colette already told you who I am. Why won't you believe her? She's the sweetest, happiest person I've ever known. And trust me when I say I've met my share of unhappy people. No. Colette's the top. She's the coliseum. She's the real deal."

"Cole, where are you?" Colette spoke.

"I'm over here in a corner, Sweetie. In a wheelchair."

"*Wheelchair?*"

"Colette, I was afraid this would happen if you kept calling my name. I wish you hadn't. I wish you weren't here. I was hoping our last tryst with Irving and George would have sufficed to send you on your merry way, but you came back. Why? And this time you brought your psychiatrist friend." Cole sulked in the dark mumbling incoherent thoughts as though he had grown quite stupid. "You came at the worst of times. This is my dark period when I was at my lowest. It was after the horse accident. I was in so much pain. You know, they eventually amputated my leg. That's when I truly fell apart. It's when I wanted to cease living. So, here I sit. Here I waste. No more parties. No more friends. No more light. Only darkness and depressed feelings. I can't tell you how many times I wanted to end it all. To kill myself just like you tried the day you were going to fling yourself off the bridge. If anyone knows suicidal thoughts, Colette, it's me. I could have taken my life a thousand times if I wanted. I'd wake up in the morning and ask myself, 'Is this the day you do it? The day you kill yourself?' But I didn't. I suffered to the very end, but I didn't do it."

"But, Cole, you have all of those wonderful memories. Why would you feel this way?"

"Despair. Despair can ruin the heart, dear girl. It certainly kills happiness. My life experience was scattered over decades with happy moments but littered with stupidity. Wasn't it Nietzsche who said, 'Even great spirits have only five fingers breadth of experience; beyond that, thinking ceases and empty space begins'? I was empty. In the end I was totally void of happiness."

Rube spoke up. "Are you listening to him and what he's saying? Are you soaking up his experience? Learning?"

"Listen to me, Colette," Cole continued. "You are so young. Your best memories are just beginning. Whatever pain you've experienced so far is simply life at its infancy. You haven't reached five fingers, yet, let alone two. More importantly, a lifetime of memories is about to unfold. Don't sell your life short. Make memories, good memories, and be happy."

Colette and Rube listened as Cole's wheelchair wheels squealed rolling to the piano and as he groaned to reach the keyboard. Rube could finally make out the shadow of a man and the image of his ghost. Cole strummed a chord and the room seemed to brighten. "This was my favorite song. Some people thought it was about Linda or one of my lovers. Truth of the matter, it was about holding onto life when life turns darkest. It's about seeking light in the still of the night. May I sing it to you both?"

"Of course," Colette responded.

"♫ In the still of the night as I gaze out my window at the moon in its flight, my thoughts all stray to you. In the still of the night while the world lies in slumber, oh, the times without number when I say to you—do you love me just like I love you? Are you my life to be, that dream come true, or will this dream of mine, will it fade out of sight like that moon growing dim way out on the rim of the hill, in the still of the night?.... ♫"

When he finished, Cole moved to where Colette stood and gazed up at her. "Be like the bluebird who never is blue, for he knows what singing can certainly do. Sing and be happy, sweet Colette. Seek light."

"Another Nietzsche?" Rube queried.

"Nope. That one is all me," Cole replied with a sad half-smile. "Colette, I won't be here the next time you sing my name. It's time for us both to move on and regain memories. As for me, I'm going back to 1930. No, wait. 1927. No,

1917. Well, as you can tell, there are so many moments with so many good memories.... just like there will be so many good memories for you. Au revoir, ma Chérie."

Predictably, Cole placed the flat of his hand on their chests and shoved them backward. They fell and fell and fell....

CHAPTER ELEVEN

The mood at Arthur Metcalf's office was anything but lighthearted. The night before, when he called Dr. Meriwether Rubottom, Rube seemed out of sorts and disoriented. How was the esteemed doctor going to simultaneously represent Colette and Jennifer Garfield, now Garfield-Thomas? Arthur asked. "You can't have it both ways." Did he not understand the legal ramifications of 'conflict of interest' when it came to probate? Did he not understand the term 'objective impartiality' as it applied to declaring someone sane or mentally un-sound? In that one-sided conversation, Rube managed to eke the word "breakthrough" about Colette's afternoon session, but he refused to discuss anything more or anything about the incident in any detail. Oddly, poor Rube sounded both excited and confused. Really? *Confused*? "You psychiatrists are supposed to be cool, calm, and collected under fire. Not confused," Arthur ballyhooed. "What the hell is going on?" Upset, Rube hung up on him. This worried Arthur. Truly worried him.

When the trio of Colette, Conrad, and Dr. Rubottom entered Arthur's office, Freddie and Jennifer already had seated themselves facing Arthur's massive table-desk. The pair had refused to acknowledge each other and sat with their backs positioned to emphasis the point. The chairs had been pre-arranged in a giant semi-circle permitting no one closer than six feet apart, what Arthur termed 'safe social distances.' Jennifer found it strange how her hired gun, Dr. Rubottom, seemed to already be acquainted with her half-sister but she brushed off the familiarity as coincidental or that, perhaps, the two had met in the elevator on the way up. In any case, once she spied Jennifer walking through the door, she spent the first thirty seconds forming a first impression. Did the girl resemble her? Was the Thomas genetic lineage at all obvious? Did the girl appear crazed as rumor suggested? *And just why did Colette have duct tape plastered over her mouth*?

"What the hell is going on, Arthur? Why does Colette have tape covering her mouth?" Jennifer pressed.

If there had been a breakthrough as Rube stated, obviously the taped mouth was not a favorable sign. Sensing a catastrophe in the making, Arthur bent over his desk and beat his forehead against it. We're screwed. Totally screwed, he told himself. Frustrated, he straightened himself and repositioned his tie and cleared his throat to regain decorum. "Excellent question, Jennifer. Dr. Rubottom, would you please explain the duct tape covering your patient's mouth? This appears very odd in light of the importance of today's meeting."

"His patient?" Jennifer barked. "What is going on here? I want—"

Arthur signaled Jennifer to hush so Rube could answer.

Once everyone sat, Rube addressed Jennifer's concern. "Ms. Garfield or Garfield-Thomas or whomever, Colette has been my patient for the past four weeks at the Riverside MHMR facility in Wabash. When the Indiana APBN assigned you to me, I received the request late yesterday afternoon via email, didn't have time to thoroughly look over the request until this morning, and, frankly, have been a bit preoccupied. I didn't realize a conflict of interest existed until a few hours ago and by the time I put one and one together, well, it was too late. So, here I am with Colette. I'm sorry but if anyone knows the details surrounding her condition, it is me. I can answer anything you'd like regarding her condition and still maintain my objectivity. It may very well prove my being here on your behalf plays to everyone's advantage."

"Her condition? Is she nuts or something?"

"Yes and no. She has a condition that causes her to sing continually. It's the reason for the tape. It keeps her mouth shut because, once removed, she loses control and sings show tunes non-stop. What she suffers from is a well-known clinical psychosis labeled 'musical hallucinations.' It began roughly four weeks ago when Colette attempted to take her own life but failed. You see, a lightning bolt struck her down and rewired her brain before she completed the act. She suffers from amnesia with musical aphasia. In a way, singing became her way of coping with manic feelings surrounding a world spinning out of control—the tragic loss of parents and many other depressing issues. Four weeks ago, she was extremely depressed but, I must confess, she's now quite the opposite and quite euphoric. She's happy and delightful and definitely not her old self. My staff and our patients at Riverside love Colette. She sings to them with her lovely voice and she has an uncanny ability to remember lyrics to old tunes harkening to the 1930s and 40s. She serenades us all ad nauseam. But we do have a drug called Valproate at our disposal. I have a dosage with me. It can be injected into her blood system at any time and can permanently restore her lost memories in less than a minute and put an end to this condition."

"Then, why haven't you administered it?" Jennifer pressed.

"Because she'll no longer be the sweet happy soul you see in front of you. She'll revert back to her old mopey self and, more than likely, attempt suicide again. She'll no longer sing. She'll no longer be happy because her memories are too painful. I think our mission today, Jennifer, is to maintain her happiness. Don't you agree?"

Skeptical, Jennifer chuckled, nonetheless. Everything Rube described meant Colette was a borderline schizophrenic and definitely not of 'sound mind'. It meant everything she hoped for—the Thomas fortune, Thomas Enterprises, the house, the stock, everything—would be exclusively hers for the taking. "Remove the tape," she blurted. "I've gotta hear this for myself."

As instructed, Rube reached over and peeled away tape from Colette's mouth; the girl ignited belting out a Cole Porter song, unchecked. "♫ My story is much too sad to be told. But practically everything leaves me totally cold. The only exception I know is the case is when I'm out on a quiet spree, fighting vainly the old ennui, and I suddenly turn and see you're your fabulous face—"

Upon hearing her old Cole Porter burlesque song, Jennifer stood as if shot from a canon and, without thinking, vocally accompanied Colette. The woman may have stopped working the Des Moines men's cabaret circuit, but her feature song had not stopped working her. The duet sounded fabulous, as though Cole had written the song exclusively for them. "—♫ I get no kick from champagne. Mere alcohol doesn't thrill me at all. So, tell me why it should be true, that I get a kick out of you ♫...."

Thoroughly enjoying the performance, Arthur and Freddy began to clap in rhythm with the song. Rube, however, stroked his chin, confused, while pondering the bizarre spectacle. What is happening to me? Have I gone mad? Did my encounter with Cole Porter honestly happen? Was it my imagination? What if it did happen? Does it mean Colette is, indeed, mentally competent or is she some sort of spiritual vessel channeling Porter's music? "Stop!" Rube screamed. "All of this is just plain screwy. Do you two realize you are sisters? Isn't that what this is all about? Two lonely people finding each other. Family helping each other. Being happy together."

Of course, Jennifer knew they were related by blood, but Colette did not. The announcement jolted sweet Collette back to reality as much as a lightning bolt had subdued her four weeks earlier. And for the first time in four weeks, Colette spoke without singing drowning out her vocalized thoughts. "Sister? You're my sister?" She asked straightaway.

"Yes. Yes, we are sisters. It's why we're here. So Arthur can read us our father's last will and testament on your eighteenth birthday," Jennifer replied. "We're connected because of our father. Technically, we're half-sisters."

When Colette heard those words, she threw herself onto Jennifer in a stranglehold embrace and began to sob. "Oh, my god. I've always wanted a sister. I'll settle for any half any day of the year. I'll take your half. As far as I'm concerned, half is almost a whole. And you're so, so beautiful and smart. I am the luckiest person in the whole wide world to have found you. Where have you been dear sister?"

Startled, Jennifer wanted to back away, but Colette would not let her go. She pondered how best to pry away her newfound sibling's arms and soon realized freshly minted eighteen-year-olds possess a great deal of strength. She grimaced capitulating to a never-ending hug, for Jennifer had never been hugged by anyone without strings attached. In fact, Jennifer would have to return to memories of Keokuk and her grandparents twenty years earlier to recall those feelings. This girl genuinely loves me, she thought. *And unconditionally.* Why? Why would she feel this way about me, a complete stranger? Is having a sense of family that important? And then, as if by some miracle, something inside Jennifer stirred her heart to the emotion of the moment. The hug felt reassuring and genuine and pure. Lightly patting Colette's shoulders in an awkward reciprocal acknowledgement, she glanced at Rube and next Arthur in a 'what in the world is happening' stare. Arthur mouthed, "She adores you. Adore her back." Maybe his words resonated. Jennifer shrugged her shoulders as if surrendering to the moment, exhaled, and whispered to Colette, "Where have I been? You ask. I've been lost, sweet Colette. That's where I've been. Now, I'm found…. by you. I've always wanted a sister, too. Look, why don't we amscray out of here and get to know each other. Get a cup of coffee. How does that sound?"

"It sounds absolutely wonderful," Colette answered between sobs. "I want to know everything about you. Everything."

Jennifer turned to Rube. "I think I like my sister the way she is. She's happy. Maybe some of what she's got will rub off on me. Forget the Valproate. Got it?"

Rube nodded his head he understood loud and clear. Arthur smiled for the first time in days and high-fived

Freddie. "Happy days are here, again," he crooned. He and Freddie linked arms and twirled in celebration. Rube cast a sad smile to his patient. His work was finished.

Late that night Rube sat in his office, alone. Lights had been turned off and he wallowed in a mood aptly described as a 'blue funk.' He had lost his favorite patient to a bout of sanity kindled by sisterhood *redécouverte*. Now, sitting in the dark, he questioned his own sanity after conjuring Cole Porter's ghost the day before. He reached in his desk and pulled out a bottle of Jack Daniels and debated to drink it straight from the bottle or pour it into a red Solo cup and drink it neat. He opted for the Solo cup. His hands shook attempting to pour whiskey while recalling the unforgettable, irrational moment when he communicated with a dead man courtesy of Colette Thomas. Could he do it again? He wondered. Without her? On his own? He struck the metronome pendulum and listened to it tick back and forth, back and forth. Light from an outside streetlamp diffused inside his office and provided enough luminescence to watch the pendulum sweep hypnotically from side to side. He remembered the two words Colette used to summons Cole and he repeated the man's name three times. Nothing. He smiled. Such a stupid idea, he told himself. At least you're sane for another day, buddy, he mused. He glanced at the photo on his desk of himself and his favorite dog, Elvis. The dog passed away unexpectedly a few months before and its passing broke his heart. He missed his dog friend and smiled softly. "Here's to you," he said, toasting the dog. "I sure miss you." He remembered the love he felt for his deceased pet and sad memories weighed heavy on his thoughts. If he could only glimpse the animal one last time, he told himself. Just one more time. Perhaps, another stab at conjuring might summon the dog's apparition. Why not give it a try? Listening to the soothing tick-tock of the metronome, he uttered the words, "Elvis. Elvis. Elvis." Suddenly, his chair fell back as though a truck plowed him from behind. He felt himself falling and falling and falling.

When he landed, he crashed headfirst onto florescent green shag carpet. When he turned to look up, a young man dressed in white and sporting sunglasses had already moved to help him stand.

"You okay?"

"I think so," Rube replied.

"Where'd you come from, friend? You one of Pricilla's invites?" The man asked. "You know, the party ended a long time ago."

Rube stared at the man and took a step back. "*Elvis*?" he asked.

CHAPTER TWELVE

All of this happened years ago. Fortunately, with my sister's help, I was able to slowly regain memories of what sent me spiraling downward into that depressed state as a seventeen-year-old child and, fortunately, I was able to deal with those ill-gotten feelings. Jennifer and I attended many family counseling sessions together and within a year I reapplied to Yale and was admitted. I graduated a few months ago and just in time to help Jennifer run the family business. No, we did not sell the shoe apparel line. In fact, we opened a new factory in Iowa outside Keokuk and also, here, in good old Pee-roo. Dr. Rubottom began dating Jennifer a week after they met. She inspired him to open a private practice. He calls it Graceland Behavioral Center. For some strange reason he took on an Elvis Pressley persona, Vegas-style, as his medical shtick and his patients love it. I mean, who can't unload their baggage on Elvis? Jennifer certainly did. I guess it's why they married and now have two baby boys with a third on the way. Apparently, there was a huka-huka burning love during their courtship and, I suspect, there still is.

My friend, Conrad, and I kept in communication almost every day while I was away at Yale. He's still my BFF. Did I mention we're engaged? I finally did remember what those high school naysayers said about the two of us. How we were so different that we would never become a real couple. *Ha.* They were so-o-o-o wrong. Yes, we are lightyears apart on many things but not our values and certainly not the one thing we thrive doing together—*singing.* A Captain & Tennille we are not but we do have our own unique voices as the C&C Music Machine; we're the spotlight duo on Friday nights at the Peru Holiday Inn. We love old standards taken from the great American songbook. We specialize in Gershwin, Berlin, and Porter. Even better, we nail karaoke performances like it's nobody's business and to a packed house.

The first year after recovering from my aphasia, there were moments when I needed to converse with Cole. I tried a few times to summons him, but he never answered my calls. Heck, I even tried to reach George but uttering his name fell on deaf ears, too, so to speak. I have since learned to share my concerns with my BFF and my other BFF, *God*. Between the two of them, I know that I'll always have someone watching over me.

Jennifer and I started a family tradition five years ago. Every July 1st, my birthday, we pick out a song that says something about our lives together and we perform it for our men and our friends. This is our latest. Here, have a listen....

"♪ I was born with my feet in motion but since I met you, I swear, I could be happy anywhere. Any mapped-out location, you're always my destination. You're the only thing that I'm chained to. I could be happy anywhere. I could find happiness anywhere with you.... ♪"

On that note, I say move over Blake Shelton. You don't have a corner on happiness. I do and so does my big sister.

I'm twenty-three years old and have a new outlook on life and new-found words to live by: *Dream a while, scheme a while, and you're sure to find happiness.* Alright, I know what you're thinking. You're thinking is this another one of those catchy Frederick Nietzsche sayings? Nope. Absolutely not. These are the words straight from my friend, Cole Porter, and he said all these wonderful things to me.

My name is Colette. This is my story. And Cole and I wish you a happy, happy life☺.

Cole Porter, circa 1940

<u>HUNTING SNIPES</u>

For Bailey

HUNTING SNIPES

Snipe Hunt – noun; plural noun: ***snipes*** 1) An act of hunting wild snipes.
2) A practical joke in which an unwitting victim pursues something that does not exist.

CHAPTER ONE

(August 2000)

"And at the top of the hour, here are the latest headlines from the Utah News Network: The El Diablo Serial Killer has claimed another life. The victim, a Salt Lake City man, was hiking in Glen Canyon National Recreation Area where he was gunned down. The murder marks the sixth such incident in the four-state region since January, leaving a trail of death that—" <click> "State troopers in Torrey have not released the name of the latest El Diablo fatality, the sixth gruesome serial killing involving a hiker in the Four Corners area. The victim, a Caucasian male in his early thirties, was mortally wounded by rifle fire over the weekend. The headless body was discovered by passing— "<click> "Because of the threat to campers and hikers alike, the FBI and Utah CSI are warning tourists to avoid all state and national parks in the area until they've had time to finish sweeping the Glen Canyon basin, this after a grizzly execution-styled murder of a hiker southeast of Torrey...."

Edna Prichard jabbed desperately at selector buttons on her vintage console radio. She hoped a soothing ballad might provide an antidote to the latest rash of murders, but music hid between headlines. To make matters worse, a few seconds earlier she detected the unmistakable drone of an aircraft. Now, with a sputtering engine echoing off nearby canyon walls, practicing a *Doctor Laura* speech grew more difficult. "Perhaps, one more recitation will do the trick," she whispered to a full-length mirror. Indeed, while one more rehearsal could potentially bolster Edna's self-confidence, it would definitely provide an alternative to the depressing news. As the aircraft buzzed overhead, it occurred to Edna how in a matter of minutes the man she loved would be throttling down his Cessna and landing for another hurried postal stop. Emotion yielded to panic. "What if he doesn't want to see me? What if he doesn't want to come inside? And if he won't come inside, how will I ever be able to confront him?" She asked the reflection. Instinctively, she glanced at a hijacked mailbag stashed in a corner. "Oh, he'll come in, alright," she spoke reassuringly. "He has to come in to retrieve the mail I stole."

Edna also realized if the pilot rejected her ultimatum, she would be forced to bring closure to an affair of the heart lasting far too long. Unfortunately, at her ripe old age *redos* rarely happen. Few men of quality survive beyond age seventy, or so Edna convinced herself. Then again, there was always Sheriff Sam Blalock—good old hefty-pensioned Sam. While the feelings for the sheriff had always been amicable, the man did not possess the same mystical aura shrouding her handsome pilot.

Contrary to an August heat wave, Edna's forearms raised in goose bumps. If the confrontation went poorly, she knew moving on with life would not come easily. After all, running a cafe ninety miles to the nearest town of any size made for a lonely existence. Furthermore, with the nearest covey of senior men over one hundred and fifty miles away at Bryce Retirement Home, finding suitable male companionship in the middle of *nowheresville* seemed out of the question. She gazed, again, at her mirror and a freshly ironed poodle skirt dug out of a storage box dated 1958 and repositioned an orange neck scarf hiding seasoned leathered wrinkles and a slight wattle. Not bad, she told herself while turning sideways and flattening her stomach. "You still got it, girlfriend," she boldly announced. Ultimately, however, she capitulated to pent-up melancholy and sighed at the prospect of being alone. She rubbed her arms for warmth and for the twenty-seventh time recited the 'put-up-or-shut-up' speech inspired by a Dr. Laura radio episode:

"Precious William: I thought eight years ago you'd finally be mine, but you said you needed more time. While I understand your reluctance to buy the cow when you're getting free milk, eight years is just to long for me to wait. So, it's either Dorothy or me. You need to make a choice, today."

As the plane roared in the distance, she turned off the radio and groaned aloud, "William is coming. He's almost here. He's almost here."

Like all of William's landings, she felt compelled to witness the event heralding his skill as an aviator. Flying a Cessna remained the last vestige of his glory days as a fighter ace. Whenever he landed the craft, she transformed into a giddy teenager with an adolescent crush. Landings stirred her lovelorn imagination and perpetuated an unfaltering hope they would wed.

He's a proud matador. Yes, a matador, she fantasized. Let's see, that would mean the plane is his cape and the wind a deadly bull. And, pray tell, what would a matador be without his beautiful lady in waiting to witness his death-defying feats? But fearing insanity had overshadowed sensibility, she recoiled on these absurd thoughts and refocused on the here and now. Oh, brother, I must be out of my mind. It's just William in his Cessna for Pete's sake. If there is a deadly bull in our lives, it's the line of bull manure he feeds me twice a week. Get a grip, Edna. Get a grip.

Lately, reality had eluded her with more and more regularity. It had become far easier to daydream about the stagnant romance than face reality. The truth is her rationale had waned as years passed without resolution to their relationship. Today, however, disappointment was serving a wakeup call for long deceived eyes. Today, her reality in a sweltering August heat wave was how this landing might prove to be the last one she would ever witness.

Despite this uncertainty, she continued to gaze with mixed feelings out a picture window and onward to high mesa brush a quarter mile away. She glanced at her wristwatch. It was exactly 9:01 AM. Such a predictable creature, she thought. On time every Tuesday and Thursday since 1973.

As expected, the Cessna dipped its wings back and forth checking lower elevation air currents and dust plumes for wind direction. It swooped a few feet above a caliche runway and plowed headlong into a prevailing westerly and slowly but confidently touched down, first one wheel and, then, the other, with its tail resting firmly on an aft tire. Gravel and dust kicked in the air upon impact. The plane's fragile tricycle-styled struts flexed under the stress of weighty mail parcels yet, despite a bumpy touchdown, the goods survived the landing. Naturally, this feat was not accomplished by some mere random skillset. Rather, the great William Bartholomew Snipe, Korean War hero and ace-without-equal piloted the craft.

Once on the ground, the Cessna coasted unchallenged for two hundred yards because William refused to place too much stress on a leaky hydraulic brake system. Reaching the end of the runway, he swung the craft left in a one hundred eighty-degree tailspin, revved the engine, and taxied to where a pickup truck with two postal carriers awaited. Rumbling to a stop, dust swirled past both young men and the six-room inn adjoining the cafe, and sandblasted a corrugated roof sheltering a concourse between the two buildings. The remote outpost had survived since the 1930s and the completion of a WPA highway project; the road looped from Blanding past Fry Canyon and onward to Torrey, a three-hundred-mile route William shortcut diagonally from the air. Still, despite dust and a perpetual breeze, not much else had changed at the oasis since the completion of the highway—not even Edna.

With the plane parked, the propeller and prevailing wind turbulences proved too much for onlookers. One of the men grabbed his cowboy hat fearing it would blow away into unending prairie and never be seen again. The pilot ignored this comical spectacle and slid open his side window. Blast furnace air poured inside the cockpit. William batted at dust as his jaws chomped staccato on three-hour-old Juicy Fruit gum. A few seconds later, the propeller feathered to a lazy stop. "Looks like we've got ourselves a scorcher. Aye boys?" The mustachioed flyer yelled through the window.

"No shit, Gumby. Why do you think this place is called Fry Canyon?" The younger of the two postal workers screamed back, grinning ear-to-ear.

William frowned. His jaws ceased for the first time in hours as he stared at the young man. Sliding gum between upper molars and his right cheek, he wagged a finger at his carrier friends. "I wish you boys would quit that foul language. You know how much I hate cussing. Especially with women around."

The two looked at each other not the least bit upset by the remark and laughed hysterically. While they had trouble comprehending how their everyday vernacular could be so caustic to William's intolerant ears, they still found him quite amusing. William was the oddest person they had ever dealt with, regardless of the fact they rarely interacted with anyone in this remote outback of southern Utah. It was the second man, the older of the two, who next spoke. "Sorry 'bout that, Gumby. We sometimes forget your rules. Don't mean to be disrespectful of the womenfolk."

William eyed them both, not sure if they were purposely teasing him or were trying to be sincere. Unbuckling his seat belt, he climbed to the rear of the plane and decided to accept their apology for the time being. He unlatched the cargo door and jumped down, forcing a painful but agile move for a man approaching seventy with arthritic knees. "So, tell me, boys, how was your weekend?"

"Not bad considering all the fuss about the killer running around free as a jailbird out there," the older carrier answered, pointing to painted sandstone cliffs off to the northwest.

"Shoot, Manuel, I wouldn't worry none about it if I were you."

"And why's that, Gumby?"

"Because that El Diablo fella seems to only go after hard-working ambitious sorts. You know—hikers and mountain bikers. Guess it all but rules out post office employees."

"Oh, yeah, Gumby? Does it rule out skinny old post office contractors?" The man countered.

"First, I am not skinny. You are sadly mistaking being physically fit for skinny. You boys would be in much better shape, too, if you jogged everyday like yours truly instead of eating frijoles and tortillas all the time. Second, I'm not fool crazy enough to set foot in the park until they flush old El Diablo the heck outta there. Sabe? So, this brings me to the third and most important point. Your disease."

"What disease?" The younger man asked.

"Dunlops."

The younger man scratched his head. "Never heard of it. Didn't know I had it."

"Oh, you got it alright. It's when your belly done lops over your belt." William cracked a mischievous grin. "It's about time you two fellas get on an exercise program and lose some weight."

The two ignored William's unfiltered rhetoric in a much-ballyhooed attempt to avoid an argument. They hoofed to the pilot's side of the airplane and began tossing bags into the back of the pickup. Smartly, they avoided eye contact with William lest he further ruffle feathers. The younger man with the cowboy hat glanced inside the plane between tosses and paused briefly to tip his Stetson, pinching its brim. "Good morning, Ma'am," he said softly.

William appreciated the man's sincere attempt at civility and smiled. "Not sure which one you're talking to, Tom Little Feather, but if it's Trixie, she's asleep. That's what old pups do. Sleep. You know, she'll be twelve years old next month. Why, that's nearly equivalent to seventy-two human years."

"I wasn't talking to your dog, Gumby. Do you think I'm an idiot or something? I was talking to Mrs. Snipe. I was paying her my respects."

"Oh? Well that's awfully—*awfully adult of you*, Tom. Thank you kindly." William lowered his voice to a whisper, pointing to his own ear. "But she's a little hard of hearing. Only listens to me. Besides," he chuckled, "she's snoozing along with old Trixie. I'll be sure and pass it on to her. 'Bout you paying your respects and all. You know, she tells me she thinks you've become quite the gentleman over the years since we started making pit stops together at Fry Canyon."

"She does?"

"Yup. At least more of a gentleman than old Manuel."

The younger man beamed. Manuel mumbled an obscenity and gave his partner a dirty look.

"Tell her I appreciate that, Gumby," Tom replied.

It was Manuel who noticed an oil drip cascading below engine cowling. "I thought you were supposed to have the gasket replaced?" He barked.

"I am but the part hasn't come in."

"Uh-huh. Sure you are. You're just a cheap son-of-a-gun. I'll bet it's not fixed a month from now."

"Am not cheap."

"Are, too."

"Am not, Mr. Chubby."

"What'd you call me old man?"

While the childish razzing continued, the younger carrier stepped back to study the aircraft's worn exterior. "You know, Gumby, I think this plane could sure use a good mechanic."

"She's already got one—*me*. I am A&P certified or have you both forgotten that little fact?"

"We haven't forgotten how you lied to the FAA about her airworthiness," Manuel stated dryly, tossing the last bag in the pickup.

"So, when are you going to trade this bucket of bolts in for a new 675?" Tom asked.

"Don't plan on it. The 170s are the best Cessna has ever made."

"Oh yeah? Says you," Manuel interjected. "I read where all contractors are supposed to switch over to 675s or lose their routes."

"Well, this contractor would just as soon lose his route than switch over. How 'bout them apples? Changing airplanes would be like, like being unfaithful to a good woman. I'm too old and too set in my ways to change and the 675 costs too much money. And I've got a conscience and don't cheat on Birdie. Besides—"

"Besides what?"

"Birdie and me both learned to fly at the same time. We're kindred spirits. When she quits flying, I quit flying."

"Uh-huh. And when was that, Gumby?"

"When was what?"

"When did you and the 170 learn to fly?"

William thought for a few seconds while chewing wildly on Juicy Fruit until his memory kicked in. He tousled his silver mustache. "Korea. Nineteen-fifty-two. It was the year I mastered the F86 and Birdie churned off the assembly line in Wichita, Kansas. We got our wings at the same time."

The younger carrier slapped his partner on the shoulder. "Stop pestering Gumby. He's got more pressing matters to attend to."

"Like what?" Manuel asked.

"Like Edna. *Remember?*"

The two men looked at each other. "She wants to see you, Gumby, before you take off."

"Yeah, that's right," Tom added. "She's got coffee and biscuits and eggs ready for you inside."

William looked at both suspiciously. "I don't think so. I'm getting the heck outta here as soon as you two load me up with the outgoing to Torrey. Edna will have to wait until Thursday."

A sickened look crossed Tom's face. "That's part of the problem, Gumby. She's got the mail and won't give it to us.

'Says you gotta go inside and get it yourself. 'Says there's something real important she needs to talk to you about."

"What the—? She can't do that. Why, why that's a federal crime. It's blackmail. It's—"

"It's *personal*. Involves you two and only you two," Manuel interrupted. "Just do it, Gumby. Okay? Quit pissing people off and none of this would ever happen. Tom and me, we have deliveries to make and can't leave until you're airborne. So, go," he barked again, pointing to the front door of the cafe. "*Go*."

William let out a deep breath, nervously swirling his gold wedding ring. His jaws reignited violently on chewing gum. Grinding teeth woke Trixie. Tom noticed the dog stir. Its ears perked for an instant before rolling over and closing its eyes. He placed an index finger to his lips for quiet and pointed at the semi-awake canine. William looked inside the Cessna through the opened pilot's window. He was not as concerned about Trixie as much as Dorothy. If his wife heard the conversation outside the fuselage, how Edna Prichard insisted on seeing him privately, she would be furious. "Okay. Okay, dag-gum it all. Keep your voices down," William muttered, throwing a quick head jerk toward the cockpit. "I'll go get the mail but if Edna ever does this again, I swear I'll leave it, here, in Fry Canyon to rot. Sabe?"

Both carriers nodded they understood. Meanwhile, William stomped off toward the cafe and kicked up dust with the toes of his boots.

Edna watched his approach and had already drawn shades. By the time he entered the cafe, the room pitched gray except for a ray of sunlight filtering through a crack in the front door. William barged in slamming the door shut.

"What's this about you holding up the outgoing?"

Edna cleared her throat and tried to smile politely but her lower lip quivered out of control. She bit it before beginning the speech. "Precious William, I thought eight years ago you—"

He held his hand flat signaling her to be still. "Like I said, the boys tell me you've hijacked the mail. Now what on earth is going on?"

Edna closed her eyes and continued where she left off. "Eight years ago, I prayed you'd finally be mine but you—"

"Don't you know, Edna, how stealing mail is a federal crime?"

"But, but you said you needed more time and—"

"And blackmailing me so I'd have to come in here is almost as bad. Maybe even worse." He paused. "More time? More time for what? What in blue blazes are you talking about, Edna?"

"Us. I'm talking about us, William."

"Us? The only us I'm talking about is the 'US' in the U.S. mail. What does *us* got to do with anything?"

"Eight years, William. Eight long years ago it happened to us. Don't you remember?"

He twirled his wedding band squinting at her suspiciously. "Nope."

"It was eight years ago when you kissed me. It was eight years ago I told you that I loved you and I'd wait for you but now I'm tired of waiting—*goddamn tired.*"

"Dag-gum it all, Edna. Quit your cussing. You know how I hate cussing."

"Yes, I do. I also know how much you love Juicy Fruit gum, old dogs, and that ranch of yours. I know you prefer your eggs over easy with biscuits, how you play with your wedding ring whenever you get nervous thinking about us, and how it takes you fifteen minutes to pass water in the early morning hours."

"The prostate's all better. Doc gave me a clean bill of health."

"Well, I wouldn't know about that, William, because it's been eight years, eight months, and ten days since you kissed me. It's been over eight years since we've done anything privately together."

"All that kissing stuff was a mistake. A bad mistake."

"Fine. It was a mistake back then but what's the excuse now?"

Nervously twirling the wedding ring Dorothy gave him forty-four years earlier, William stared at Edna's eyes. Not having a handy explanation, he refused to answer the question altogether.

"William, precious William, there are no excuses now. We're not getting any younger. They say these are supposed to be our golden years. Let's make them the best years of our lives. Let's give it a try. Okay?" She studied his face for an answer. He continued to stare at her with a blank expression. "I'm not waiting any longer, William," she stated after a few seconds of silence. "I'm tired of waiting and Dr. Laura says three years is more than enough time. If you haven't noticed, it's been eight."

His jaws began attacking gum. "Well, Edna, I'm sure sorry you and Dr. Laura are tired of waiting. I can't blame either one of you but I'm still not ready."

"And just why not?" She pouted.

"Because Dorothy wouldn't understand. It would kill her."

"Dorothy? Oh, no, you don't. Don't you dare bring her into this. This is strictly between you and me and the love we share in our hearts."

"And Dorothy's heart. Don't forget she's got one, too. It would kill if I left her for good."

Edna buried her face in her hands and began to laugh hysterically. The laughter soon turned into a pitiful wail. "Jesus Christ, William. I've wasted all these years on you, you crazy jackass."

"Quit your cussing, Edna."

"Do you know how badly you piss off the people around you, William?"

"Yes, I do. I get told that quite often. Once already today, as a matter of fact."

She shook her head and began to cry. She knew any hope the two of them would run away together played a pipe dream. "Then, what is it you want, William? What? WHAT?" She yelled.

His jaws ceased moving about the time Edna screamed the second 'what.' He turned to look out the window and peek from behind a drawn shade at his airplane. He hoped Dorothy heard nothing. "What do I want?" He whispered. "I'll tell you exactly what I want. I want to go home to Little Zion, hold my wife in my arms, and make sweet love to her. That's all I ever really wanted in life, you know. To make love to Dorothy."

Edna hung her head realizing she had lost to her rival. The line she drew in sand had washed to sea. Now, there was no turning back. "In that case, I guess we're finished, William Snipe."

"I suspect we are, Edna."

"Then, it's good-bye."

He turned to grab the mailbag, but she held onto a shirt sleeve to thrust a gold cigarette case into his chest.

"At least take the Christmas gift I bought you."

He looked at the present and memories flooded back. "Get that thing out of here, Edna. I told you eight Christmases ago I didn't want it and I still don't." He brushed her hand away, seized the satchel, and stormed out of the cafe.

Edna drew up the shade and watched him climb inside the Cessna. He never saw her blowing a kiss or heard her parting words of how she would always love him.

John David Johnson awoke to a distinct thumping of helicopter blades plowing through thick morning air. He knew authorities hovered dangerously close to his cabin, but he also knew camouflaged netting made it nearly impossible to detect his one-room hideaway butted against a canyon wall. Unconcerned, he yawned and strode barefoot across a dirt floor to open a window and watch the aerial commotion. Oblivious to his whereabouts, two aircraft passed within a thousand feet of his hideaway but continued onward in their search for the elusive serial killer. Mockingly, he waved at the helicopters not the least bit worried they might have spotted him. It had been eight months since his first victim tasted death and he began eluding authorities. Both Utah CSI and FBI authorities failed to locate him in the vast forests of southern Utah. Feeling haughty over his ability to outsmart high-tech poses, the swarm of flies flooding inside his cabin was not so impressed. Having forgotten to clean the remains of victim number six's head impaled on a pike outside, he slammed shut the window. Twenty-four hours after the fact, the decaying head had become a magnet for flies. As the window crashed against its sill, two framed pictures fell from nail supports and onto the floor. One frame remained miraculously intact. He picked it up and read aloud a news clipping taped under glass. "Mr. Abuse Sets School Mark: John David Johnson of Brigham Young High School has set a new Utah state record for most quarterback sacks in a single season. Johnson, nicknamed 'Mr. Abuse' by teammates, eclipsed his own state record set a year ago as a junior. Johnson is a sure bet to make first team all-state honors as a linebacker. He has announced his intention of attending Brigham Young University next fall...."

When he finished reading the clipping, he attempted to hang the framed picture on the same nail by stretching to reach the location from where it had tumbled, and he winced in pain. Instinctively, he reached to stretch a knee backward; the same knee had kept him from completing his senior year at the university. Like most mornings, the knee throbbed. He knew stretches loosened scarred tendons, that and daily hiking.

The second picture frame fared less fortunate. Glass shattered upon impact; cracked runners spiraled from its center. He stared at the photograph of his mother and stepfather and himself taken before New Year's Day. The faces of the two men had been meticulously razor cut out of the photo months earlier but today the sight of his mother smiling behind broken glass upset him. And, like the photo, the men in his mother's life were missing—one in hiding and the other dead because of a cruel past.

"I'm sorry, Mom," he said softly. "I had to do it."

He laid the picture on a table and pointed index fingers at the two missing heads. "Bada-bing?" he shouted at his stepfather, waiting for an answer. "Bada-bing? Bada-bing?" Ultimately, he finished the question with the same answer used every day since the first murder, "Bada-boom."

Hurriedly, he dressed and threw a hunting rifle over a shoulder. He knew the best time to hike was early in the day. Cool mornings also offered the most opportunity to find sporting game. Maybe today, he could find a new head to fill the void left by his stepfather's murder. He stepped outside and swatted at flies and set off toward Bullfrog Creek Valley and gaited toward the sandy arroyo backpackers frequented.

By the time William's plane became airborne, Trixie had awoken to sniff mailbags. The old German shepherd slid on the Cessna's slippery floorboards, especially when they encountered air pockets on their ascent to a 10,000-foot cruising altitude. During a notable turbulent episode, the dog crashed against the cargo hatch. William gave a quick come-hither hand signal, not completely sure of the door's ability to withstand a jolt by a seventy-five-pound dog. Trixie obeyed the command, moving clumsily between the cargo and two front seats, and sat next to him with her head on his lap. He patted her with a free hand while eyeing ground below.

The steep ascent, while breathtaking, also grew nerve-racking climbing out of Fry Canyon and over jagged hills and cliffs. William never tired of the view of canyons or the surrounding countryside still unblemished by human hands. Ground colors slowly melted as they stair-stepped from the Grand Canyon basin to upland desert prairies. In between these landmarks hid a series of uninhabited canyons. The canyons are what drew him to the area before his retirement from the Air Force—that and the opportunity to be his own boss flying postal deliveries as a contract carrier. He remembered in the late 60's when he flew cross-countries as squadron commander, he always preferred those exotic routes taking crews over this particular expanse of Utah. Someday Dorothy and I will hike those old canyons, he told himself. Someday we'll own a piece of Utah turf and build a cabin and explore this sweet corner of planet earth to our hearts' content.

He never regretted the direction his life took with the decision. How could he with so much natural beauty beckoning from his skyward vantage? From white to yellow to red and white again, each change in ground hue represented millions of years in the earth's geological timespan. He marveled at the colors, not wanting to waiver from these breathtaking sights but, begrudgingly, checked the navigation compass and landmarks to make sure he was on course. Without an onboard GPS or a local VOR beacon to serve as guides, finding Torrey from air became a matter of dead reckoning and years of experience.

The Fry Canyon highway now veered due north underneath him; he would take a northwesterly beeline for Torrey. The highway would be the last semblance of man traceable from air for the next sixty minutes. Soon, he would be buzzing the Colorado River and the Glen Canyon basin. Directly below his position Castle Butte hovered. Ahead twenty miles and slightly to the left, at 11:00 o'clock, the Henry Mountains chain would appear with Mt. Hillers first in the series. From there, he would pass Mt. Pennell, also to the left, and, then, swoop toward Mt. Ellen, the halfway point on the flight. With some luck, they could skim close enough to his ranch, Little Zion, to spot it off the right wing and soon, thereafter, the jaunt would be over with a quick landing at Torrey. He placed his head against the side window and looked down. Castle Butte stood directly below; ahead was Mt. Hiller as planned. From this point onward, scenery changed drastically. A red ribbon Colorado River cut through silicate cliffs, only to fall into plateaued flats gouged by winds. With each step along the route, land ebbed higher and higher toward the aircraft. Mesa desert eventually gave way to mountainous foothills and a verdant cedar and pine forest. He smiled peacefully at these sights before gazing right and boasting to his second most favorite companion. "So, what do you think, Trixie? Am I still the best pilot you've ever had the pleasure of flying with?"

Trixie's head cocked upon hearing her name called. Her tongue retracted as her eyes focused on his. He blew into her nose and stroked her ears hoping for a response. "Does Trixie-wixie love her Gumby-wumby?" He cooed. Trixie furiously wagged her tail but, this day, tail wagging was the only answer William could expect from his canine friend.

Finally, after hours of non-stop chomping, his gum had turned stale. He spit out the wad and rolled it into a ball with his fingers smearing it behind a Plexiglas framed photo of Dorothy and Trixie when Trixie sprouted a mere three months of age. Without softened pre-chewed gum to serve as adhesive, the photo would eventually vibrate off the craft's instrument panel. The photo of his two girls had always been his favorite and assumed a prominent position between the altimeter and the heading indicator. When he finished thumbing the frame back in place he smiled, kissed a finger, and pressed it lovingly to Dorothy's image. The routine culminated with a nervous twirling of his wedding ring.

"I'm glad to see I'm still number one," Dorothy announced after what had been a conspicuously long dead silence.

William was relieved she was finally talking to him and hoped the snooze improved her temperament.

"Who else is there, Sweet Cakes?"

"Well, Trixie for one."

He turned to face Dorothy, this time with a wry smirk. "Never. I gave up on dogs a long time ago."

"Uh-huh. Then, how do you explain your ten-minute episode with Edna?"

His cheeks puffed. He glanced away.

"That's right. Don't say anything that might get you in trouble, Gumby. Do you know how long I waited here, baking in this cockpit while you did whatever it is you were doing? *Too long*. You know how I hate to be forgotten. You know how important it is to be on time. Don't you ever learn?"

"I'm sorry, Sweet Cakes. It'll never happen again. I promise."

"I hope so."

William desperately wanted to change the subject. His jaws began gyrating on fresh Juicy Fruit thinking about her uncanny ability to know his deepest thoughts. It was as though she had telepathy. The more he thought about this ability of hers, the more violently he chewed gum. Saliva welled and he swallowed hard. "You do have an uncanny gift, Sweet Cakes. You know me all too well. Better than I know myself."

"It's nothing, Gumby. It's simply woman's intuition. That's all. Not everything I do is hocus-pocus. Remember my stock picks? They weren't made with magic."

"I don't know how you did that, neither. We sure shootin' made a lot of money off old Mr. Wrigley."

"Well, my goodness. We had to. You spent a fortune on his gum."

William chuckled. "A thought just occurred to me. Did you buy the stock before or after my monthly errands to the grocery store?"

"Before, of course," she said.

He chuckled longer.

"Well, Gumby?"

"Well, what, Sweet Cakes?"

"How was Edna today?"

"Her normal demanding self. I don't think she's gonna make biscuits and eggs for me anymore. I told her you were still my love interest. It didn't sit well with her. I believe we are a thing of the past."

"Good riddance."

"And I don't think she's gonna watch me land Birdie on the runway anymore."

"Even better. Maybe now Sam Blalock has a chance with that old hag."

"Well, he'd better grab his wallet cuz if Edna gets ahold of it, she'll buy out half the town of Torrey."

Dorothy smiled at the prospect.

A thought occurred to William and he scratched his head feigning inspiration. "I hope you realize Edna's wanting me can't be all her fault."

"You mean you're finally admitting to some of the blame? That's a first."

"Now, we've been through this before, Sweet Cakes. I'm not accepting any more of the guilt than I did before. It's just that she may have been smitten by this old pilot's charm and debonair style. You know, *the curse thing.*"

Dorothy's sarcastic smirk resurfaced. "Oh, Gumby, you're so-o-o-o right. That had to be what started all of it. The infamous curse of the Snipe men. Why didn't I see this earlier? It's so clear to me now. None of it was your fault. It was the darned old curse."

"That's right, Sweet Cakes. Yuk it up all you want but everyone knows how once you kiss a Snipe man, you might as well hang it all up. Worked for Daddy on Mama. Sure shootin' worked on you."

She shook her head and laughed. He watched her and was pleased she still maintained a sense of humor. He turned to look out his window to spot Mt. Pennell. While he surveyed their position, Dorothy glanced at the instrument panel.

"Gumby, is the oil pressure gauge working?"

His ears perked at the question; his head spun toward the panel. The gauge indicator had dropped dangerously close to zero. He thumped the glass a few times. No change. He checked other gauges. Everything seemed to be operational except the engine temperature gauge. It stoked red.

"Doesn't look good, Sweet Cakes. I think we've finally blown a gasket."

"Can we make it to Torrey?"

"No."

"Can we land?"

William ignored the second question. After years of flying his mail route, he had prepared himself for such an emergency as would any experienced pilot, but there was no easy solution to a forced landing. He knew they were in serious trouble because the Henry Mountains had unforgiving terrain. If he lied to her, she would intuitively know; she could see through him just like she saw through the affair with Edna. Honesty was the best policy, he told himself. "As long as we can do a glide, keep Birdie above 65 knots into the wind, we'll be able to land. Don't you worry none."

"But can we land *safely*?"

He ignored her third question, having already begun the emergency landing routine. Furiously, he tried to hail anyone within earshot on the radio. By now, the engine sputtered erratically. The Cessna shook in waves and vibrated cargo loose from holds. William turned off the ignition switch and made sure fuel selector valves shut off. "Brace yourself, Dorothy. And don't expect one of my famous three-point landings. We'll be lucky to get a two-pointer outta this."

Once the engine stopped, vibrations ceased. Air dragging against wings and fuselage provided a soft whooshing sound. William pitched the nose down without flaps until he achieved the airspeed needed to glide. The steep attitude gave him better visibility to look for a landing site. He fumbled with the transponder, tuning it to the emergency frequency. "Mayday. Mayday. This is Cessna niner-one-five-five-foxtrot. Am attempting to land under emergency situation in Henry Mountains north of Mt. Pennell. Repeat, this is...."

From an altitude of ten thousand feet, the plane fell quickly into a valley nestled between the crests of Mt. Pennell and Mt. Ellen with each peak towering at an elevation of nearly twelve thousand feet. Dorothy watched altimeter needles spinning. She knew the valley floor stood at slightly over seven thousand feet. Her voice accelerated as ground rushed to meet them. "Nine thousand four hundred.... nine thousand three hundred.... nine thousand two hundred. Damn it all, Gumby, I don't see any place to land. All I see are rocks and trees. Nine thousand one hundred...."

"Now quit your cussing. You know how I hate cussing, Sweet Cakes. Don't you worry. I can land this old bird on a buffalo's hinny if I have to."

While his jaws exploded nervously on gum, Dorothy grew more frantic. "Oh, my God. Eight thousand nine hundred.... eight thousand eight hundred...."

The plane twirled into a slow downward spiral when William spotted a dried gorge with a sandy arroyo off to the north. From his limited vantage, the short flat stretch of dried creek bed spread a hundred yards in length before opening to a boulder-strewn field and a scattering of cedar. Getting safely through the boulders and trees would be tricky but getting to the gorge itself meant clearing a ridge of junipers and pinyons and, then, dropping to a speed of less than fifty knots into a stiff crosswind. It would be a dangerous maneuver because the nose of the craft would have to pitch skyward to attack the steep approach. William would be flying blindly into the ground during the stall. Worse, the final descent would be at less than fifty feet above ground, not the customary three or four the 170 handled routinely. He knew such an impact would be the end of Birdie and potentially cause serious injury to his precious cargo.

He looked first at Dorothy, then at Trixie. "Well, girls, this could be it. Wish us Godspeed."

Dorothy remained preoccupied with sweeping needles on the altimeter. William began to sing, hoping to calm her.

"It's very clear, our love is here to stay...."

"What are you doing, you old fool? Have you lost your mind?"

"I'm singing. I'm singing our song. Remember? *Not for a year, but ever and a day.*"

"Of course, I do. Of course, I do. Just shut up," she said, still watching the altimeter. "Seven thousand seven hundred.... seven thousand six hundred Do something, Gumby. Do something. It's not time. It's not time."

"Time for what, Sweet Cakes?"

"Time to die. It's not supposed to happen this way. Seven thousand five hundred. Oh, Jesus, do something. Seven thousand four hundred...."

William aimed for the ridge. An unexpected gust of wind hit the plane head-on and lifted it above a fast-approaching tree line. A pinyon's limb teased the underbelly as the Cessna passed overhead.

"Seems the Man upstairs heard you, Sweet Cakes," William yelled out. "Now I get to show you both how I shot down those MIGs in Korea."

He yanked back hard on the yoke. The plane's nose pitched up. "Flaps down. Check. Master switch off. Check. Seat belts tight. Check." He reached across Dorothy's lap. "Passenger door unlatched. Check." He winked at his two girls. "There's nothing to be afraid of. Like I said, I could land Birdie on a buffalo's hind side if needed. Oh, yes, one more thing. The patented Snipe mid-air stall is how I killed all those MIGs."

Nose-up, the plane hesitated and on cue, stalled only to tumble into the sandy flat before crashing in the center of the arroyo. Struts bowed but held with the first impact. Lurching forward, the craft bounced ten feet in the air with its nose pitched downward before the second impact. Dust and rocks kicked up with the third impact until wheels solidly contacted ground. At over forty knots, the craft's landing speed exceeded the one-hundred-yard stretch of arroyo.

"By golly, I think we've made it, Sweet Cakes," William yelled as he slammed the rudder right.

Crying, Dorothy shook her head 'no' and pointed at a looming boulder at the end of the flats and less than forty yards ahead. "I'm sorry, William. It wasn't supposed to happen this way—"

William swung the rudder left. The plane's tail spun one hundred eighty degrees as front wheels dug into sand, flipping the craft on its back, shearing the right wing, and slamming Birdie against the boulder. The craft split in half and threw mailbags fifty yards in the air. Caught by the valley's gusts, bags crashed hard against rocks and shredded. Loose parcel swirled up and over the juniper and pinyon ridge the craft eclipsed earlier and vanished with the wind.

CHAPTER TWO

(Forty-five years earlier)

"So, what are you waiting on, Captain Snipe? You've been standing there gawking all night. Make up your damn mind."

"No need for cussing, Sir."

"You're right, Captain. This is 1955. We're not barbarians. So, are you going to go on the attack or be content in a stall?"

The young captain looked at his squadron commander, unsure how best to answer the question. He drew a deep breath while nervously straightening medals on his uniform. He primped hairs on his mustache. At loss for words, his tongue searched for chewing gum tucked under a right cheek. Once fished out, he began chomping for a solution. "I have no earthly idea, Sir," he finally replied, rolling the gum over to the other cheek. "You know, I'm not into all this USO dancing stuff," he re-stated. "I think I'll just stand here and look at all the pretty women. Thank you kindly."

The seasoned officer shook his head. "Just look? Are you out of your mind, Captain? You'll never find a date standing on this side of the room while all the lieutenants take swoop in." No sooner had the colonel finished lecturing than a slow ballad filled the room's PA system.

♫ *It's very clear, our love is here to stay....*

"Do you hear that, Captain? It's called a slow dance. Anyone, I repeat, *anyone* can do a slow dance. Now go over there and ask one of those women. If she says yes, hold her tight, ask her to put her head on your shoulder, and blow in her ear. By midnight and with a little luck, she'll be *nice* to you, if you know what I mean."

Over fifty young women, all costumed in full-length formal gowns, nervously awaited against a far wall. Clustered in small circles, they peeked demurely at handsome young aviators striding their direction across the dance floor. One by one, unabashed lieutenants whispered in their debutantes' ears and whisked their partners away to the gymnasium's center, thus beginning the ritualistic first dance at the USO sponsored event.

...♩ *Not for a year, but ever and a day....*

"Well, Captain. Go on the attack. That's an order."

William grimaced, convinced his feet would never cooperate on the dance floor but reluctantly obeyed his superior officer. He shuffled across the gymnasium, slalomed between dancers, and silently prayed his tongue would untie by the time he reached three attractive women in a far corner. As he approached this stray group, he noticed a buxom redhead standing next to a talkative attractive friend. The pair smiled coquettishly and turned to greet him.

"Well, Captain, which of us is the lucky one?" The talkative one asked.

William nodded to both and smiled. "Ma'am. Ma'am." Reaching between them, he extended a hand to a shy younger woman sitting in a chair. This third woman paid no attention to his approach and seemed lost in a dream-like trance watching couples twirl. "Excuse me. Ma'am. Up here," William said, pointing to his face.

Startled by her suitor's presence, the young woman made cursory eye contact before resuming her study of dancers. "May I, may I help you?" She stammered out of a corner of her mouth.

"Why, yes, Ma'am. I was wondering if you would care to dance."

She smiled uneasily before glancing his direction but, just as quickly, resumed watching couples sway effortlessly to music. "I'd enjoy dancing with you but as you can plainly see, with these hideous leg braces I'm afraid I won't be doing much dancing tonight."

William continued to extend his hand. "I saw the braces on my way over here, but you know what I spotted first?"

"No. What?"

"The most beautiful eyes I've ever seen. Azure-blue, right?"

Embarrassed, the woman blushed and looked down. He placed his hand under her chin and raised it to glimpse her eyes a second time. She smiled but only reluctantly.

"Yes. I do believe they are azure-blue," he continued. "Kinda hard to see in this dark dance hall. Well?" He persisted.

"Well, what?"

"Would you give me the honor of this dance or will I have to return home a man with a broken heart?"

"I'm afraid my polio hasn't been forgiving enough to allow me to dance quite yet. Maybe someday when I recover and I'm stronger."

"Oh, really? It appears to me you're strong enough now. Why, your polio can't be as bad as what I've got?"

"And what's that, Captain?"

"Two left feet. It's a terminal disease, don't you know."

She laughed. Her curiosity stoked. "And what name do you go by Captain? You are a Captain, right?"

"Yes, I am and I'm also the best fighter ace in the U.S. Air Force. 'Should be a brigadier general by now but they need me in the air. Generals aren't permitted to fly."

"I'm impressed. Do the other fliers here know about your prowess?"

"Yes, they do but everyone of 'em is in denial. You see, they're egomaniacs," he stated. "I'm the only honest one of the bunch."

She laughed, again, feeling more at ease with the stranger. "So, you never answered my question, Captain. What's your name?"

"Name? Why, I'll take any name you'd like me to have if you'll give me this one little dance."

"Any name, huh?"

"That's right. You name me and then you dance with me. Those are the rules."

She watched his lips nervously smack against chewing gum. The longer she hesitated, the more anxious he became. His jaws picked up pace.

"I think I'll name you *Gumby*."

"Gumby? You mean the little cartoon character?"

"That's right. You did say I could name you anything I wanted. Right?"

"Well, sure but—"

"Then, Gumby it is," she finished.

Squeezing the chair's sidearms, she pushed herself to a stand and wobbled without crutches for support. He gathered her in his arms and lifted her to where her toes barely touched planks.

...♫ *In time the Rockies may crumble, Gibraltar may tumble....*

"Do you hear that?" She asked. "That's Nat King Cole. Isn't he wonderful?"

"I suppose he is if you're into old Gershwin tunes. Personally, I prefer Patti Page songs."

"Honestly? Which ones?"

"*How Much is That Doggie in the Window.*"

She giggled. "I had no idea dashing aviators liked children's' tunes."

"Well, it's only because I love dogs."

"Me, too."

"On the level?"

"Sure. I've lived my entire life with dogs. Big dogs. Bird dogs. Retrievers. My father's an avid hunter so there were always Britney's and English pointers around the house. And you?"

"Shepherds. I always had a German shepherd back on the ranch to keep me company."

"That's nice, Gumby. I think I like you already. It appears we have something in common—*dogs*."

"In that case, are you ready to give it a go?" He asked, his head nodding toward the dance floor.

"Okay but don't have any expectations."

William moved his right foot back slowly. She mimicked. He repeated with his left, next his right, and unexpectedly twirled ninety-degrees to his left but hesitated before pushing his luck and slowed to a crawl. She followed each of his unconventional moves.

"Why the quick turn left, Gumby?"

"I was told it was always a safer direction to go. 'When bereft, throw her left.' At least that's what Mama always used to say." He winked.

"I see. Do you feel bereft with a poor cripple in your arms?"

He slid his cheek against hers. "No. For the first time in a long time, I feel anything but. Actually, I feel a little frightened."

"Frightened? An aviator frightened? I'll tell you what, Gumby," she said. "You get me through this dance, and I'll get you through the rest of your life. Is it a deal?"

"Yes, Ma'am." Feeling more confident, he began breathing slowly in her ear.

"Stop that," she shrieked, laughing. She slapped him playfully on the shoulder.

"No?" He asked.

"No," she said. "Good girls don't. I'm a good girl. Good girls have reputations. They'll be no breathing into this good girl's ear tonight."

"Yes, Ma'am," he replied disappointedly.

She laid her head on his shoulder and they continued to move around the dance floor, this time covering every square inch available.

When other officers first heard her infectious laughter, they ceased dancing altogether and spotted their clumsy friend with the young polio victim. Almost immediately, they formed a tight circle with their dates around the pair, applauding the couple's efforts with each awkward sway to music.

"You know why they're cheering for us, don't you?" William whispered.

"No. Do tell, Gumby."

"They know I can't dance worth beans. They think it's a miracle, you being able to teach me."

"You think?" She teased.

"Sure. That and the fact the prettiest girl in the place would take pity on these two left feet of mine."

They continued to dance in William's unique unorthodox style—three scuffled steps at a time, forward for her and backward and bumbling for him, culminating with an exaggerated twist to the left while onlookers chased after them. Dance floor couples mimicked their last awkward move with an obnoxious hop. He ignored the charade being more preoccupied with her earlier rejection of his advances. Ultimately, he decided to try a different tactic. This time he sang softly in her ear in unison with the song.

"♫ They're only made of clay, but our love is here to stay...."

She responded by tightly pressing closer into him. He reciprocated, placing his cheek against hers.

"And what name do you go by, Ma'am?"

"Why, Gumby, do you think I should tell? After all, we just met," she said, toying with a ribbon on his uniform.

"And, after all, you are a good girl," he countered.

"That's right. I am."

"Fine. But I think it would be nice."

"Nice?"

"Yes, nice. I think it'd be nice for our children's sake if I knew their mother's name."

This time she belly laughed. "Okay. You win. I'll tell you but one day you must christen me with a special name. After all, you have one, *Gumby*. I should have one, too."

"Not tonight?"

"No. Not tonight."

"Okay. It's a deal. Somewhere down the line, I'll give you a really good name Indian-style."

"Indian-style?"

"Sure. Remember the movie Davy Crockett? When Fess Parker gets his Indian name from the Cherokee tribe?

Because of a distinguishing feature. You know—the coonskin cap?"

She drew blank stares. "No, but someday you'll have to explain it to me. I can hardly wait. For now, my Christian name will have to do. It's Dorothy. My name is Dorothy."

"Dorothy? I love the name Dorothy. Dorothy, Dorothy," he shouted. "*I love the name Dorothy.*"

He had been talking aloud while dreaming.

"For heaven's sake, Gumby. I love my name, too, but if you don't shut up and unbuckle your lap belt, you'll pass out again. Now unbuckle it this instant."

He turned to look at her. "You're upside-down, Sweet Cakes."

"No. You're upside-down. Trixie and I got out safely, but we couldn't get to your seat belt. You've been hanging there for over fifteen minutes bleeding all over the place and shouting my name. Now pull the latch, you old fool or you'll end up dead for sure."

William felt his forehead. Where his head crashed against the instrument panel, it felt wet. Blood had dripped and pooled beneath him. Fumbling with the latch, he yanked on it and instantly tumbled on a headliner. He groaned when a shoulder crashed and splashed in blood. Pivoting on his back, he gathered enough strength to pull himself through the fuselage window and crawl to where Dorothy kneeled coaxing him toward her. When he reached her side, he pulled himself to his knees and felt his forehead a second time. Most of the blood around the wound had already coagulated but there was a huge welt the size of an egg where forehead met scalp. He looked at his wife, relieved they were together. "For a moment there, Sweet Cakes, I didn't think we'd make it. You must have worked some of your good luck hocus-pocus."

"Nope. It was all your doing, Gumby. You landed it and got us on the ground, alive. Nobody could have anticipated that boulder, not even you."

She was right, he told himself. Few people could have made a last second maneuver as well as he did and survive. None the less, her flattering words did not help how his head ached. When he touched the spot a third time, he flinched. "Ouch. How's it look, Sweet Cakes?" He pouted, pointing to the goose-egg bump. "It smarts."

Dorothy leaned forward and peered at it, wrinkling her nose. "Pretty nasty cut."

"Must be. Blood's everywhere inside the cockpit. Knocked the living daylights outta me. That's when I must have started dreaming about us."

"Oh, really?"

"Yup. About the first time we met at the USO dance in San Antonio."

"That's when I couldn't walk. Remember?"

"Sure do. Also remember you were one heckuva dancer that night. Lighter than air, you were."

"And that's because you lifted me all night long. It's before your back went bad. Before the irritable colon. Before the enlarged prostate. Before you couldn't—"

"I get the picture, Sweet Cakes. It was before I got old. But you know what I still have that works?"

"Do tell, Gumby."

"A pair of good eyes. Twenty-twenty they are." He used them to study her appearance. "Speaking of which, you don't look any worse for the wear."

"Nope. I'm fine. So is Trixie. Birdie's not so good, though."

"*Birdie*? Oh, no, Birdie," he wailed.

He spun to look at the Cessna. The plane spread in pieces, crumpled beyond recognition. Cargo and tail sections remained intact on one side of the boulder, and the cockpit, fuselage, and left wing on the other. The right wing lay thirty feet away in a shallow trench where it flipped the plane on the last second turn. "Poor old Birdie," he moaned. "I hope she didn't feel any pain."

Dorothy shook her head. "William Snipe. You show more empathy for that old airplane of yours than for the two survivors."

He didn't respond to the remark. Instead, he walked straight to the bent propeller. Kneeling next to the engine, he said a prayer for all to hear. "Dear Lord: Please take care of Birdie. She was a good old bird who took care of me to the very end. And Lord, if you could, maybe in the next life she could return as a falcon or an eagle. I know she'd enjoy it a lot. Amen."

"You old fool, Gumby. It doesn't work like that. Planes don't have souls," Dorothy spouted.

"Says you. I say Birdie had real honest-to-goodness spirit and if she had spirit she had a soul and I don't wantta hear any more of your lip about her, old woman."

Dorothy startled. Only once before had he ever talked to her with a stern tone of voice. "Gumby, I'm sorry. If you think He'll make Birdie an eagle or a falcon, I'm sure He will."

William did a quick Hail Mary but suddenly became dizzy and fell back to his knees. Dorothy and Trixie moved closer to help.

"Poor thing. Here. Trixie found the first aid kit. Inside are gauze and iodine. You need to dress your wound and tie gauze into a tourniquet around your head. 'Sorry I can't do it. When it comes to hands-on medical attention, I'm afraid I'm not of much use with these worthless hands of mine."

"That's alright. You've always been squeamish when it comes to blood," he replied, smearing iodine on the gash and wincing as antiseptic took hold. Next, he wrapped gauze around his crown.

"Gumby, when you finish doing that, you need to go through what's left of the cargo hold and find our canteen. Oh, yes. How about the radio? Do you think it's still working?"

"I don't know. I'll check her out in a second. First there's something else I wantta look for." Feeling less woozy, he stood and gazed lovingly into his wife's eyes and at her face and smiled for the first time since the crash.

"*What?*" She asked.

"Nothing. Everything. You're still the prettiest gal in the joint."

"I'm the only one."

"Makes no difference. You're a sight for these sore eyes and head. Ouch." He paused to feel the bump through bandages. "You know, you always were good in crisis situations, Sweet Cakes. You always liked to take charge."

"Well, I must admit, I wasn't too good in Birdie a few minutes ago. It's only because I was frightened for you and Trixie."

"I could tell you were. But I still think you're one-in-a-million when the chips are down."

She hesitated. "I wasn't so one-in-a-million in the fire. Was I Gumby?"

"No. No, you weren't," he said, his smile capitulating to the recollection. His mouth abruptly puckered. "Guess none of us are perfect."

"Not even yours truly. Why, if it weren't for me, Little Zion would still be in one piece," she added with a sigh. "Tell you what. While you're doing all the salvaging, I'll go scout around and get a better fix on our location."

"Why bother scouting? You might get lost. And Little Zion can't be more than a six-hour hike around Mt. Ellen, over yonder," he stated, pointing north.

"You don't want to hike all the way over there do you?"

"Yup. I sure do. It's been over eight years and I miss the old place. And, it may be the only spot with good drinking water for miles around."

"I just don't think it's a good idea to drum up the past."

"I don't care, Sweet Cakes. There's not a day goes by when I don't stare the past right dab square in the face. The past isn't our enemy. It's the future. Besides, it's not gonna hurt nothing to see the old place. Once we get to Little Zion we can rest and walk the entrance road back to the main highway."

"Fine. You're the captain of this ship but I'm moving to higher ground to see if we're where you think we are. I trust you, Gumby, but you're not infallible."

"I'm telling you, I'm okay. And I'm correct about our location. You know how good I am at directions, especially when it comes to the Henry Mountains. Having a good sense for direction is a man thing. A Snipe thing."

"Well, I don't care what you say, *Mr. Man.* I'm still going to scout around. It certainly won't hurt anything. Maybe I can spot a chimney or a road or something with two legs not named Sasquatch. In any case, I'll return within sixty minutes. Oh, and one more thing. I'm leaving Trixie with you," she said, walking to the ridge toward the east.

"Hold on there a minute, Sweet Cakes. I wouldn't go if I were you. 'All alone without me to protect you. There could be wild animals out there. What about bears? Do you know what to do in case of an attack?"

Without breaking stride, she spouted sarcastically from the corner of her mouth, "The same thing you've told me to do a hundred times before. Don't move a muscle. Lay perfectly still. Play dead."

He laughed nervously. "That's right, Sweet Cakes. Play dead."

He watched her disappear from sight. When she had successfully climbed out of the gorge, he began rummaging through debris and found a compass kept as a spare in case the Cessna's navigation system ever went out. By the time he crawled back inside the cockpit, Trixie had already hunkered inside the remains of the fuselage as an escape from intense sunlight.

"Well, old girl, we both made it didn't we? The Grim Reaper will just have to wait a bit longer, won't he?"

Trixie whimpered, softly licking his forehead and the gauze wrapped over the gash.

"There. There. I'll be fine. Don't you worry none." He patted the dog's head and kissed her wet nose and set about salvaging whatever he could find. He quickly discovered the main radio, like everything else electrical on board, was shorted out by the impact. The battery-operated transponder would be the only beacon working for a search party to locate the craft.

Soon, the oppressive heat inside the cockpit took its toll, making his work more exhausting. William began sweating profusely with perspiration drenching his Mexican wedding shirt. His head still throbbed when he leaned against a cabin wall and closed his eyes. Trixie fell asleep with her head on his lap while he dreamed.

"I'm not enjoying this honeymoon game, Captain Snipe."

"Why not, Mrs. Snipe?"

"Because my legs are still weak and I can't run fast enough and you've got an unfair advantage."

He grinned. "That's the idea."

"Whoa. You said *Mrs. Snipe*. Oh, I do like the sound of it. It has a rather honest ring to it, doesn't it, Gumby?"

"Yup. Awfully honest. Speaking of ring, I sure like this new fancy wedding ring of mine."

"You never looked at the engraving."

"Haven't had a chance."

"Well, go on. Look."

He twisted the ring off and held it under light. "It says Remember Us, January 2, 1956. That's nice, Dorothy. Very nice."

"Truthfully?"

"Yes."

Dorothy suddenly became melancholy. "Gumby, do you remember the first time we met? At the dance?"

"How could I forget."

"Remember what I told you?"

"Yes, I do. You said you'd take care of me the rest of my life. I'm holding you to your promise, Dorothy."

"I meant every word of it, Gumby. I do love you."

"In that case," he said, casting a one-eyed wink, "let's get to it."

"I know what you want but I don't feel comfortable playing this childish game of yours."

"Now, Dorothy, you promised me if I could wait until our wedding night, you'd make it all worthwhile. Now, I lived up to my part of the bargain. Guess whose turn it is now?"

"Fine. But this dogfight game is a little bizarre if you ask me."

"It's just the thing we need to get you over tonight's first-time jitters."

"Okay. Fine. I said I would, and I will. You win. So, tell me, again, what I'm supposed to do."

William straightened his two hands and held them out in front of her with his right hand positioned behind his left. He maneuvered hands to and fro in broad sweeps, one hand pursuing the other as they twirled acrobatically in the air in a high-speed chase. "Here are the rules: You're a MIG15 and I'm an F86. I'm on your tail, pursuing you, and you're trying to get away but can't because I'm an experienced American fighter ace. And what happens next?" He prompted.

"You have a new secret weapon."

"Which is?"

"The heat seeking missile," she stated, glancing at his pajama bottom.

"That's good, Dorothy. See. You're even making wisecracks. It means you're relaxing. Relaxation is what we need. Here, have some more champagne."

He poured her another glass. She consumed it in two quick gulps.

"I do feel a little tipsy, Gumby. You will be a good flight instructor tonight, won't you?"

"Of course, I will. And from now on call me *Captain*."

"Sure thing. And when you're finished, Captain, you won't fall asleep will you? You will hold me all night long and talk to me?"

"Dorothy, sweet Dorothy, I don't plan on sleeping at all tonight. Do you?"

"Oh? You mean we'll be doing dogfights all night?"

William nodded his head in the affirmative. She smiled uneasily.

Once again, he reviewed their rules of engagement. "OK. Here we go. Arms out and swept back," he said, positioning her arms. "If you're gonna be a MIG15, you gotta look the part of a MIG15. From now on, your arms are wings. Ready, set, go," he continued, nudging her forward and watching her glide away. "Now, bend more at the waist, accelerate, and prepare yourself to experience how I shot down those MIGs in Korea."

She shrieked running ahead of him in a full-length but sheer white negligee. He chased her throughout the Palmer House Hotel's marquee suite with both their arms outstretched in mock combat. Over the bed, in and out of the bathroom, and around a coffee table she ran trying to outmaneuver the Saber jet and the ace pilot. Nevertheless, he was too skilled at his craft and attacked from behind, only to press her tight against a tenth-floor picture window overlooking downtown Chicago. Light from nearby streetlamps bounced off falling snow and illuminated darkness into an iridescent kaleidoscope of gray hues. She radiated beauty and he became consumed by desire.

"Stop, Gumby, 'er Captain. Someone will see us."

"Who? We're on the tenth floor. The lights are off and there's a blanket of snow on the other side of the window. It's just you and me."

She knew he was right. The storm blinded everything outside but not his wanton eyes inside. He ran his hand down to the fold in her back and kissed her gently on the neck. When his fingers reached below the fold, he squeezed her buttocks firmly.

"Why'd you do that?" She asked, startled.

He laughed but said nothing.

"Sometimes you can be so cruel, Gumby," she pouted.

"You've got the wrong idea, Dorothy. I'm only laughing because I thought of a good Indian name. Remember? I promised to give you a name months ago."

"I'm almost afraid to ask."

"*Sweet Cakes,*" he announced.

"Sweet Cakes? Never."

He kissed her on the neck. "Never say 'never.'"

"But why Sweet Cakes? People will know it's something crude."

"Oh, horse feathers. No one will know. Only you and me. Besides, it's merely a term of affection." He kissed her once again on the neck and, then, on the shoulder. She gave into his touch. Slowly, he slid his free hand between the cold glass and her warm body. She spun to face him head-on. "Remind me someday to show you how I vaporized those MIGs," he whispered. Gently, he hoisted her in his arms and carried her to their bed. "It's a classic maneuver, like this next one."

"I will, Captain," she responded.

"Promise?"

"Yes. I promise."

Trixie stirred William from sleep. Less than sixty minutes after the crash, the cockpit had turned into an oven. His dog friend awoke him with wet sloppy kisses. He pushed her away. "Stop it, Trixie. I'm awake. Stop it." Unable to breathe, he crawled out the fuselage window and gasped on cooler air. Once again, he dodged death with the help of his dog companion. He rolled over on his back, sat up and hugged Trixie. "Thank you, sweet girl, for saving me," he said.

"I was wondering if anyone was alive," a voice quipped, hollering from a distance. "It appears you made it," the stranger added, laughing hysterically. "Bada-bing, bada-boom?"

William froze. He watched the stranger's approach along the arroyo.

"Yes, indeed. I was wondering if anyone could survive that horrendous crash. Looks like you pulled through with flying colors. Ha. Get it? Flying colors." John David Johnson chuckled, flashing finger quotes. "Anyway, it's a good thing, right? You pulling through and all. It tells me you're a survivor. It tells me you're a fighter. That's what I'm looking for. An adversary who'll give me a good fight."

William stretched his neck to better glimpse the stranger. Morning sun radiated about the man's shoulders and briefly shrouded a clear view. From a distance, his rescuer appeared to be quite formidable—tall and stocky, well over six-foot, muscular, perhaps a body builder, youthful, and early twenties at most. The man wore baggy camouflaged pants tucked into army boots. A hunting knife strapped to an ankle and a khaki camouflaged vest crisscrossed with ammunition belts. As he drew nearer, the man casually flipped sunglasses on top of his head. It was the moment when William noticed his eyes. The man's eyes glared angry and void of feeling or of a soul dwelling within.

"Who are you, mister?" William asked.

At first, the stranger did not respond but, instead, walked straight to the old aviator to help him stand. It was obvious from the ease with which he lifted William that he pumped weights. Bald and shaven, the man's clean-cut appearance clashed with a brazen tattoo of a devil on his right shoulder. A lever action Winchester 30-30 with a scope slung over a shoulder. The butt of the rifle accidentally smacked into William's ribs when he bent over to help. "Sorry about that, Pops," the man said, re-hitching the rifle. He reached out to Trixie. The dog sniffed his hand and cautiously backed toward her master, growling. "I guess your dog doesn't appreciate me." He paused to study William's fitness and overall heath. "By the way, I saw the whole thing. I was south, above the draw, when your airplane cleared the ridge. I watched it buckle in half and smack into that boulder over yonder but, somehow, it held enough together to save you."

"Yes, she did," William answered, holding out his hand for handshake. "William Snipe is the name. This here's Trixie. Don't mind her. She tends to be overly protective if she doesn't know who you are. She's really a pussycat."

"Snipe? Did you say Snipe?"

"Yup."

"I bet you get a lot of razzing on a name like that?" The man grinned.

"Hardly. Everyone around these parts has got used to it. And I didn't catch your name."

"That's because I didn't throw it," the man replied with a smug smile.

William hesitated before giving up on the idea of a handshake. After a few seconds with his arm outstretched, he reluctantly lowered it. When the man saw him retract the hand, he reached for it feigning sincerity. William went to shake it a second time but missed as the man deliberately yanked his own hand back, swirling his thumb behind a shoulder hitchhiker-fashion.

"Fooled you, Pops. You'll need to be quicker."

William scowled.

"Say," the man continued, "have you heard the joke about the old woman and the old man? Seems Wilma wanted her boyfriend, George to take her out on a date. She says to George, 'How bout we go the movies?'. George says, 'Nope. Agnus is already going to take me'. Wilma thinks about it and says, 'Well, I'll buy you popcorn.' And George says, 'Nope, Agnus is buying me popcorn'. 'How about this,' says Wilma. 'I'll play with your thing while you're watching the movie'. And George says, 'Nope. Agnus said she'd do the same thing'. Now, old Wilma is pissed. She says, 'I don't get it. I'm prettier and smarter and younger than Agnus. What's she got I don't got?' to which George responds, 'The palsy'. Get it?" The man asked, twitching his hand. "The palsy," he said laughing hysterically.

"I do get this," William replied. "You appear to be one of those new breed of young people with a disturbed sense of humor."

The statement agitated John David. "You're one of those young people with a disturbed sense of humor," he mimicked, pouting in falsetto. "What the hell is that supposed to mean, old man?"

"It means you must be the kind of person who likes to make fun of everything at others' expense. It means being insensitive when a man and his dog's lives are hanging by a thread after a traumatic airplane accident and you're telling jokes, and bad ones, I might add," William retorted.

The counter did not sit well. John David glared. Muscles surrounding his chiseled jawline bulged. It was when his knuckles popped, a result of clinched fists, the man realized he was losing control and began counting aloud. "One, two, three, four, five.... all better." He sighed.

"So, you won't shake my hand, huh?" William continued. "How about a name. Your daddy did give you a name, didn't he, boy?"

"Your daddy did give you a name, didn't he, boy? Wow. Are you ever a hick. I'll bet you're from Bumfuck, West Virginia or some backwoods third world country. In fact, I'll bet you don't even know who your daddy was. Did he run white lightning? Did he fight the revenuers?"

William stepped back, troubled by the deranged tone of voice. He reached in his shirt pocket for the one thing that could bring him solace at a time like this, a stick of Juicy Fruit. He methodically unfolded the wrapper and slid the stick in his mouth. He closed his eyes hoping the man would somehow dematerialize with the sweet taste of Juicy Fruit but when they reopened, the man appeared as intimidating as before.

"So, Pops, you think it's important for me to have a name? Fine. Give me one."

"Name you? What in tarnation are you talking about?"

"I'm talking about the rules to our game," the man answered. "Give me da name and we can start da game. Hot-cha-cha-cha-chaw."

"Start the game? Look, my head hurts and I'm a little confused right now. Stop talking in riddles."

"Here's the deal, Pops. I'll tell you about the game after you name me, but you have to follow the rules. You want to be a player, don't you?"

"I don't know if I do or not. What kind of name do you want?"

"Any name you want to give me. Here are some ideas." The man's shoulders began to gyrate up and down; his hands and fingers fanned air robotic-like in pike positions. Imitating a rhythmic beat of a base drum, his mouth exploded with percussion.

"You having a conniption, young fella?"

"Quiet, old man. I'm getting ready to do a rap...."

> *Some people call me Johnson,*
> *But they all know my name;*
> *Some people call me Johnny,*
> *But they don't know my fame;*
> *Now, you can call me Lucifer,*
> *Or you can call me Loose;*
> *You can call me Beelzebub,*
> *Or Mr. Abuse;*
> *You can call me Dark Prince,*
> *Or Satan's Messenger;*
> *But I prefer The Devil,*
> *It's far more cleverer.*

...And you doesn't has to call me Johnson."

William threw the gum wrapper on the ground, applauded, and whistled for more hoping to placate the man's ego. The man bowed, ran behind a nearby boulder, and returned for encore hand clapping.

"Thank you. Thank you very much," he said, bowing and blowing kisses to a make-believe audience in a misguided attempt to impersonate Elvis.

Ultimately, the man's eyes told William everything he needed to know—his rescuer stewed angry insane and on the prowl. William guessed he was the prey.

"So, which name do you prefer, Pops?"

"How about a different one. A good old-fashioned Indian name?"

"Indian name? That's fine. Just hurry. It's getting hot and the games must begin. Let the games begin."

"How about *Mr. Killer*?"

The man smiled, shrugging his shoulders. "Why not? It beats the hell out of El Diablo. I never liked El Diablo."

William nodded his head. "Thought it was you. News folks said you were somewhere in these parts. Actually, I had a different name all picked out. Would have fit you even better."

"Well, Pops, don't leave me in suspense. What is it?"

"*Mr. Crazy.*"

The man scowled. "One, two, three, four, five, six, seven, eight.... *All better.*"

"And you can count, too. That's impressive. That way you can keep track of how many people you murder."

"I never murdered anyone. They were all poor losers."

"Oh, really? Seems to me it can't be a fair game when someone who's crazy as a loon carries a gun to use against an unarmed victim."

The man exploded. "Screw you, you old fart. I've tried to be nice. Now, you've gone too far you, you shit head."

"Hey, don't you go cussing. I hate cussing."

"Oh, yeah? In that case—"

William placed his hands over his ears to block a tirade of profanity.

"I know you can hear me, old fart. You can hear everything I'm saying. Know what I'm going to do? I'm going to give you an Indian name, too. One I'm sure will piss you off. It's *Dead S.O.B.*," he shouted. "Wantta know why?" He asked, jabbing his finger in William's chest. "Because you remind me of my stepfather and he's one dead S.O.B. When I was a kid, he used to dunk my head in the water trough on the farm. He'd hold my head under, torturing me up and down for punishment. Bada-bing, bada-boom. Bada-bing, bada-boom. Bada-bing, bada-boom. Get it? If I yelled out, he held my head under water longer until I couldn't breathe and I'd pass out. When I got older and could fight back, he stopped doing it. Then, he went after my mother.

Years later, he thought I forgot about what he did to me. That I blocked it out. That it was too traumatic for me to conjure and deal with. But I remembered. Oh, did I remember. I shot the son-of-a-bitch in his sleep New Year's Day. Welcome to the millennium, Daddy Dearest. Now, the same thing is going to happen to you, Dead S.O.B. You're now part of the game."

William slid his hands away from his ears. "And what if I don't want to play this stupid game?"

The man moved to within inches of William's face. "Oh, you'll play alright," he said, "or I'll kill the dog. Wouldn't want that to happen to man's best friend, would we?"

"No."

"I didn't think you would. And who knows? Maybe you'll be my lucky number seven." With those words spoken, the killer removed his belt and looped it around Trixie's neck.

"So, what are the rules to this game of yours, Mr. Killer?"

"Quiet, I'm thinking. We need something special. Something different for you." Then, John David smiled slyly as inspiration struck. "You ever go snipe hunting as a kid? You know, with a flashlight at night?"

"Can't say as I have."

"Well, the rules are pretty simple: The hunt takes place at night. I'm the hunter. You, being a Snipe, get to be the snipe." He laughed obnoxiously. "Bada-bing, bada-boom."

"So, how does one win at this snipe hunt?"

"Well, I win if I shoot the snipe while it's still dark, in which case I get to cut off the snipe's head and carry it to home base in a bag."

"Home base?"

"A cabin not too far from here."

"I see. And if the snipe makes it to daylight, does it win? Does it win the dog back?"

"That's right. The hunt's over. I let the snipe go. I let you both go." He shrugged, looking at the dog. "Unless the snipe wants to keep playing, upping the ante. More than likely, the snipe will want to quit while it's ahead," he guffawed. "Get it? *While it's a head.*"

"I get it. I also get that you are one very disturbed person who needs to be on medication. Preferably, the kind where they give it to you with a three-plunger injection and you never wake up."

The remark infuriated the man. "One, two, three, four, five, six, seven… eight… nine… ten… to hell with it," he screamed. "Here's something to help you sleep until nightfall, Dead S.O.B."

The killer unslung his Winchester and with a free hand gripping the barrel, slammed the rifle's butt against William's forehead. Stunned, William tumbled onto creek sand. The tourniquet turned red where his gash reopened. The man wasted little time and stepped over William's semi-conscious body to check William's pockets for booty.

William rolled over on his back and gazed at his assailant. The pain was so intense he had trouble keeping his eyes open. When he looked to his left, at Birdie, he thought he saw an eagle perched on the propeller shaft. The bird suddenly flew to the east toward a ridge and over a faraway figure. "Sweet Cakes," he moaned.

"What the hell do you mean by that?" The man asked.

"My wife, Dorothy."

"Oh, yeah? That's a funny name, Sweet Cakes. Bet it's one of your dumb-ass Indian names, huh? You'd be surprised how many of my players think about their wives or girlfriends before they die. They always seem to call out their names. Well, she'd better get used to her new one."

"Her new name?"

"Yeah. *Widow Snipe.* Bada-bing, bada-boom."

Defiant, William flipped off the man, but the man ignored the gesture, too preoccupied with what was in William's pockets. He glanced at the pilot's dilated pupils knowing his victim would soon fall into unconsciousness.

"Hey, Dead S.O.B., did anyone ever tell you that you have a knack for pissing off people?"

"You're the third one today," William mumbled, closing his eyes. "Third one today."

CHAPTER THREE

When the phone rang at the San Juan County Sheriff's office, the lone on-duty deputy had disappeared across the street to pick up two takeout orders. The other receptionist, a fill-in, preferred to respond to the call rather than listen to endless twittering. "San Juan Sheriff's Office. May I help you?" A disguised male voice prompted in falsetto while pinching shut nasal passages.

"Yes. I need to speak to Sheriff Sam Blalock."

"And what is the nature of your call?"

"It's an emergency. *I think.*"

"You think? Can you be specific? We get lots of emergency calls in San Juan County."

"Be specific? No, not really. I just have a bad feeling about something. Look, I know Sam is busy, but I need to speak with him anyway. It's personal."

"Not without specifics, Miss. I suggest you call back in thirty minutes and speak to Deputy Slim Young. He can process your complaint."

Upset by the put off, she took a deep breath. When she exhaled, an explosion followed. "Now, looky here, lady. I don't have time for all this run-around crapola. You put the frigging sheriff on right now. Tell him Edna Prichard is on the phone."

The voice should have recognized Edna. Fortunately, she didn't recognize his. He immediately swapped the handset to the other ear, cleared his throat, and spoke in his usual baritone minus the nasal deception. "Sam Blalock. May I help you?"

"Sam, thank goodness it's you. This is Edna."

"Edna Prichard, the prettiest girl in the county. How are you gorgeous?"

"Sam, you need to get rid of your receptionist. The woman seems to have a perpetual cold and gets on my nerves."

"I'm working on it, Edna. I'm working on it." He laughed uneasily.

"Good."

"So, when can I take you out to dinner? Lilly's Cafe has a two-for-one senior special tomorrow night. Interested?"

"Look, Sam, this is not why I called."

"It's not?"

"No. And I don't have time for your malarkey, either."

"Oh?"

"It's William. I'm worried about William."

"Old William Snipe. That William?"

"Yes, Sam. That William. He left here around 9:30 this morning for Torrey and never made it. They called less than ten minutes ago wondering where he was."

"Well, it's only noon. Maybe he's doing a little sightseeing."

"Listen to me, Sam, and listen good. William doesn't sightsee. He's only been late to Torrey once his entire life. He should have landed by 10:45. That's his routine. That's what he's been doing for over twenty-seven years. Something went wrong. I know it."

"I hear you, Edna, but we can't start running around like chickens with our heads cut off. We need more to go on."

"Okay, try this on for size: The boys said when he took off this morning, he blew oil all over the runway. Said he had a bad gasket. Tom Little Feather said William spends most flights looking out the window and not watching his gauges and probably wouldn't know his oil is missing until the engine locks up."

"How far did Tom think he could have gotten?"

"Halfway. A little more, maybe. But he also had a full load."

"That's not good. That would put him over the Henry Mountains and too heavy to glide. He'd drop like a rock. There's no place to land out there."

"I know, Sam. Now you can see why I'm worried."

"Any passengers on board?"

"The usual."

"Oh, great. Tell you what. I'll get Slim and we'll drive out to Starr Spring Road and take a peek around. I'll notify the boys in Garfield County. This thing probably falls in their bailiwick. In the meantime, I want you to call the FAA in Blanding. If William is down, he'll have an emergency transponder and they should be able to pinpoint the plane's location. Have them call me on the car radio if they pick it up."

"Thanks, Sam. I owe you."

"All you owe me, Edna, is a dinner."

"It's a deal. And one more thing."

"What?"

"When I get off the phone, I plan on meeting you at the Starr Spring entrance. This is my search, too."

"No problem. Slim and I'll wait for you," he paused. "You know something, Edna? William is probably fine. He's always been lucky."

"Lucky?"

"Sure. He's been loved by two women. Most of us never get a chance with one. In a way, that's the most any man can ever hope for—to be loved."

It had been both a vivid memory and a somber recurring dream. He remembered her laying naked on top of the bed as he stuffed the last items into a duffel bag. His flight to Saigon departed in less than an hour and the Los Angeles traffic promised to delay his arrival if he did not leave soon. The new wing commander could not be late, or so he told himself. Lieutenant Colonel William Snipe had to set the example for all young officers on their first tour in a war already winding down for Americans. He remembered sighing heavily and wanting to crawl in bed next to Dorothy and hold her in his arms and make love one more time. She was a sleeping temptress beckoning him to stay but he could not. Just minutes before, he told her he would return to California in six months and back to their cozy wood frame house. Six months was a mere blink of the eye, he said. And he knew she would forgive him soon enough for volunteering. Life would return to normal. Thinking on these things, he nervously wadded a fresh stick of Juicy Fruit and bit down. Right now, the taste of gum seemed to be the only thing capable of diluting his concerns. Watching her sleep so peacefully, he began to twirl his wedding ring.

This would be his third tour to Vietnam flying Phantoms and probably the last time he could perform as a combat aviator. He found the prospects terrifying. Flying had always been his life's calling—the Air Force his family and the young officers his children. A non-military life offered him little. What good was the psychology degree? One could not land a decent job with a diploma in psychology.

If you're going to be stuck behind a desk, might as well do it as a general, he tried convincing himself. Yet, he found himself too often preoccupied over a boring staff promotion when he should have focused on Dorothy. After they made love, she cried herself to sleep and he felt horrible for being so aloof. So many things had changed in the sixteen years since their wedding night—most for the best but some for the worst. An overpowering sense of guilt seized him as he watched her sleep. He took a deep breath and kissed her gently on the forehead. The touch stirred her. She rubbed her eyes and sat up.

"Are you leaving?" She moaned.

"Yes."

"You were leaving without saying good-bye? Is it that easy for you?"

"It's never easy. I just didn't want to wake you. I knew you were tired and, and—"

"And what?"

"Nothing."

"No. Say it, goddamn it all, Gumby. Say it."

"Don't cuss, Sweet Cakes. It's not ladylike."

"That's the best you can do. Don't cuss. It's not ladylike? You can do better. How about, I love you more than this goddamn Air Force?"

"We've been through this before. This is my life. It's who I am. What I do for a living."

"Yes, we have been through this before, countless times, and you know what? I can't take it anymore. I can't take being an Air Force widow. Being alone. I can't take not having roots. And I especially can't take living every day in fear how you could get shot down and tortured to death at the hands of barbaric animals."

"I'll be back. I promise."

"Fine. Then what happens? The same thing over and over again? When does it end? When does it ever end?"

"When I get home."

"Oh, really? What's going to be different?"

"We'll start our family like you want. I'll buck for promotion and quit flying."

Her face soured at the suggestion, melting into a sobbing frenzy.

"What? What did I say, Sweet Cakes? Is it about children? Having a family? What?"

"Yes," she wailed, burying her head deep in her hands. "I feel so, so worthless."

"Tell me what's wrong," he pleaded.

She swatted away tears between sobs. "I went to the doctor last week. I wanted to find out why I haven't been able to become pregnant."

"Pregnant? I thought you were on the pill?"

She shook her head 'No.' "Oh, Gumby, I've been so lonely. I wanted children so badly. I haven't been taking the pill for over a year."

"*A year*? Why didn't you tell me?"

"Because I knew you didn't want children right now. You wanted to wait but I couldn't. I'm thirty-six years old. If we wait much longer, I'll be too old."

"Well, what did the doctor say?"

"He said I couldn't have children because of the polio. It's all related to the polio."

"But you're over polio. You've been strong for years."

She shook her head 'no,' again. "It's just…. I've been losing sensation in my legs for weeks. I tried to ignore it hoping it was temporary but when I fell down the stairs, I knew something was wrong. The doctor ran tests and said I was regressing. He said I'm experiencing the same symptoms as his multiple sclerosis patients. He said because of the disease, my uterus is rejecting eggs. As far as my legs, he said it could go either way. If it got worse, I might be confined to a wheelchair."

"I am so sorry. This is all my fault. I was selfish. We should have had children years ago when you wanted. When we had the chance." He collapsed next to her and buried his head in his hands. She ran her fingers through his hair, laying her head next to his. "Lord, what have I done? What have I done?" He wailed.

"It's alright, Gumby. We will get through this thing. It's just a small imposition. That's all. I have you. You're all the children I could ever possibly want."

They held each other for minutes, neither saying a word. Eventually, he spoke. "I can't leave you. Not this way. Not now."

"I'll be fine."

He studied her eyes for the truth. Dorothy's eyes always told him answers to what lay in her heart. "You're a pretty bad liar, Sweet Cakes. You know that?"

"I don't lie."

"But you are now. No, it wouldn't be right for me to go and leave you alone, not this time. I just wish you had told me sooner."

"I've managed without you before. I can do it again, Gumby. I'm simply feeling sorry for myself."

"Sorry for yourself? Not my Sweet Cakes. That's not your style. No. I think this is a long overdue wake-up call. I think maybe it's time for us to move on."

"Move onto what? To where?"

"To a new beginning. The Air Force has served its purpose in our lives. We're way overdue on establishing the permanency you want. You know—roots. How would you like to move? To live in Utah until we're old and gray?"

"Utah? Why Utah?"

"Because there's the most beautiful piece of heaven I've ever seen waiting for us there."

"But when have you been to Utah, Gumby?"

"Never. I've never set foot in it. Only seen it from the air. Maybe a dozen times or so flying cross-countries but I've never tired of the view. You see, there's this place in southern Utah. A range called the Henry Mountains. The land there is the prettiest wilderness I've ever seen. From the air it's a green oasis of pine trees and cedars all surrounded by red hills and white sandstone canyons. The more I've flown over it, the more convinced I've become our future is somehow tied to that stretch of earth. Kinda weird, huh?"

"No, I don't think so. Not if you've felt this way for years. But Utah? How would we live? It's so remote."

"I'll take my retirement and get a job."

"A job doing what?"

His eyebrows rose mischievously; he grinned for the first time. "Flying a mail route for the post office. They contacted the Pentagon last month looking for retired flyers. It seems they have a need for airmail contractors in remote regions of the West. You know, it could be just what the doctor ordered. We could hike, explore canyons, climb mountains and make those legs of yours stronger."

"But I don't want you to give up your career, Gumby, or your dreams."

"Look, Sweet Cakes, my career is about to be shifted to a desk. Do you realize how I dread that prospect? Do you realize there are only two things in life that keep me going—you and flying?"

"I didn't know you hated being on the ground so much."

"Not the ground, the inability to fly. The world is completely different at 10,000 feet with your head in the clouds."

"Are you sure your head's not in the clouds right now?"

"Positive."

"And that's what you want to do the rest of your life? You've really thought long and hard about this. About flying a mail plane for the post office in the backwoods of Utah?"

"Well, that and the other thing," he said, looking away, slightly embarrassed.

"Do tell, Gumby. Don't leave me in suspense. What other   thing?"

He returned her gaze and became quite serious. "To hold you in my arms and make sweet love to you until the end of time. I guess I'm just a simple man."

"You're anything but simple," she said, touching his cheek.

"Then, is it a plan? We move to Utah and you let me take care of you? Nurse your strength back?"

She laid her head back on his shoulder. "It's the best plan I've heard in a long, long time. I love you."

They sat on the bed for minutes saying nothing. Dorothy finally broke the silence. "A penny for your thoughts."

"Oh, I wasn't thinking about much. Maybe about our song. I felt like singing it."

"Singing? Now? Have you lost your mind?"

"No. As a matter of fact, I think I've rediscovered it. Come on. Sing with me."

"Our song?"

"Yes, our song. We should always sing our song when the chips are down."

"You'll have to sing without me, Dearest. I can't carry a tune. You know that."

"Fine. Here goes another solo performance by William Snipe," he said, clearing his throat. "*It's very clear, our love is here to stay. Not for a year, but ever and a day....*"

"Wake up, Gumby. Wake up."

He blinked repeatedly trying to focus. When he realized where he was, stranded in the wilderness, he jumped up. He patted the swollen egg on his forehead and pinched his arms and legs.

"Whatever are you doing, Dearest?"

"I'm checking. Am I dead, Sweet Cakes?"

"Heavens, no. A little bruised and bloodied, perhaps, but definitely not dead. You were even singing in your sleep. Horribly, I might add."

"Singing?"

"That's right. That dreadful old song you enjoy so much."

He looked into her eyes and smiled. "That's because I was having one of those dreams about us. Must be the bump on the head."

"These dreams are becoming a habit with you, aren't they?"

"Yup. Three in one day. So far they've mostly been about good things."

"Just mostly?"

Wrinkling his mouth, he studied her face and suddenly became pensive. "When did I first make you unhappy?"

"You? You never made me unhappy."

"Somewhere along the line I must have. Tell the truth."

"Why do you ask?"

"Because you never have sung our song. You always acted angry when I asked you to sing it. Something must have been bothering you."

"Don't be ridiculous."

"I am not being ridiculous. Are you?"

"You're delirious and out of your mind. It's the jar to your brain that's done it."

"Maybe it knocked some sense into me. I'm finally seeing things clearly."

"Look, Gumby, this isn't the time or the place to bring up the past. There's a killer lurking out there somewhere. I've had this horrible premonition, a bad hocus-pocus, he's getting ready to come back here and finish you off. We need to leave now."

"That's because he wants to hunt me—hunt me like a snipe."

"He said that?"

"Yup. My crazy young friend, Mr. Killer, is none other than El Diablo, himself."

"I thought that's who he was. Fortunately for us, there's a full moon. We should be able to see our way out of this mess with a little luck."

William looked at a beautiful night sky. With no humidity, stars appeared more bountiful than normal and shimmered in endless white specks across a black canopy. The moon hovered above the eastern horizon, peaking above the ridge and casting long shadows off juniper and pinyon trees.

"Dag-gum it all. I must have been unconscious for quite a long time, Sweet Cakes. It's already night."

"Hours. You were out cold for hours. I watched El Diablo go through your pockets. I felt so useless hiding like a coward. I wanted to run out and club him over the head."

"Why didn't you?" William smirked.

"Don't be silly. He had a gun. And, yes, I was scared, Mr. Man. I was mostly scared for you and Trixie. I thought you both were goners but when he dragged you out of the sun and into the shade and propped you up, I knew he wasn't going to kill you—at least not right away. He also left water," she said, pointing to the canteen lying next to the tree. "I found his goodwill gesture a bit odd."

William picked up the steel flask and twisted off the cap. "Mighty generous of the young fella. Guess even bad boys have a good side." He gulped half the water.

"Don't be silly, you old fool. He's fattening you for the kill."

"Probably, but don't forget, I'm the player he needs to finish his sick game. It wouldn't be any fun for him if I couldn't put up a good hunt. Can't be dehydrated and still put up a good hunt."

"So, is that how he does it? He kills people in a game. Treats them like they're hunted animals?"

"Yup. Made a special game just for me. Calls it a snipe hunt."

"My, that is quite clever of him, Mr. Snipe."

"Isn't it though?"

"Yes, indeedy."

"And here's the twisted part. Each of his victims has his daddy's face written all over their rigor mortised kissers. It's why he cuts their heads off. You know, that boy' is about two French fries short of a Happy Meal."

"Well, what should we do?"

"There you go again."

"What?"

"Using the *we* verb. We shouldn't be seen together. He doesn't have a clue about you and that's the way we are gonna keep it. You need to stay clear of me. I'm the one he's after. Well, me and old Trixie. Said he'd shoot her if I didn't play his little game, but I think I can beat him at it."

"How?"

"The element of surprise. Two against one. We'll go on the attack."

"Do tell, Dearest. I'm all ears."

"Piece of cake. You see, in Korea we used to lure MIGs after one of us while the other one crept from behind and blasted 'em outta the sky. I'll show you. Give me your hand." He straightened her hand out and, then, slid his right hand in front, with his left hand behind hers. He had her chase his lead hand as he moved it in and out, to and fro. "See what I'm talking about. You're so intent on the Saber in front, you don't see the one from behind—Rat-atat-tat. Rat-atat-tat. You're dead, sucker. I'm the bait and you just got shot down from behind."

"Damn it all, Gumby. Not dogfights, again?"

"Why not? My plan will work. And quit your cussing."

"Then, enlighten me on this tactic of yours. How is it going to work out here in the wilds?"

"Simple. I'll have him chase me all the way to Little Zion. He doesn't know how well I know these parts. He sure as heck doesn't know about the ranch. Now, I still have tools in the barn. I'll lure him inside and when he's not looking, you'll attack from behind and knock him clean on the noggin. *Whamo*," he exclaimed, slamming his hand on a make-believe head.

"You know I can't do that. Take a human life."

"Fine. You distract him and I'll club the rascal."

"Why club him? It may not do the deed with the first blow. And clubbing is so primitive—*so Neanderthal*. Why not stab him with a pitchfork? It's what they did to Wolf Man."

"Good idea, Sweet Cakes. The pitchfork it is."

"Outstanding. It seems only fitting someone named El Diablo should die impaled on a scepter."

"By golly, you've got a point there, too. I do love you, Mrs. Snipe, I can always count on you to come through. Like at the Palmer House Hotel." He winked.

"Don't go there, Gumby. I'm warning you."

He smiled. "You know, if we can't lure him inside the barn, I suppose we can always wait him out."

"Wait him out? Whatever do you mean?"

"I mean by sunrise if he hasn't caught me, the boy's game is all over. Kaput. He lets me go. He loses. I win. He gives Trixie back."

"Gumby, you old fool. You're so gullible."

"You don't believe he'd follow his own rules?"

"Never trust the devil, Gumby. He's a trickster, that one."

"I suppose you're right." He paused with eyes suddenly exuberant. "Then, the pitchfork plan it is. He's as good as dead, sweet wife."

"Death to the devil," she proclaimed.

"Death to Mr. Killer," he beamed.

CHAPTER FOUR

When John David Johnson returned to untie his prisoner and begin the snipe hunt, William and Dorothy already had a twenty-five-minute head start. Normally, a one or two-minute lead was all El Diablo ever allowed a prisoner. Even short head starts provided what he termed "a sporting chance" of survival. But, at this point, he had no idea how long his newest captive had been on the run. He hoped it would not matter and the old man would tire and become disoriented in darkness. He also knew the night vision goggles strapped to his head would be of little use tracking prey with a luminescent full moon. The low humidity seemed to intensify moon glow and nullify his high-tech advantage. The backup flashlight became his main instrument of visual pursuit—that and Trixie.

Like most canines, Trixie picked up her master's scent and became quite eager to find him—almost as eager as John David. The dog tugged on the hunter's belt-leash with her nose to the ground; she dragged John David along the arroyo and past the cedar and boulder strewn wash that emptied into Bullfrog Creek. When the oddly matched alliance reached a narrow stream, Trixie abruptly lost the scent. It became the moment when John David realized he might actually lose the game, thereby tarnishing his perfect record. Now, he faced a monumental dilemma. Go upstream northwest or downstream southeast. It was a decision that could break his string of victories. He looked upstream deciding William Snipe had to know the heading to Torrey forty miles away. Upstream it would be. If correct, eventually the old pilot would have to abandon the creek and head for higher ground. That's when Trixie would detect a scent and the chase would go more to his liking. Knowing he could not be far behind, he yelled out hoping to intimidate the hunted. "Dead S.O.B., you cheated. No fair. Cheaters never win."

John David's voice echoed off the valley's walls and bounced its way three hundred yards to where his prey sloshed through a stream. The old pilot froze. His ears perked attempting to unscramble a muffled human voice. Panic overtook his rational side, and he began panting.

"Pipe down, Gumby. Don't you hear that?"

"Heck, yes. It sounds like our little friend is onto us, Sweet Cakes."

"He's close, alright. How close would you guess?"

"No telling with these cliffs."

"How in the world did he figure out our direction?"

William grinned. His teeth shone white with the aid of the moon. "I believe our four-legged canine is aiding and abetting the enemy."

"Trixie? That Benedict Arnold dog of ours."

"Now, now, Sweet Cakes. Don't go bad-mouthing the old girl. This is probably the most fun she's had in a long time."

"Hush, you old fool. Trixie will be your undoing."

"Maybe. Maybe not. We'll just have to outthink her, that's all. She can't track us as long as we're in water."

"Yes, but even you said we have to cross over Mt. Ellen's lower face. That means blazing a trail out of this valley."

"I'll figure something out. Don't you worry none."

She looked at him skeptically. "That's the second time today you've said that. Look what happened the first time."

He gave her a dirty look. "I'll make a deal with you, Sweet Cakes. You keep that tongue of yours from wagging and I'll get us out of this mess."

"Oh, and I suppose if I do keep talking you'd stubbornly plop here on the rocks and let Mr. Killer catch us? What would you say to him then? 'I could have gotten away, Mr. Killer, sir, but my wife wouldn't stop pestering me. So, I decided I'd take a bullet to the head, instead. Please put me out of my misery, kind sir.' Is that what you'd say? Is that what you'd do? I think not."

Losing patience, William shook his head. Rather than risk a long-winded counter, he simply gave Dorothy the patented Snipe pipe-down command—flicking thumb against fingers in a hand gesture resembling a snapping dog. "Nip it."

"What did you say, William Bartholomew Snipe? Don't you dare—"

"Nip it."

"How dare you. I'm a free thinker and I don't appre—"

"Nip it."

"Why can't I just say—"

"Nip it."

She puffed her cheeks knowing to continue would prove a useless undertaking. "You win," she muttered, throwing her hands in the air.

"Fine. Let's go."

"Fine, yourself," she retorted.

"Fine."

"Fine."

Slowly skirting boulders and fording rocks in the stream, they pushed ahead. William guessed there was at least a fourth of a mile to go before they could set off over the foothills of Mt. Ellen. Once out of water and in woods, their speed would more than double provided night sky remained clear. On the other side of the mountain, Little Zion nestled in a valley. The trek would be less than two miles with a shortcut or four without. During daytime and in the best of conditions, the journey would have taken a minimum of six hours. Now, groping and stumbling in an eerie moonlit twilight, they would be lucky to reach their destination by dawn.

"What time do you have?" She asked.

He squeezed a night-glow button on his watch and squinted to read the display.

"It's almost ten."

"When will the sun come up?"

"Around six. Why?"

"I was wondering if we could get to the ranch by then. That's why."

"Great minds think alike, Sweet Cakes."

"You don't say. You were wondering the same thing?"

"Yup. I was thinking we might have to take the shortcut and scale down Snipe Cliff to reach the barn in time. It means we could have an hour or two wait for Mr. Killer if he doesn't follow us the same way. Are you up for it?"

"Of course."

"How are your legs holding out?"

"They feel heavenly."

"Good. I can always count on you when the chips are down."

"Gumby, what if we don't make it? What if Mr. Killer and Benedict Arnold catch up with us? Before we get to the cliff. Or what if he ignores his own rules and hunts us after dawn?"

William thought for a few seconds on the likelihood. "We'll make it," he finally muttered.

"But what if we don't?"

"First, I don't want to hear any negativisms. It doesn't do a lick of good to be pessimistic, but—but if they somehow manage to catch us before we get to Little Zion, we'll have to split up. Remember, he doesn't know anything about you. I'm the one he's hunting. If he catches me, he catches me. I'm not afraid to die."

"Oh, my. You're much braver than me. I was scared to death when the fire broke out."

"I understand. Fires scare the living daylights outta me, too, but you're here now. That's all that matters. You take living one day at a time and do the best you can with the cards you're dealt. When time runs out, it simply runs out."

"You are a perceptive man. That's a good philosophy, Dearest. I want you to remember everything you just said."

"Anyone can come up with philosophical gibberish after the fact. You know what they say?"

"No. Do tell, Gumby. Do tell."

"Hindsight is twenty-twenty."

"That's true. Especially if you're blind to the future." She nodded assuredly.

As she spoke, he noticed for the first time her reflection mirrored in water. Even now, after so many long years, her face shimmered magnificently beautiful. Her profile seemed to glow against the backdrop of the moon.

"You're doing it again, Gumby."

"Doing what?" He asked, dodging a huge rock.

"Gawking. Thinking. Maybe, thinking too much."

"I'm always thinking. When I stop thinking, I might as well be dead."

"Okay. Then, what were you thinking about?"

"I was thinking how drop-dead gorgeous you still are."

"Oh, go on."

"Nope. I was honestly thinking that and how under other circumstances, being out here under the moon and stars, we'd probably take advantage of what otherwise would be a tempting carnal setting."

"And do what?"

"You know what."

She paused, wrinkling her face. "*Men.* That's all you ever think about. Here we are fleeing for our lives and you're thinking about fooling around."

"It's what keeps the world turning, Sweet Cakes."

"Uh-huh."

"Think about it. What good is that flat boulder, over yonder, good for?" He asked, pointing up stream. "Except to have two naked bodies crawl on its backside and celebrate life like two primitive animals."

"Says you."

"Says me and half the male population on this planet of ours."

"It's all wishful thinking."

"Wanton. Wanton thinking."

She giggled. "Too bad. You'll have to wait."

"Seems as if I've been doing a lot of that lately."

"Believe me, Gumby, the next time we get intimate, it'll be worth the wait."

They continued to compete with the noisy creek, babbling nonstop as they waded upstream. Rapids swept over their ankles as the stream narrowed with higher elevation and its velocity picked up. When William spotted the outline of Mt. Ellen silhouette against night sky, he knew the time was ripe to veer from the protection of Bullfrog Creek.

"This is where we're gonna confuse Mr. Killer," he boasted.

"You know. I really do love your plans, Gumby. What's this one?"

"We split up."

"Oh? I don't like the sound of that."

"Don't worry. We'll meet soon enough. It's just to throw the rascal off. You're gonna go left from here and circle around, hooking back with the creek about a hundred yards upstream. You're gonna hike back down the creek fifty yards and we'll reconnoiter right and climb the hill north. There's a lookout point up there, a place called Widower's Ridge. We should be able to spot our hunter and see if he took the bait and continues to follow the stream."

"You mean if Trixie took the bait?"

"That's right." He grinned. "If the smart one took the bait."

"Well, I hope it confuses them both."

"It will. Trust me."

A thought occurred to her. "Say, just one minute. How come I'm the decoy? That's not fair."

"Simple. My head hurts. My feet ache. And you're smaller. You won't have all the problems fighting tree limbs I'd have."

"Oh, aren't we chivalrous?"

"Look, under normal circumstance I'd have—"

She interrupted him mid-sentence with the Snipe hand command. "Nip it."

"What I meant was—"

"Nip."

"Fine. Be that way—"

"Nip."

He shut up.

They parted company as Dorothy made a sweep clockwise away from the creek. At first, she had trouble managing alone in the wilderness, but she eventually found the creek, again, and located William downstream. He greeted her enthusiastically. "You sure made that look simple, Mrs. Snipe."

"I did, didn't I."

"Like a walk in the park."

"Best we get out of here, Gumby. I have a feeling our dynamic duo will be upon us very soon."

He climbed the steep bank and was the first one on the hill. She followed his lead, being somewhat more light-footed and not sinking in mulch-covered terrain. By the time they reached the ridge, he felt exhausted and gasped swallowing air. By comparison, she remained energetic without any signs of shortness of breath.

"However do you do it?" He asked. "I'm the one who jogs, eats three square meals, and has a daily constitutional. But you?"

"Yes, Gumby, you are quite the regular fellow, but you lack something I have."

"And what's that?"

"Female self-control. I've learned to pace myself."

He was getting ready for a comeback when she suddenly spotted the faint glow of a flashlight in the creek valley. She brought her finger to his lips, signaling for him to be still, and pointed toward their pursuers. They peered over a rock outcrop as the killer and Trixie neared the diversionary takeout point.

"Will they, or won't they?" He whispered.

It did not take long for an answer. Trixie hovered around the spot where Dorothy stepped out but seemed blind to her mistress's scent; the dog continued upstream.

"What's wrong with that dog? She acts like the only Snipe worth tracking is her precious daddy."

William smiled, not the least bit upset by the failed diversion. "That's my Trixie-wixie," he beamed.

"She always liked you best."

"That's because I blow in her nose and tell her I love her. You ought to try it sometime. You'd be amazed at what—"

"Hush," she interrupted, pointing to the trackers.

They watched a flashlight beam stop upstream from the previous spot and begin frantically scanning the ground and adjoining hillside. They could not see Trixie through the brush, but they could hear her barking wildly, trying to hoof her way up the bank. The beam suddenly swung high toward the rock outcrop, sweeping by their vantage, and blinding them in the eyes. They ducked.

"Oh, great, Gumby. Your lover-dog has just ratted us out."

"Now, Sweet Cakes, we can't blame the old girl. She misses us something fierce."

"So, Mr. Don't-You-Worry-None, you have any other great ideas?"

William took a deep breath, but the killer's voice stopped him short of a reply.

"Here snipe, snipe, snipe, snipe. Here snipe, snipe, snipe. I know you can hear me little snipe. Before the night is over, your head will belong to me."

William turned to Dorothy. "Yeah. I have a plan. Want to hear it?"

"Do tell."

"There's at least a hundred yards that separates us from Mr. Killer. It's about a mile from here to Snipe Cliff, to the shortcut. I suggest we run all the way there and scale its face before he can catch us. I've climbed it bunches and know how to do it. Hopefully, he'll go around the long way in which case we'll beat him and Trixie to the old barn. Then, we'll implement our Plan A."

"When we pitchfork him?"

"Right."

"I have one slight modification, Dearest."

"What's that?"

"I suggest that when we run. We run like the dickens."

"Good idea, Sweet Cakes. Good idea."

They stood and wasted little time, running northwest under a canopy of pinyons and junipers with William leading the way.

It was slightly after midnight when the helicopter landed on Starr Spring Road. Rescue trucks and county squad cars with emergency lights flashing red and blue lit the night sky. The lights served as a homing beacon for an overdue helicopter pilot and his passenger. A handful of four-by-fours flashed high beams to illuminate a makeshift helipad. Other vehicles littered ditches awaiting orders. When the helicopter finally landed, a young deputy jumped from behind a bubble-glass fuselage. He immediately began fighting vacuum gusts created by swirling rotors. He flattened the crown of his Mountie-style fedora with both hands, barely keeping hold of the hat. He spied a supervisor's automobile, ran toward it, threw open a door and jumped inside headfirst. In the front seat Sheriff Sam Blalock and Edna Prichard sat studying a map of the Henry Mountains. The deputy casually knocked dust off his shoulders and hat, forgetting for a second where he was or why he was there or the message he was supposed to convey.

"Well?"

"Well what, Sam?"

The sheriff glared before clearing his throat and eyeing Edna. Slim noticed the not-so-subtle signal.

"Oh, excuse me. I mean, *Sheriff.*"

"Well, damn it all, Slim, what the hell did you find out there?"

Edna tapped Sam gently on the shoulder. "There's no need for cussing. I don't like cussing."

"You're right, Edna. It's just a bad habit," he replied politely, turning to look at his deputy with a not-so-subtle sour face. "Well, don't leave us in suspense, man. Did you or did you not find the plane?"

"Sure did. It was right smack in that gorge where we thought it'd be."

"*And?*"

"Done split clean in half. U.S. mail scattered all over that arroyo. Looky here what I rescued," he said, grinning wide as a schoolboy. Slim pulled out a Playboy magazine from the liner pocket of his D.P.S. jacket and fanned through the pages showing his boss.

"I'm talking about casualties, Deputy. Were there any?"

"Don't know."

"Why not"

"Couldn't find none."

"You mean all you found was a broken airplane and a bunch of mail?"

"That's right." He paused. "Well, and little blood."

"Where?"

"Inside the cockpit. Probably a head gash. Couldn't tell if it was dog or human blood."

"Where do you think they went?"

"Can't say." Slim shrugged.

"Any ideas?"

"Well, there were at least two sets of human footprints and some dog prints, but it was too dark to follow 'em. We'll have to go back when the sun's up."

Edna finally spoke, interrupting the interrogation. "No. That won't be necessary"

"No?" Sam responded. "You don't want us to search for him?"

"Of course, I want you to search for him, but not there. That's not where William would go."

"Then, where?"

"His ranch. Little Zion. Here," she said, pointing to the location on their map. "That's where he'd go."

Slim leaned forward over the front seat and eyeballed the map. "I know where that is. About five miles from the crash site. Eight miles off Starr Spring Road. 'Been hunting in those parts for pronghorn many a time. It's awfully thick, though. Lots of trees and scrub. Best if we wait until daylight before tackling the road."

Sam looked at Edna. "That okay with you. To wait until daylight?"

Her face puckered not liking the idea but knowing it was for the best. "Yes, Sam," she said. "I can wait. I'm used to it."

When William and Dorothy reached Snipe Cliff, they only had a fifty-yard lead on their hunter. Had it not been for a thick wall of trees, John David would have been able to fire off a round at his prey. The same protective underbrush also wreaked havoc on William, beating him with every branch-laden step. His arms and face tore up while running full speed into low hanging limbs. His prized Mexican wedding shirt shredded into rags. Dorothy, on the other hand, appeared unscathed.

"I don't know how you managed to run through the woods and still come out smelling like a rose?" William panted, pausing to gather breath.

"It's because I drafted off you, Gumby. You forged the trail for me. Thank you, Dearest."

"Well, you did good to keep up, Sweetie. We wouldn't want to mess with that pretty mug of yours, would we?"

"I should say not. It could hurt my modeling career with Cosmopolitan magazine."

He chuckled at the remark and peered over her shoulder as a flashlight caught his eye. Trixie was barking hysterically knowing her master stood only a few bounds away. "Best we hightail down the cliff," he said, waving along Dorothy to follow him.

Having scaled the cliff he named after himself and having hiked it a dozen times before, William easily locate a hidden entrance to the trail. Once he found a huge sandstone arch, they were able to squeeze through an opening and begin their descent. From there, a shallow ledge wound its way along a vertical wall and a drop of roughly two hundred feet. Over years, herds of pronghorn antelope and wild sheep beat a path into the side of the precipice as a part of an annual migration to the valley's rich springs. It also became the safest route for herds to elude predators. For a human to scale the wall became a matter of surefootedness—holding onto craggy rock facing, balancing weight forward on toes, stomach flat against wall. Still, following the narrow pathway was most dangerous in the dark, especially since the cliff's wall faced the leeward side of the moon. Nevertheless, William remembered how to traverse the ledge, feeling the mantel with his left foot, then, sliding his right to catch up until both feet touched; the entire time he never looked down. He repeated the movement over and over and gained confidence with each awkward sidestep. Dorothy followed his lead.

"You know, Gumby, I always did love your unorthodox manner of dancing."

"So, you think this is a dance, huh?"

"As long as you don't twirl left, it'll be one of the best ones we've ever done together."

He rotated his head to catch a glimpse of her face. He could tell she was smiling and unafraid. To bolster her spirits further, he began to coax her closer to him. "Nothing' to it, Sweet Cakes. It's the old one-two, one-two."

"Let's call it the Snipe two-step."

"I like that," he remarked. "Our own death-defying waltz."

"A waltz is a three-step, Dearest."

"*Oh?*"

Given the starlit night and serene romantic pale of the valley, William began to croon in rhythm to their sidestepping motion while singing their song. Dorothy hummed softly to the melody, a first for her. Fortunately, they rounded the bend in the trail as their hunter, Mr. Killer, approached cliff's edge, and screamed into the chasm and disrupted an otherwise tranquil moment.

"Here snipe-snipe-snipe-snipe. Here snipe-snipe-snipe. I know you're out there, Dead S.O.B."

John David peered through darkness and down the precipice. His bad knee swelled from chasing after William and he knew scaling the cliff posed an impossibility. He decided to circle around and hoped what little speed he could muster would outweigh William's slow descent. Besides, his bloodhound, Trixie, refused to go anywhere near the trail.

"Hey, Pops, I may not be able to see you, but I know you're out there. I know what you're doing. You won't get away with it. I can get there from here, too. Then, I'll head you off. Get it? *Head you off.* Bada-bing, bada-boom."

Dorothy gazed up searching for the hunter but the rock facing projected outward above her head and hindered her view. "Oh, darn. Double darn," she said.

"What's wrong, Sweet Cakes?"

"I was hoping I could see what Mr. Killer looks like. That's all."

"My, oh, my. Aren't we curious?"

"I've always wanted to see what the devil looks like."

"This devil of ours doesn't look a whole lot different than most young people nowadays. The main difference is his eyes. They look possessed."

"Well then, he doesn't scare me anymore. I'll know exactly what to do when we confront him."

"And what's that?"

"Avoid eye contact. Treat him as if he's Medusa."

"Now wait a cotton-picking minute. Medusa was a woman with snakes in her hair. Men turned to stone looking at her. How do you come up with comparing Mr. Killer to a she-devil?"

"Easy. I've always had a theory Medusa was a man impersonating a woman and—"

William stopped her mid-sentence. It was too dark for her to see his scowl but she could hear the words, "Nip it."

"You don't think that Greeks were a little—"

"Nip."

"Fine. I'm still not looking at his eyes."

"Fine."

"Fine."

The rest of the way down the cliff they said nothing and tried their best to concentrate on the trail and task at hand. William's head began throbbing, again, and exhaustion lessened his sure footing. He tried to take his mind off their predicament and his need of sleep by thinking about the two of them and their past.

"Say, you never did answer my earlier question, Sweet Cakes," he finally uttered.

"Which one?"

"The question about when I first made you unhappy."

"What makes you think you ever made me unhappy?"

"Well, for one thing, you stopped smiling. But, maybe, it had more to do with you sending me bad vibes more than anything you actually said."

"Like what, for instance?"

"For starters, your continued refusal to sing our song."

"Not that, again. I thought I already answered that."

"Well, you pooh-poohed the question. You said you couldn't carry a tune."

"I didn't pooh-pooh anything. All I said was that you had a much better voice than me and how I couldn't sing on key if my life depended on it and how much I loved to listen to your rendition."

"You said all that?"

"Yes. Don't you remember?"

He thought for a second or two. He cast a blank stare through darkness. "You honestly think I have a good voice?"

"The best."

"Okay, okay. Then, how about the fact that when I go to bed you won't hold me. You never want to hoochie coochie?"

"Not so."

"It's true."

"It's probably because my disease wore me out and I lost a lot of sensation. Intimacy isn't enjoyable. Besides, you have a rabbit's libido."

"Not so. When I turned sixty, I decided that once a week was plenty."

"Oh, is that what happened? You decided? Well, you'll be seventy next month. What's the quota then?"

He thought for a moment. "Twice a week?"

"Twice a week?"

"Yup, I'm not getting any younger. Like kids say, use it or lose it."

"My goodness, we wouldn't want that, would we?"

"No, I've always told you, practice makes perfect."

"After forty-four years, Dearest, you can't call it practice anymore."

"Sure it is. It's practice for the old fogies Sexual Olympics."

"Not that again. So, who's our main competition this year?"

"The Petoskeys—Igor and Svetlana. A Russian couple out of Moscow."

She giggled. "Don't forget, their practices are subsidized by their government."

"Well, we certainly don't need subsidies. We're enterprising Americans. We practice for the thrill enjoyment and satisfaction of it. We go for the gold."

"Yes, we do. Yes, we do."

He laughed aloud before becoming serious, again.

"But there were other things, too."

"I suppose there were. I'm sorry, Gumby. But you always did say that talking to me was like—"

"*Like making love.* I know. I know. I also said that—"

"That you could talk to me for all eternity and you'd still be a happy man. That if you had only one wish in life, it would be to spend the rest of your life making love by talking to yours truly."

"I did say that didn't I, Sweet Cakes?"

"Yes, you did. All the time. Did you change your mind?"

"No. Never."

"Then, what other complaints do you have on your list?"

"How about all the nasty facial expressions when I'd push you in the wheelchair. I hated those dirty looks you'd give me. Still do."

"Now, Gumby, even the young people today have an expression to answer that one."

"What?"

"Duh-h-h-h."

"You mean I'm acting stupid to the obvious."

"Yes. What woman would have been happy-go-lucky losing the ability to walk? Having to depend on her husband to push her around in a wheelchair?"

"Probably none."

"Exactly. Look, I had good days and bad days like any woman. I'm sorry if I was insensitive to your feelings but I had major problems of my own to cope with. The good news is my legs don't bother me anymore. And I'm obviously having a good day with you right now. That should be worth something."

"You think this is a good day, Sweet Cakes?"

"Sure. Why not? It could end up being our best."

"You think?"

"Yes. Sometimes a little adversity pulls people closer together. As far as I'm concerned, it doesn't matter if Mr. Killer wins this game or not. He can't take the memory of this day and this night away from us and that's more important."

"I can tell you right now, he's sure as heck not gonna win."

"That's the spirit, Dearest."

"If I have anything to say about it, he's gonna get a pitchfork right smack dab up his keister."

"Yes, he is. He most definitely is."

It was after 4:00 A.M. when they reached the bottom of the cliff. William guessed they were an hour and a half ahead of John David and Trixie. The ranch made for an easy forty-minute hike along a spring-driven creek and through open pasture and knee-high grasses. When they finally arrived at Little Zion, all remaining of the once proud estate were the log barn he built by hand, a windmill, and the burned-out shell of a cabin. The moon had positioned well past its zenith but still managed to illuminate charred skeletal timbers.

Fearing the sight might rekindle old memories, sad memories, William skirted around the cabin without making eye contact. Farther out, he knelt next to a cottonwood he and Dorothy planted years earlier. The tree had grown enormous in size. Silently, he crossed a quick Hail Mary and brushed debris away from an assortment of handmade grave markers. Where had all the time gone? He wondered. It seemed only days before when they planted the tree. In reality, it had been nearly fifteen years.

"You miss them, don't you, Gumby?"

"I miss all my pets."

"Well, you certainly buried them with dignity."

"They provided me years of comfort, like old Trixie does now. They're the ones who gave me dignity."

"Is this where you'll lay her to rest someday?"

"Yes, and it's where I plan on being buried, too. You know, if this old head of mine doesn't start feeling better, I may soon be joining everyone." He felt his head. The swelling had gone down but the never-ending throbbing was of migraine proportions. "Sweet Cakes, would you mind being the lookout for our young friend while I take a quick snooze in the barn? Let me know when he gets close?"

"Of course. In fact, it's kind of nice having you depend on me for a change."

"Thanks," he said, still feeling his forehead. "You're one in a million. I can always count on you when the chips are down."

He stumbled toward the barn, collapsed inside by the door, and fell asleep on top of musty straw bales stacked three high.

CHAPTER FIVE

For years, William tried to suppress the recurring dream. Most memories of Dorothy stoked happy thoughts and pleasant dreams but not this memory. This one became more a hideous recollection of a past he tried to tuck neatly away with all things painful. It was a nightmarish reminder of a moment in time he despised. He remembered the incident happened in December shortly before Christmas eight years earlier. He remembered it had been cold and the wood-burning stove needed stoking. Like most winters in southern Utah, temperatures rarely exceeded forty or forty-five degrees; cold enough to keep their cabin perpetually chilled and Dorothy's paralyzed legs constantly icy.

"Do something, Gumby. I can't feel my legs," she wailed.

"I've already put fresh wood in the stove, Sweet Cakes. The place will warm in due course. Give it a chance."

"Look at these crippled legs," she said. "They're dead. I can't feel anything except the cold." She slammed her fists hard against thighs. "I can't even maneuver this wheelchair through the front door. I'm a prisoner in this goddamn wilderness."

"Now, quit your cussing. You know I hate—"

"Shut up. Just shut up. You're not the one strapped to this chair. You're not the one suffering,"

He closed his eyes. If only she knew. "I'm sorry you're cold," he said. "It'll warm up shortly."

"That's not good enough. It's too slow. Put kerosene on the fire. Jump start it."

"It's too dangerous."

"Just do it. If you won't, I will."

Reluctantly, he seized a metal gas can and twisted open its spout. Swinging the stove door open, he slowly poured kerosene on smoldering wood logs. The combustion was instantaneous, igniting wood with an explosive woosh.

Flames leapt out of the stove. He slammed the door shut almost setting himself ablaze. "There. Are you happy, now?"

"Much."

"Good, because it's time for me to go."

"But I don't feel good. Rub my shoulders."

He moved behind and massaged her neck and her back the way he always did. She pointed to spots he missed with nothing quite satisfying her pain. He glanced at his watch. "I need to go, Sweet Cakes. I can't be late."

"Why do you have to go? You know how I hate being alone here while you're gone."

"I'll be home by noon, like I always am on Tuesdays. If you're feeling better on Thursday, I'll take you with me. How's that sound?"

"It sounds good for Thursday but how about today? By the time you return I'll be frozen stiff."

His patience taxed; his reply became curt. "Look, when I get home, I'll stoke the damn fire."

"Fine. I don't care if you're late. I don't care if you ever come back. I'm tired of all this, anyway."

"All what?"

"You leaving me in this cramped excuse for a home. I'm beginning to hate it here."

"You don't mean that. You love Little Zion."

She thought for a moment before capitulating to a grimace. "You hate the idea that I could be this way the rest of my life and you'd have to wait on my every beck and call. It's true isn't it?"

"No."

"Yes, it is."

Exasperated, William fell on his knees in front of her and seized her hands. "I want you to listen to me, Sweet Cakes, and listen good. I love you. There's nothing that can stop that feeling. Not your anger or this bad mood you're in right now. I plan on honoring you in sickness and in health."

Dorothy began to cry. "Then, don't leave me. I hate being left alone."

"I'll be back. I promise. Don't forget, this is what I do for a living. Flying is my life. It's the second-best thing I do."

"And the first, Gumby? Remind me again."

"The first is loving you."

"Then, stay."

"No."

He stood and moved toward the door.

"Damn you, William Bartholomew Snipe. Come back."

"I can't be late, Sweet Cakes. I'll be back by noon. Don't you worry none."

He moved outside. She followed him as far as she could, to the door. Her wheelchair wedged too wide to fit past the threshold. She sat staring at him, hoping he would change his mind, but he did not. He climbed inside his pickup truck, turned, and looked at her one last time before driving away.

When he landed in Fry Canyon four hours later, at exactly 9:01, Edna had been patiently waiting. Like most Tuesdays and Thursdays, she pre-prepared breakfast for him and, now, watched him devour her cooking. He talked nonstop and she listened to him recall his glory days in Korea. By 9:35, he moved from the table to head onto Torrey. However, on that one morning in December, Edna stopped him on his way out the door.

"William, do you have a minute?"

He checked his watch. "Not really, Edna. What is it?"

"Come," she said. "Follow me."

She grabbed his hand and led him to a back room and her private living quarters. He had never been beyond the wall posted 'Employees Only' and appeared baffled by her insistence.

"I take it, this is where you live?"

"Oh, yes. This is where I live, sleep, and dream."

He smiled uneasily. "Maybe I should go," he said, stepping back.

She held onto his hand and tugged him inside, shutting the door behind him. "Come here, William. Sit next to me," she said, patting her bed. "Don't worry. You're safe. It's the only spot to sit in this room. Besides, I've got something for you."

"For me?" He gulped.

"Yes, silly. A Christmas present." She reached under a pillow and pulled out a small, neatly wrapped box. He took the gift in his hands unsure if he should take it.

"Oh? This is sure nice, but I didn't get you anything."

"It's okay, William. I'm not offended. It's just that when I saw this in the store window in Salt Lake City, I knew it was the perfect gift for you. Well, don't sit there. Open it."

He obeyed, tearing into the paper and the bright red ribbon, hastily throwing scraps on the floor. When he removed the box's lid, he pulled out a gold cigarette case.

"I know what you're thinking, William: Why in the world would Edna buy me a cigarette case? But it's much, much more. I got the idea the minute I saw it."

"What idea?"

"A marvelous idea. You can use the case to store your sticks of gum. Isn't that keen? And look, here," she said, grabbing it away from him. "It has a spring latch that flips the lid open. I counted and you can store thirty-three sticks inside." She pointed, where a pack of cigarettes would normally insert. "And here's the best part," she continued, turning the case around. "I had it engraved. It says: To William from Edna, Christmas, 1991."

She handed the case back to him. He studied it closer. "I like this, Edna. It's very thoughtful of you and, and I—"

She pressed her finger to his lips. "Like I said earlier, William, I don't expect anything from you. I don't mind."

"But I feel guilty. I wish there was something I could give you."

"Maybe there is, William."

"What?"

She drew a deep breath. "How about a kiss?"

He peered into her eyes and knew a kiss crossed over the professional boundary they shared for years but he also considered her a close friend and, so, he kissed her gently on the lips. When he pulled back, her eyes told him she wanted more; he kissed her a second time, this time pulling her into him in a passionate embrace.

She moaned. "Make love to me, William."

He began to take off his shirt but when his eyes met hers a third time, he noticed Edna's eyes were not azure-blue and guilt swept over him. "I can't do this," he said.

"Why, William?"

"Because it's not right."

"Right? For whom? You? Me?"

"Everyone. Especially Dorothy."

"William, precious William, do you know how long we've known each other?"

"Almost twenty years."

"That's right. Twice a week for nearly twenty years you've been coming into my cafe. For nearly twenty years I've been feeding you, listening to you, sharing your thoughts and feelings, and slowly falling in love with you. You're like a relentless cancer that languishes until one day you discover it's too late. When that happens, it becomes as much a part of you as anything else. Bad mixing with good. Good mixing with bad. Don't tell me what's right."

"But this is wrong."

"Is it? So, I guess it's right for a wonderful man to waste the rest of his life with a woman who no longer feels. Who's angry. Who treats him as if he was a hired nurse and who denies him happiness?"

"I shouldn't have told you those things. They were private."

"But you did tell me, and many other private things, too," she responded, throwing her arms around him. "I can make you happy in ways Dorothy can't. Make love to me. Here. Now."

"I can't. I just can't."

"But you want to. I know it."

"Yes."

"Then, why not?"

He removed her hands from around his neck and returned the gift. "Because Dorothy needs me."

Edna shook her head. "Not nearly as badly as you need her."

"You're probably right. I need her worse."

"So, how long are you going to continue the charade and deny what your heart desires?"

William smiled a sad smile. "As long as it takes. Until death do us part."

He turned and walked away. She ran after him.

"I still love you. I can wait. She won't be around forever, William."

He nervously twirled his wedding ring while his legs picked up pace running to the plane. It would be the first time he had ever been late to Torrey.

"William. William, wake up," Dorothy gently murmured.

He sat up and tried his best to focus on her eyes.

"Sweet Cakes? Is it you?"

"Of course. You didn't think I was Mr. Killer, did you?"

"No," he replied, feeling his forehead and trying to forget the nightmare.

"I spotted our hunter friend walking this direction. Trixie was dragging him to our hideaway. They'll be here any minute."

William cocked his head listening to Trixie's distinctive yelps. "Are you ready to do this, Sweet Cakes?"

"Ready and willing. Just tell me what you want me to do."

"Here's what I have in mind. You're gonna hide behind these bales. I'm gonna stand over on the other side of the barn where the pitchfork is hung. It'll be concealed behind my back. Now, when I hear him rustling around outside, I'll holler out to let him know I'm inside here. He'll come marching through the door looking for me and I'll lure him further inside, say, within ten feet or so of me."

"Gumby, what makes you think he won't shoot you on the spot?"

"He's not the impetuous type. He'll want to see the expression on my face, watch my eyes when he squeezes the trigger. Otherwise, there wouldn't be any thrill in the chase for him."

"What happens after he gets close to you?"

"Well, you'll be behind him and I'll give you a signal for our diversion."

"What kind of signal?"

"Dag-gum, I don't know. Why do you ask so many questions?"

"Because I don't want to blow it."

"Fine. I'll say 'nip it' and, then, you jump up and start yelling."

"What should I yell, Dearest?"

Frustrated, William shook his head. "How bout, Mr. Killer, over here. Behind you."

"That's good. It should startle him enough to turn around. That's when you'll jab him?"

"That's right. I'll spear him in the heart."

Dorothy giggled before scurrying behind the bales while William assumed his position on the other side of the barn. When he heard Trixie scratching on the door, he was about to yell out and give away his location, but he didn't have to.

"Here snipe, snipe, snipe, snipe, snipe. Are you in there little snipe?"

"Yup. Sure am, Mr. Killer."

"Can I join you in your snipe nest?"

"Be my guest."

"John David slowly swung the door open and peered into the darker niche of the barn. His flashlight instantly locked onto William's eyes. He turned the flashlight off, satisfied with early morning twilight pouring through rafters. Unaware Dorothy stooped behind hay bales, he limped forward after tying the dog to a post. Trixie yelped furiously trying to get to her master.

"Well, well, well. Mr. William Snipe, also known as Dead S.O.B. We finally meet again." John David gloated, unslinging his Winchester.

William said nothing but kept his eyes glued on his hunter while waiting for the perfect moment to pounce. Meanwhile, Trixie stopped barking and began a frenzied tug on her leash.

"You played the game well, Pops, but obviously not well enough. Any last wishes before I finish our game?"

Groping for the pitchfork, William slyly grasped the handle behind his back. "Just one wish, Mr. Killer. The same one I always wish for."

"Oh, really?" The hunter responded, noticing William's defensive posturing. "So, what are you going to do, Dead S.O.B.? Throw that pitchfork at me? The one behind your back. Try to kill me?"

"Maybe."

John David took aim, cocked the firing hammer, and wrapped his finger around the trigger. "So, do you think you're fast enough? Do you think you've got what it takes, punk?"

"We'll see, won't we, Mr. Killer?"

"Then, go ahead. Make my day."

William stared at the man's finger on the trigger, then, quickly to his left. Trixie had almost pulled herself free. He glanced to the right. Dorothy was now standing on the tallest bale and awaiting his signal. It was now or never. He blurted the command words, "Nip it."

Dorothy responded, "Oh, Mr. Killer. Over here."

The hunter didn't flinch. Instead, his face drew a puzzled expression studying William. William's forehead began to break out in sweat.

"Do it again, Sweet Cakes," William shouted out of the corner of his mouth. "Nip it."

With that, Dorothy started jumping up and down, flapping her arms wildly, and screaming hysterically. "Mr. Killer, over here. Over here. Boo. Boo-o-o-o."

Unfazed, John David slowly tilted his head away from the scope. "Are you supposed to be talking to someone, Pops?"

"Yes. Of course, I am. Don't you hear her?"

"Hear whom?"

"My wife, Dorothy. She's behind you screaming her fool head off. Dag-gum it all, how come you didn't turn around? Are you deaf or something?"

John David's eyes opened wider. "Your wife? Oh, I get it. You thought your wife would distract me and, then, you'd toss the pitchfork when I turned around to look at her, Right?"

"Well, yes. Something like that."

John David began laughing hysterically. "It's a good plan, old man. It's clever and lethal. You know, I have never had a player fight back. It's a first. But you had better get a new accomplice."

"What the heck are you talking about?"

"I'm talking about Dorothy, your wife, you crazy old fart. Why do you think I didn't hear her?"

William's face cast a blank stare.

"It's because she's not behind me. She's not even in this room," he said. "*She's dead.* Buried outside. I read the epitaph on the tombstone under the tree. It said she died eight years ago in a fire. So, what is she? Like a ghost or something?"

Frustrated, Dorothy hovered from the bales and flew to William. When she passed through John David, he shivered from a brief sensation of netherworld chills. Once she reached William's side, she closed her eyes to avoid glimpsing the devil in the face.

"Did you hear what rude Mr. Killer said about me?"

"For Pete's sake, open your eyes."

"You think it's safe?"

"Of course, it's safe—*for you.*"

She opened one eye keeping the other shut. "Well, Gumby, are you going to let him talk about me like that?"

"I don't have much of a choice, do I, Sweet Cakes? He's the one with the gun."

"In that case, I'll pitchfork him," she said, trying to grasp the wood shaft of the weapon. With each attempt, her transparent hands came up empty. "What on earth is happening, Gumby?" She asked, holding her hands in front of her face.

"I'm afraid he's right. Your hocus-pocus won't do us any good here. Least on him. I'm the only one who knows about you. You're here because of me. It's because I can't live without you, Sweet Cakes."

"*It's because I can't live without you, Sweet Cakes,*" John David mimicked in falsetto. "I think I'm going to barf," he grumbled, uncocking the rifle and slinging it over a shoulder. "You know, Pops, that's the trouble with snipe."

"And what's that?" William asked.

"They're like ghosts. They only exist up here," the man complained, pointing to his brain. "I should know. I've been living with one for eight months. Frankly, I'm getting the hell out of here before our ghosts get us both killed. Don't think it hasn't been fun."

"Wait a minute, there, young fella. Aren't you going to shoot me?"

"Nope. Rule number one: Never shoot one of your own,"

"Your own?"

"Never shoot a bona fide crazy. It's bad luck. Besides, the sun's up. You win."

The two men eyed each other for a few seconds saying nothing else. The old pilot cautiously laid the pitchfork on top of a workbench and wedged it against a support timber. It was the exact moment when Trixie broke loose and leaped at her master. Caught in between, the collision caught John David off guard. His bad knee buckled, and he crashed backward against the bench into pitchfork prongs. The prongs penetrated through his rib cage and impaled him on the scepter.

At first, the hunter struggled to stand but within seconds blood loss from a torn aorta rendered his legs useless. He collapsed on the floor convulsing with the pitchfork propping him in a forced sitting position. Blood regurgitated as he attempted to speak a few last words. "Bada-bing? Bada-bing?" he wheezed, looking desperately at William.

William knelt beside the dying man. "Bada-boom," he answered. "Bada-boom."

Then, John David smiled. He reached out to William and touched him gently on the cheek. "I like you little snipe," he said before drawing one last breath and slumping into silence.

Dorothy fell to her knees to stare John David in the face. "Maybe I was wrong about this one, Gumby."

"And how's that?"

His eyes don't look anything like the devil's eyes. These are the eyes of a frightened child."

It was later in the morning when William and Dorothy decided to rest and sit on the front porch of what once was the entrance stoop to their log cabin. The sun perched squarely above the hills east of Mt. Ellen and the day promised to be another scorcher. William plucked a blade of tall grass and placed a stem in his mouth and chewed aggressively on it—anything to satisfy Juicy Fruit withdrawal. He leaned against a cedar post supporting the last span of standing porch. Trixie laid her head on his lap. Dorothy moved in front of them both. She still appeared upset.

"So, what do we do now, Gumby?"

"Now, as in right now, or as in later this morning?"

She shook her head 'No.' "Why do you have to make things so difficult? I meant, what do we do now about us?"

"I'm not sure what you mean, Sweet Cakes. I think us is just lucky to be alive. I think us is hunky-dory."

"What I mean is we can't go on existing like this. You do realize that, don't you?"

He became somber and sat up straight to gaze in her eyes to read her mood. "All I know, Sweet Cakes, is that I love you. That's all that matters to me."

"And I love you, too, but this has to come to an end."

"Why, dag-gum it all? Why does everything have to end?"

"Because that young man was right. I almost got you killed back there. We can't have that, can we? It's simply not your time to leave this world."

He looked away at the burned out remains of the cabin. "Eight years ago, you left this world because of me, when I left you alone. When I didn't come home by noon like I told you I would. It sure as heck wasn't your time."

"But it was. That's how fate works."

"That's not so. I caused your death. It was my fault."

"Nonsense. I'm the one who was angry and impatient. I'm the one who poured kerosene in the stove when you didn't come home on time. Besides, I pushed you away from me. I pushed everything I loved away. That's why you were late. That's why you were with Edna. But your love pulled me back. Your love saved me from anger, and we've had eight wonderful years to heal and get over the past. I love you for that. I'm the luckiest woman alive." She hesitated. "Well, the luckiest woman, anyway." She winked.

His lips pressed together, pouting. "Then, why do you have to leave me again?"

"Because it's part of the plan, Gumby. A plan where I'm not in the picture. You have a lot of years left. Years to grow and learn. I would hate for you to spend them with me. I'm just a memory. I'm the past."

"But you promised to take care of me the rest of my life."

"And I shall if that's truly what you want but I think it's time to let someone else take care of you. It's time to let someone else share your life. It wouldn't be fair for a ghost to squander the love of a wonderful man, would it?"

"I don't know if I'm all that wonderful."

"Oh, I think you are."

He nervously twirled his wedding ring. "Remember Us. That's what the ring says. That's what I promised you I'd do, Sweet Cakes."

"And you have and I'm sure you always will. As long as you remember me, Gumby, I'll never really be dead, but it is time to let me go." She paused, lowering her voice. "You've got to stop twirling the ring, Dearest."

He noticed a sparkle in her eyes. Her lips pressed in a capitulated half-smile. It was the same type of sad smile a mother gives her little boy when sending him off to a first day of school. It reflected love steadfast and pure. He knew she would be seeing him off and he began to sob. "Don't cry, Dearest. There's someone else who wants to share your future. There's nothing to be afraid of. She'll see you through this life just like I did."

"You mean Edna?" He fussed.

"Yes. She's coming. It's the old hocus-pocus premonition, don't you know. She'll be here in a few minutes. She loves you very much."

"I guess eight years is a long time to wait for a person."

"Not if you love them. Love can make it worth the wait. I know because I'll be waiting for you."

Dorothy stood and moved inside the burned out remains of the cabin. "This is where it all started, Gumby. This is where it will end."

He stood on the stoop and watched her glow slowly fade. As she disappeared, she began to sing. Her voice sounded beautiful and on key. "*It's very clear, our love is here to stay. Not for a year, but ever and a day.*" Then, she paused to look at him one last time. "I always loved this place, Gumby. It was our bit of heaven, wasn't it?"

"Yes, it was," he said. "It was our Little Zion."

She blew him a kiss and vanished.

William sat back on the stoop. He heard a search party approaching and knew his few moments of solitude would not last long. In a way, the commotion was a welcome relief. He was hungry and missed his chewing gum. Civilization and a cozy bed would be gladly welcomed with open arms. No doubt, Edna would be leading the pack to drag him to Fry Canyon and cook him biscuits and eggs the way he liked. He knew life without Dorothy by his side would never be the same—different but not the same. He nervously began to twirl his wedding ring. When he realized what he was doing, he looked at the finger bearing the ring and twisted it over the finger's joint and dropped it in a shirt pocket.

It was the second woman in his life who suddenly craved attention. Trixie pressed against him, whimpering and distracting his thoughts. He gently rubbed her ears and blew in her nose the way he always did. "Does Trixie-wixie love her Gumby-wumby?"

Trixie's tail wagged furiously. The brief show of appreciation was the most he could ever expect from his canine friend. But as for his sweet wife, he realized her love and fond memories would sustain him the rest of his earthly life and he smiled a smile of contentment.

<u>JESSICA COLLECTOR</u>

For Siena

JESSICA COLLECTOR

Rick first heard the song or, rather, *the beat* to the song as a prepubescent child. Whenever anxiety struck, the song reared its head and distracted his emotions to the point of full annoyance. The song also served as a mental diversion and, eventually, as a catalyst for change. When his father backhanded his mother, when a girlfriend dumped him, when a neighbor killed his dog, or when school grades dipped egregiously below a C- range, he huddled in a quiet corner of his bedroom where he rocked back and forth and sucked a thumb while clutching a *blanky* with the song playing nonstop in his head. Now, as a forty-year-old adult, he had yet to totally eliminate Gene Krupa's *Sing, Sing, Sing* or at least that first Benny Goodman version, but he had learned to suppress it with positive energy and redirected thoughts and, only on few rare occasions, called upon his tattered childhood blanket. The curious reason for this evolved state is the fact Rick no longer needed Krupa to drown out angst on a full-time basis. Nevertheless, ridding himself of the song's constant cadence had not been easy. *No? Don't believe me?* Try Googling the song and listening for yourself. Listen to the insidious jungle rhythm and try turning it off as though you never heard it in the first place. Try suppressing its siren-like wails and provocative rhythm. Then, as you lay in bed attempting to fall asleep, see if the song repeatedly plays in your head. See if an Ambien or Benadryl squelch the vibes rat-a-tat-tatting from Krupa's incessant snares and claps. But, more importantly, see if you begin to appreciate poor Rick's psychosis.

Fortunately, the methodology Rick developed to accomplish this masking technique anyone could learn. You see, over years, Rick attended the best seminars and listened to the world's foremost gurus—Tony Robbins, Les Brown, Dr. Deepak Chopra—to help him cope with Krupa and arrive at a happy place, what he termed his "inner nirvana." And once he attained this state of wellbeing, he knew his life calling was to help others achieve what he had achieved. He would become a 'motivational coach' for the despondent and seasonally indifferent. Rick knew this calling ran akin to Christian pragmatism shrouded in Hindu-like philosophy and he felt good about it and, using his own words, "pleased as punch." His favorite sayings were "It is far better to conquer yourself than to win a thousand battles. With God's help, you can do it" and "God helps those who help themselves. You can do it." Of course, almost all of Rick's catchy adages sprinkled capriciously with "You can do it" because other than that one tried-and-true phrase, Rick's depth as a motivational human ran a bit shallow.

Ironically, he had grown a faithful following who clung to these simplistic words. As of this date, midway through a national pandemic crisis, over two hundred forty-seven believers attend his weekly webinars emanating from the Ankeny La Quinta and the glittery Hawkeyes Ballroom. Granted, only twenty or so faithful attend in person and these stalwart few space themselves at socially acceptable six-foot intervals sporting KN-95 masks, but Zoom teleconferencing sign-ons easily exceed two hundred souls and most of them survive the one-hour Monday night spots broadcast from *Doctor_Rick_Believes_In_You.com* to the bitter end, this despite NFL games competing for viewership.

And while the 'doctor' title had over time become more honorary than factual, two hundred forty-seven followers never once questioned their leader's credentials. *Why would they*? If it ain't broke, why fix a lie? After all, the *white* lie had been fabricated for the common good and attracted lucrative donations. *Yes*, there were only a handful of super generous donors to support the cause but the vast majority of faithful paid a mere $50 a month and seemed quite pleased with Rick's soothing mantras and one-liners. When the time approached to lurch forward and make a life changing plunge or, as Dr. Rick so colorfully stated, "to shit or get off the pot," student-clients would be singled-out during broadcasts and encouraged to seek their God-given purpose while the entire flock listened in.

"Mildred and Agnus Farley, are you zooming with us tonight?" Rick called out.

"Yes, we are Doctor Rick," two elderly women answered in unison, both ecstatically giddy for being hand selected. "Holy Moly, Dr. Rick. We haven't been this excited since, gosh almighty, since the Fairfield Maharishi, himself, came to Council Bluffs and blessed us," Mildred hailed.

"Oh? I don't know about that sister," Agnus spouted. "Remember when Khrushchev came to the farm and laid hands on Ma and Pa's corn? Now, that was something else, don't ye know."

Rick smiled into an IP camera and spoke in his atypical soft monochromatic manner. "Well, ladies, obviously you have truly been blessed in life. Not too many of us can speak of such endearing encounters but today we need to focus on you and your goal to become financially independent. Are you still seeking deliverance from the Maid-Rite shop you two have worked at since 1975?"

"Yes, we are, Dr. Rick," they answered.

"Excellent. And have you both been saving hard earned cash to start your rival sandwich shop in downtown Bondurant?"

"Yes, and we have over seventy-five thousand dollars saved and have been approved for a matching SBA loan. We're ready, cocked, and loaded, Doc," Mildred parlayed happily.

"Then, I say.... *you can do it*," Rick blurted, his voice rising to an excited strident pitch.

On cue, over two hundred Internet voices repeated his words, chanting "You can do it. You can do it...."

When the webinar session neared its conclusion, Rick reached out to his flock pleading for their assistance on an equally serious matter. "My friends," he said, "you all are truly awesome human beings. I am so proud of you. And I realize this horrible Chinese coronavirus attack has financially hampered your ability to support our cause, but I implore you to please send in your regular donations. This palatial facility at the La Quinta and these web broadcasts require money. Lots of money. So, please help support these gatherings. Thank you and may peace be with you."

That night, Rick attempting to fall quietly asleep played an impossibility with *Sing, Sing, Sing* rattling his brain. With his savings nearly depleted and a rent of $1,050 past due at the Raccoon Valley Apartments, he worried how to survive this latest economic downturn. Predictably, as he lay in bed, a familiar voice whispered through pitch black darkness and into an ear. The voice sounded identical to Deepak Chopra with an unmistakable north New Delhi accent. "Negative thoughts cannot be *banked* to save your business."

"I'm trying so hard, Dee, but it's difficult," Rick responded in a whisper. "Please tell me what I should do."

"Money is the root of all lust. We must learn to lust after the root of our essence. We should *coin* new horizons and *borrow* from what we know and who we know."

Rick drew a puzzled face clearly distinguishable in the dark. "I'm sorry, Dee, but I do not understand."

A long interminable silence followed with a heavy sigh wafting of curry. "Sometimes, I make things sound too complicated, my friend. *Screw it.* Just go procure a loan from your banker friend, Paul Rabinowitz. You need more cash in the tiller so you can keep spreading the mantra of life. *You can do it.*"

"Hell, you don't need a frigging loan, Dr. Rick. You need a frigging collection bureau," Harvey Rabinowitz pled. Harvey had long been acquainted with Dr. Rick's one-man enterprise. In fact, Harvey had once been a student. It was Rick's *can-do* motivational speech that spurred Harvey to take the job at Central Iowa Farm Coop Savings & Loans Incorporated and the reason the young banker prospered to become the bank president. "After looking over the financials you emailed me, it's quite clear you have impressive assets but little of it is in cash," he continued. "The truth is your accounts receivables are off the charts. The truth is your clients are deadbeats. They owe you big time, my friend, and to the tune of $86,750."

Rick mulled Harvey's words before responding. Indeed, he was keenly aware his assets' ledger reflected the hefty sum alluded to but, after, all, the virus had struck with vengeance and his flock's ability to ante up lay beyond their everyday financial capabilities, or so he thought. "We're all hurting, Harvey. People have to eat. I can't ask people who don't have the means to survive this contagion and who live paycheck to paycheck to place me as a high priority."

Harvey's cheeks puffed ready to explode as he stared at the ceiling. Words he wanted to express he could not. Decorum and deference for his guru took precedent over disrespectful thoughts, especially the one foremost on the tip of his tongue *you're so naive*. Instead, Harvey clasped his hands on top of his desk to display a sense of calm and he spoke as one might speak to an unworldly impressionable child. "I ran your list of past due accounts. Know what I found?"

"No. Do tell."

"There are some glaring inconsistencies that need your attention. For example, Drew Law owes you $1,250. He's the young man who started the chicken flavored snow cone business because of your inspiration. Today he controls twenty-three franchise huts across the state. He's making a fortune and his savings account with us is brimming six-figures. Why hasn't he paid you? Arnold and Rita Sheffield purchased a Mercedes 350 SL last week. They literally struck gold because of you. Are you telling me they can't afford to cough up the $4,400 they committed? After all, they can afford a spanking new Mercedes but can't honor the pledge they made to the humble teacher who made them filthy rich?" And for the next five minutes Harvey exhumed a list of faithful who had taken advantage of Dr. Rick's generosity and who could easily pay their respective past due accounts. "The truth is, Rick, you're too nice. You don't need a loan. You need help in the collection arena. My friend, you need *bone crushers*."

Rick wrung his hands and gazed out a window. "I hate asking people to send me money. I just can't do it. It's so distasteful."

No sooner had Rick finished his sentence when Harvey jumped on those altruistic timid words. "No worries, Dr. Rick. I've found someone who can help you. She's a pro in the business. A renaissance woman. Remember those St. Rude's commercials with the kids? Remember the Shiner charity ads spotlighting sick children? Well, she helped those organizations cash in like it was no one's business. If she can help them, my friend, she can help you."

"Well, I'm not sure if—"

"I knew you'd be hesitant. That's why I asked her to meet us, here, this morning. She's waiting outside as we speak." Harvey emitted a shrill whistle and his office door instantly flung wide as if the person of interest had been poised to barge in awaiting the signal. On cue, a young female wheeled herself over the threshold and parked next to Rick; they brushed shoulder-to-shoulder.

"Dr. Rick, let me introduce Jessica Collector. Jessica, this is Dr. Rick Gaines. This is the man I was telling you about. Dr. Rick needs your help."

Rick scooted his chair back for a better view of his "bone crusher." Upon first impression, the young woman appeared to be no more than twelve years old. She sat slouched in a wheelchair and an obvious victim of stunted growth from severe scoliosis and scads of other disabilities run amuck. Height? Probably no more than four-foot. Her dwarf legs wrapped in knee-high metal braces. Her face slid right with a dropsy mouth drooling on a cloth diaper draped over a shoulder and a neck tilted forty-five degrees searching painfully for vertical support. A hard-plastic body cast laced about her torso; Rick wondered how she could breathe with a device smothering her chest and which had obviously failed to correct the curved spine. The urchin's hair seemed matted in-place but neat and bowed in gingham red and yellow ribbon and slightly cockeyed and almost fake in appearance. All-in-all, Jessica appeared needing Rick's help more than the other way around. She held out a trembling hand and spoke with a vocal intonation resembling a high frequency screech of a four-year-old lost in a department store.

"It is so nice to finally meet you, Dr. Rick," she said impishly. "I am at your service, sir. And I've already looked over your past due accounts and I believe our first stop today resides just around the corner. Shall we go collect what is rightfully owed you?" She motioned toward the door.

Harvey by now was grinning ashamedly and flashing two thumbs up. "Jessica keeps twenty percent of everything you two can muster. How's that sound? Fair enough?"

Rick cast a *WTF* glare and turned back around to return Jessica's gaze awaiting his overdue answer. How this frail nymph could somehow squeeze money from his polished group of deadbeat clients he found somewhat baffling but, ultimately, he did not want to disappoint the child and, frankly, did not want to see Jessica break down in tears as it became quickly apparent her collection business had become her life's cornerstone. Besides, Rick sensed Krupa readying his drums and he needed clarity not escapism at that precise moment. "Okay. Let's give it a shot," Rick sputtered. "What have I got to lose?"

(Bert & Ira Modene – Midwest Med Transport, Inc. – $12,150)

Less than a block away from the bank, the Modene brothers thrived in the marque penthouse of a fifteen-story high rise. The two spinster men, now in their late fifties, founded a Lyft-like medical delivery service akin to a for-profit Meals-on-Wheels. The business specialized in delivering hospital supplies, transplant organs, and blood plasma and had grown into the largest service of its kind in the five-state region. One year earlier, the brothers considered taking their fledging enterprise public and, now, plotted to do so with the approaching cessation of the pandemic. Not surprisingly, Covid-19 proved a boon to their business. Less than four years earlier, Dr. Rick had paid the brothers a personal house call when they resided next door at the Raccoon Valley Apartments. Rick's simple words of encouragement goaded the men to move forward and pursue their business plan. Somehow in their mad rush for success, the brothers had conveniently forgotten their life coach and their monetary commitment to his cause.

Rick's collection game plan played simple enough: Rick would do the talking and Jessica would quietly observe as the maestro conducted his dirty business. Hence, the girl would only participate when prompted by her boss.

"Holy buckets of beans! Dr. Rick, what a pleasant surprise," the elder brother spouted. "And what brings you to our humble abode?"

Rick peered past the half-open door and opulent furnishings and at the stunning skyline of downtown Des Moines. He remembered when only a few years earlier he helped the brothers push start their decrepit Volkswagen Beetle as the eldest brother popped the clutch to propel it down a hill. Much had taken place since. "I knew you and Bert would always accomplish great things," Rick chimed in." I had faith in you two. You are awesome human beings with unlimited potential."

By now Bert had picked up on the conversation and strode to the door behind his brother, inadvertently blocking Rick's view. "Yes, by jingo, we did do it. We truly did. And we couldn't have done it without you, Dr. Rick. You're the one who's awesome."

"Oh, gosh darn it all, boys. You had it in you all the time. I saw it the moment I first met you. My job was simply to give you a push to find your special purpose. That's all."

"And you betcha we did. For cute's sake, it was cuzza you, Doc."

These admiration societal expressions flowed profusely back and forth for minutes until Jessica tired of the flattery flagellation and interrupted lest the manure exceed four feet in height. "Daddy, I have to pee," she abruptly interjected. "Really, really bad. Are these the men you said owe us $12,150? Can they hurry up and pay you? I need to empty my colostomy bag. Can you hurry, please? *Ple-e-ease?*" She added the second 'please' with a sad pouty face as drooled secretions cascaded onto her diapered shoulder.

Surprised, to say the least, the elder brother stepped back and for the first time noticed Jessica. "Didn't know you had a child, Dr. Rick. You never mentioned her."

Before Rick could speak, Jessica blurted, "It's because I've been living with my mother in Memphis, don't you know. She passed away last month. *Penniless.*"

Upon hearing her words and gawking for a considerable length of time, Bert snapped his fingers as his memory lit as brightly as a proverbial lightbulb. "That's it. That's why your face seems so familiar to me. You're one of those kids on the ads we've seen on FOX News."

"You betcha, I am," Jessica replied, thumbing her chest. "One and the same."

"My goodness, gravy-wavy. This is an honor. Mind if I get your autograph, sweetheart?"

Jessica cooed, "Sure thing. Okeydokey. I'd be more than happy to do it but, maybe, you can put your autograph on a check for my daddy. You know, with my open-heart surgery tomorrow, we need the money."

Bert disappeared and returned seconds later with a pad of paper, a pen, and a freshly drawn check. Without taking his eyes off Jessica, he thrust the check at Rick and handed Jessica pad and pen. "You know, we've never had anyone famous visit us. Maybe, the next time you and you father are in the neighborhood, you can come by for a Shirley Temple or something. How's that sound little girl—" He stopped mid-sentence to read her signature. "Jessica *Collector?*"

Caught off guard, Jessica backtracked. "Yes. My mother remarried and her husband, Hector D. Collector, adopted me at a very young age."

"Oh. That makes sense, I suppose."

Meanwhile, Rick eyed the check. "There must be a mistake, Bert. You made it out for twenty-thousand even."

"No. No mistake, Dr. Rick. We owe you a heckuva lot more, by golly. Hope this gets you through these bad times and helps pay for Jessica's lifesaving operation."

(Wilma Gunch – Polk County Nursing Associates (PCNA) – $4,200)

Rick summoned an Uber special needs van for their next stop. Visually upset with Jessica's shenanigans and while waiting for the vehicle's arrival, few words passed between them. From Rick's perspective, the child bordered on pathological liar or worse, *nut job*. On the other hand, Jessica clearly took command of an awkward situation and, fortunately, with a most favorable outcome. How could Rick stay angry with someone so distraught and frail and willing to put it all on the line for a helpless wimp like himself? He reasoned. Once inside the van and feeling somewhat ashamed for being upset, Rick reached over and held her hand. It was gesture of compassion for a child whom Mother Nature had serendipitously screwed over. As he squeezed her palm to confirm his support, his heart sank. Jessica's hand palsied cold and bony and void of muscle tone. He quickly altered pre-planned harsher words to reflect a softer tone. "Jessica, I am so proud of you, but we must never again—"

"Make up false stories or deceive people for our own personal gain. We must be direct and forthright. Yes?" She asked.

"That is correct, child. Please don't tell people I was married to your mother and that you're my daughter. Lies cast dispersions and negate good karma. We must never try and steer the river."

"Deepak Chopra?"

Rick smiled. He bumped her lightly shoulder on shoulder. "Exactly. I call him *Dee*," he whispered, grinning woefully. "He talks to me, you know," he added with a wink.

"And do you talk back?" She asked.

Sensing his own sanity being questioned and fearing any more disclosure on the subject might leave him vulnerable to a host of more questions, Rick said nothing else. He remained quiet the remainder of their ride to the business headquarters of PCNA in nearby booming Waukee.

Wilma Gunch, PCNA's president, wore black and gold Monday-Wednesday-Friday, gold and black Tuesday-Thursday-Saturday, and maroon and gold on Sundays. Life was no longer complicated with this simple everyday dress etiquette. These self-imposed rubrics reflected her loyalties to the University of Iowa and its nursing school while Sunday displayed support for her local Des Moines high school alma mater. Until she discovered Dr. Rick and his profound teachings and inspirational support, chaos and disorder ruled her very essence. Before Rick, her closet strew in reds and greens and putrid browns. But once she founded Polk County Nursing Associates, singularity and order supplanted daily bedlam, all because her swami told her "You can do it." These simple but insightful words changed her life and provided a path forward, which began with a daily dress code and making one's bed with square corner folds. *Yes,* her covey of nurses broke the mold and no longer wore scrub whites or greens (only black and gold) and, *no*, she only hired U of I registered nurses and never, god forbid, those uppity ISU grads. *No way, Jose'.* Nope. In short order, Wilma had it going on as much as Stacy's mom (if you know what I mean). And this current air of self-confidence and business acumen rooted from those nights spent at seminars put on by good old Dr. Rick. On this memorable day her $20,000 fighting Hawkeyes brochette highlighted a gold blazer and black pant ensemble with

Christian Louboutin gold pumps. She looked fabulous. She looked made of money.

"Oh, my, gee-willikers, it's really you," Wilma gushed. "Where ya been Doc?" She yanked on Rick's arm and towed him inside her office almost overlooking sweet Jessica planted in the hallway. "And who's your itty-bitty friend?" Wilma asked eyeing the child.

"She's, um.... She's.... Well, it's kind of hard to explain—"

"I'm his *love child*," Jessica blurted. "And I have to be honest, Ms. Gunch, he does not want me to tell people he was married to my mother. He says that's a big fat lie and only casts dispersions. In fact, he just finished lecturing me on the very subject ten minutes ago. Now, I'm sure right now you're thinking how it must hurt to be rejected by your own father. *Yes indeedy, it hurts.* But I'll survive. I'm a survivor, don't you know." A well-orchestrated tear splashed on Jessica's shoulder diaper.

Wilma stepped back startled by the revelation. She stared first at Jessica in her wheelchair and, then, at Rick standing sheepishly shrugging his shoulders. Her warm demeanor melted into a scowl. "Didn't know you were such an asshole, Doc."

"I'm not. She's making it all—"

"*Up.* I'm making up for all of the lost time without my father because, until three weeks ago, I lived with my mother in Memphis. She died suddenly, don't you know. And I had no place else to go. Look at me. I'm a wreck. I'm a frail little hummingbird. Fortunately, Rick said I could live with him, but I had to help with collections on his past due accounts. He said if we didn't collect what is rightfully owed him, he won't feed me. And, gosh almighty, I'm hummingbird hungry."

"Is that true, Doc?" Wilma pressed. "You won't feed the child?"

Rick emitted a long sigh and threw his hands skyward in an 'I surrender' pose. "That's right. If you don't pay me the $4,200 you owe me, the girl doesn't get to eat." He glanced back at Jessica who flashed him a subtle thumbs-up signal for his impromptu performance. Feeling somewhat liberated with this newfound alter ego, he let loose with a crème-de-la-crem parting shot with jive head bobbing theatrics. "No money, no food. Girl don't eat. *Boom!*"

The Uber vehicle had remained parked outside awaiting their return. The driver, an emaciated Bosnian export by the name of Daris, opened the van's rear door and slid out a ramp; he pushed Jessica inside and strapped her wheelchair to floorboard hooks. Rick maneuvered around to the passenger side, slid the door open, and hopped in next to the girl. His ecstatic grin forced a question by Daris out of busybody curiosity. "You look happy, my friends. Is there a reason for such happiness?"

"Oh, yeah," Jessica piped. "Forty-two hundred reasons."

Rick turned to face her and the two high-fived.

Four more collection stops filled the day. Nearly half of Rick's total past due receivables were collected. Tomfoolery and casting shame worked hand-in-hand; no client hesitated to ante up. The duo's shtick became more and more polished with each collection attempt and money flowed profusely with theatrics worthy of Oscar nominations—Jessica feigned hunger pangs and Dr. Rick would 'put the poor mouth' on the gravity of their financial situation with Jessica days from a lifesaving operation. Fortunately, the vast majority of Rick's clientele possessed hearts and felt guilty having regrettably overlooked their life coach and their personal financial commitments. And, of course, with little Jessica appearing ready to croak on the spot, no one wanted a handicapped child to expire on their doorsteps, not even Dorothy Brumbird, herself a multiple disabled individual unable to use her hands. Rick and Jessica waited patiently for over thirty minutes as Dorothy scratched out a check with a pen gripped in her mouth to accomplish the task. Neither felt the least bit of shame watching Dorothy struggle to fork over a paltry $1,150.

By 4:30 PM and with the next round of collections less than $1,000 each, Rick thought it best to call it quits for the day and form a new strategy. They needed a refreshed routine that could work quicker without the melodrama, especially given the size of the less impactful past due accounts. Jessica insisted they contact one more person because she recognized the name on the list.

(Junior Bernardo Capulet – Italianos R-Us Food Catering – $950)

"How do you know him?" Rick asked, mystified.

"Long story but I'll make it short. About five years ago he pledged $10,000 on one of the telethons we ran from St. Rude's and he never paid up. The event coordinator asked me to call him and see if I could get a credit card number or something."

"And did you collect?"

"Nope. He told me if I ever bothered him again, he'd break my legs. Of course, I just had new femur pins installed and was awaiting a bone marrow match. I needed a second operation and the last thing I wanted was to go through that horrible operation, again, even if it was only a threat. He was a scary person and a real butt head."

"You told him that?"

"No. I believe I said, 'You can't break what ain't fixed.'" Jessica smiled deadpan.

Rick's smile mimicked hers, not sure if she was messing with him or telling the truth. But at the next stop light, Daris, the driver swiveled to face them. Daris had been listening to the conversation. "I know this man she talks about. He a bad man. He catered my sister's wedding. When she no pay on time, he charged her fifty percent more and say if he ask her third time and she no pay, he burn down house. He is connected to mafia. Very bad men. Trust me. You should not try and collect money from him. It will turn out bad." Daris ran an index finger across his throat, from ear to ear.

Rick turned to Jessica. "What would you like to do?"

"I think…. I think we need to pay the man a visit. Get it over with. He doesn't scare me anymore. Besides, the operation was a success. My legs are better."

Rick glanced at the miniature leg braces and doubted anything coming from Jessica's mouth could be believed. On the other hand, Daris seemed forthright. Who to trust?

The long circular drive leading to the gauche Palazzo de Capulet outside Johnston littered with Romanesque statues and a giant fountain with dancing water as grand as the Bellagio in Las Vegas. Rick knew the catering business he helped foster with Junior had been profitable but never this profitable. Perhaps, Daris was correct in his assertion the man had connections to the underworld. Food catering alone in a Des Moines-sized market could never generate this amount of wealth.

When they rang the doorbell, an overweight swarthy man in his mid-fifties answered. The man had been cooking and still draped in a frilly apron. An overpowering smell of garlic wafted past them on the front porch stoop. Jessica waved the smell away from her nose as if swatting at flies. The man stared at them and they stared back, mostly at the holstered handgun strapped to his chest and prominently displayed outside the feminine apron.

"Hey-ya, Roberto, who the hell is it?" A voice hollered from the rear of the house.

Roberto hollered back, over a shoulder. "Don't know, Boss. Some gay-looking *barbone* and a midget in a wheelchair. The gay guy, he looks about forty, black and gray hair, clean cut with beautiful skin tones. The midget…. she's looks like she's ready to cry. Better come out here and see this for yourself."

Rick shook his head. Why did everyone say the same thing when describing his physical appearance? Nevertheless, he took the "beautiful skin tones" as a compliment and kept his mouth shut. Seconds later, Junior appeared beside his personal bodyguard. Two more heavyset men accompanied him. "Well, I'll be damned. 'Know who this man is?" Junior asked Roberto without waiting for a response. "This, here, is Dr. Rick Gains. He's the life coach I told you about. He's the person who inspired me to start the catering business—our ticket to becoming legit."

"No shit?" Roberto asked more as a statement.

"No shit," Junior responded. "So, Dr. Rick, I do appreciate you paying me respect by showing up at my Palazzo. And just who is this sweet little—"

"I'm his daughter, slime ball. And we didn't come all this way to pay you respect. We came to collect the money you owe my father. We came so you can *pay* my father respect. Got it?"

Upset by Jessica's insulting tone, Roberto jolted toward the girl and raised the back of his hand ready to slap her vile mouth. Junior held him back.

"There must be a misunderstanding, little girl. I don't owe your papa a penny."

"Oh, yes, you do. You owe him $950. And judging from the looks of things, you should be paying him ten times what we came to collect."

Junior stepped back for a better looksee. He eyed Jessica examining her and her sad condition. "Listen, sweetheart. Nobody collects from Junior Capulet. Junior Capulet collects from nobodies. That's the law of the jungle and I'm the mother *frigging* lion. *Capeesh?*"

By now Rick had heard enough. Daris' words still rattled inside his head and he sensed they needed to make a quick exit while they still remained upright. "I'm sure there's a simple misunderstanding, here, Junior." He took out a paper labeled 'Accounts Receivable' and ripped it into shreds and discarded tatters on the ground. "There. All fixed. We'll be on our way. So sorry for the mix up. All my fault, boys. Toodles."

He spun Jessica's chair and pushed her from what he suspected might soon become a physical melee and fast walked back to the van. Daris stood by ready at the ramp. Before he could push her inside, she yelled at the four men on the stoop, "We're not done, *Paisans*. I'm bringing back the cavalry tomorrow and we're gonna kick your asses to high noon if you don't pay up. *Capeesh?*" She finished the question flashing an Italian chin flick.

This time Daris did not secure her wheelchair to the van's floorboard. Rick dove in the passenger chair and Daris hurriedly jumped in the driver's side. They sped away with Jessica looking out the side window and shooting the bird at the four men of the Palazzo de Capulet.

They drove downtown to Jessica's hotel where she had been camped out for two weeks working as a collector-for-hire for Harvey Rabinowitz's bank. Rick announced he would escort the girl inside, that his own car parked around the corner, and they would see Daris late the next morning. Once inside the hotel, the bar beckoned, and Rick sensed he needed a drink. He also sensed Jessica still fumed over the escapade at Junior Capulet's residence and, frankly, he did not want to deal with both her craziness and bad mood. After all, her erratic behavior almost got them beat up. As he escorted her to an elevator, she saw him glance at the bar.

"Rick, you deserve a drink," she said. "How about I buy the first round?"

Rick chuckled. "The first round? That implies I buy the second round and you are way too young to consume alcohol, little girl."

The remark peeved Jessica and she slammed her hands on rubber wheels bringing her chair to a sudden stop. "Jesus H. Christ, Rick. How old do you think I am?"

"Twelve. Thirteen. Something like that."

Jessica sneered. She pushed herself upright, bent over and unbuckled her leg braces. When she stood to confront Rick, she towered over five-foot in height, a foot taller than he suspected. Methodically, she unlaced her plastic body brace and tossed it into a false seat cavity in the wheelchair along with the wet shoulder diaper. Pert young breasts

appeared out of nowhere. She swiveled her jaw back and
forth to regain a semblance of normalcy before yanking off
a wig. Her coiled hair collapsed to her shoulders; she shook
it to where it tussled as luxuriously as any hair model's
tresses. Even without makeup, sweet pathetic Jessica
instantly transformed into a beautiful young woman. "I'm
twenty-four years old, Rick, and I want a *frigging* drink.
Now, what's a girl gotta do to get one?" Her voice lowered
a full octave.

Spellbound, Rick stumbled for words. Obviously,
angelic Jessica Collector had been duping him the entire
time. "I suppose all you need to do is say the magic word
Please," he replied.

"OK. Please buy me a *frigging* drink," she countered.

That evening Rick and Jessica sat at the Savery Hotel
bar and drank themselves into a delightful stupor. Jessica
explained how the operations on her legs succeeded, how
most of her scoliosis had been corrected by spinal rods
installed during her adolescent years, and how radical stem
cell therapy had fixed her many other ills before she turned
eighteen. She admitted the drooped face had been an act as
had been other faked ailments but, in the end, those 'props'
had come in handy to facilitate collections. "Few people can
turn away a sick kid asking for money, especially if it's to
collect on a debt owed. Well, except for that *fongool,* Junior
Capulet."

"Where did you learn those acting skills?" Rick pressed.

"Mostly from the kids I worked with while doing those
fund-raising ads on TV. And, I enjoyed it so much I went to
the UCLA School of Drama. Sad thing is I never could find
a job as an actress out in California. I learned the hard way
how it really works."

"How what really works?"

"*Life*. Look, when I was a kid and truly challenged with
disabilities, when my body presented itself in beautiful
misfortune, all of those money-hungry charities wanted my
mug in front of a camera. They all wanted me to beg for

money. And I did. So did my friends. We bought into it hook, line, and sinker."

"I don't want to sound stupid but what did you buy into?"

"The idea we were of value as human beings. But the only thing those charities really wanted was to take advantage of us to make money. When my friends grew older, they were no longer the cute kids with disabilities who could generate empathy and millions of donations. As I became healthy and started to look normal and no longer pathetic, they tossed me to the street. We were all tossed away. We were no longer needed. That is until one night I listened to you. I found you on the Internet and YouTube. And you inspired me. You told me I could do anything I set my mind on. That I could start my own business and I did. And I hired my friends and we all found purpose. I mean, my team and I made over $8,000 today. Not too shabby I'd say."

Rick fell back in his chair. "Jessica…. *Jessica*? Holy Moly, the only Jessica I remember is a Jessica Montague and she lives in—."

"Memphis." Jessica grinned. "One and same. *Ta-da*," she sang with hands spread wide. "Jesus, Rick, do you honestly think my last name is Collector. Hell, that's my stage name. It's a prop like that corny shtick as the handicapped kid."

Rick thought for a few seconds before emitting a wry smile. "Say, you don't owe me any past due money, do you?"

"Nope. As a matter of fact, I believe you owe me." She paused to consider their arrangement. "And you know what else? I believe that you, Doctor Rick Gaines, have found your sea legs when it comes to collecting on past due accounts. You sure as Shinola have more confidence in doing the deed than you did this morning. I also don't believe you need my help anymore." She leaned forward and clanged her wine glass against his frozen margarita. "So, here's a bit of free advice to take to the bank—do what you need to do to survive in life, Rick, even if it makes you feel uncomfortable. Stand up for yourself because no one else will do it for you. Turning misfortune into fortune is up to you. *You can do it.*"

Rick pondered her words. "Deepak?"

"Yup and Jessica Collector."

"So, I guess as a team, we're done?"

"Nope. There's just one more collection I want to help you with and, then, I'll be on my merry way."

"That jerk, Junior?"

"Yup. Capulets and Montagues have always scorned each other. This one is on the house."

"So, you really want to go back tomorrow and kick Junior's ass?"

"You better believe it."

Minutes before arriving at Palazzo Capulet, Jessica preoccupied herself texting someone or *someones* with an intensity confounding Rick. Earlier that morning, she reverted to her handicapped wheelchair persona as her real persona remained unbeknownst to Daris to keep the disguise a secret. But, now, driving into Junior Capulet's grand compound, Rick found her preoccupation with the cell phone nervy; she should have been focused on the impending confrontation with four mobster gorillas.

For this last collection attempt, Daris thought it best to accompany his riders to the front door for their added protection. Strength in numbers is what he spouted. He voluntarily pushed Jessica up the stoop but conveniently parked himself at a safe distance behind Rick. Rick assumed command and rang the doorbell. And like the day before, Roberto answered, this time without an apron but still brazenly wearing a chest holstered handgun. The mobster stood dumbfounded gawking at the three standing meekly before him. "You *goombahs* gotta death wish or something?" He mumbled. He turned sideways and hollered down the hallway, "Hey, boss. You need to see this." And, as before, Junior showed his face with two bodyguards in tow.

"You back again?" He asked, his eyes darting to the new third person, Daris. "Like, is this human scarecrow the cavalry you promised, sweetheart? O-o-o-h, I'm scared," he mocked.

Rick swiveled around to look at Jessica expecting her to make a sarcastic comeback but, instead, she was sending off a text message. When she finished, she nonchalantly glanced at Junior and, then, out to the driveway entrance. A van was speeding past a statue of the Roman goddess Moneta and heading their direction. The vehicle painted in green with giant one-hundred-dollar bill images decaled on its sides; huge lettering advertised *Bone Crushers – We Collect*. The van screeched to a stop in front of the stoop and a hydraulic ramp rapidly unfolded.

"No. Our Uber driver is not the cavalry. They are," she replied motioning to the van.

Two young men and a woman awkwardly tumbled out and down the ramp. The trio dressed identically in green jumpsuits. First out of the chute strode Bobby 'Bling' Rodriquez. Bobby shuffled clumsily with arm walking braces dragging along crumpled useless legs. He shook involuntarily from cerebral palsy. Next came Susie 'Wheezy' Yang. Susie puttered in a motorized scooter with movement facilitated by forced breath-puffs into a directional turning 'straw.' A spinal injury had left the young woman virtually numb below the neck ever since a horrific semi-truck rear-ending accident as a ten-year-old. Last shuffled a giant of a man, Waldo "Sasquatch' Jones. Void of eyesight since birth but towering at 6' – 4", Waldo managed his way with the use of a white cane and repeated tapping on Susie's scooter, following her lead.

"This is the cavalry I promised, Junior. This is my dream team. They all work for me. They're called 'Bone Crushers' and I suggest you pay my friend, Doctor Rick Gains, right now before things get ugly. Real ugly. *Capeesh?*"

A few seconds later the three dream team members stood in line with Daris and behind Jessica. Waldo pulled out a short metal baseball bat and wacked it repeatedly in the flat of his palm. Susie revved the motor on her scooter and threatened to charge into the men blocking the doorway. Bobby grabbed the end of a walking brace and pitched it skyward and ready to tomahawk anyone not complying with Jessica's collection threat. Junior and Roberto stepped back, speechless.

"Well, boys, what's it gonna be? This Montague girl and my bone crushers lay waste to your nifty little house or you pay up?"

Junior turned to Roberto and spoke out of the corner of his mouth. "Go make out a damn check." He turned to face Jessica, again, this time with a soured look of capitulation. "Montague, huh? Our two families, like, they go way back to the old country. Yes?"

"Yup."

"So, little girl, you're Italiano? Right?" Junior pursued.

"Yup."

"That explains everything, *Paisana*. Let me be the first to say you gotta big set of shiny brass ones." He turned to Rick. "Sorry about all this, Doctor Rick. I've been a little preoccupied of late. Seems we're expanding shop to Omaha next week. Roberto is learning the family recipes. He's gonna run the new operation. This is a big move for him and me both. It means we finally go legit and no longer gotta deal with family scum. We can start bein' real upstanding citizens." He paused to study Jessica's crew of miscreants. "You kids look familiar. Have I seen you before?"

Susie spoke up. "I'm sure you have. We used to work with Jessica. We did the fund-raising spots that went nationwide on TV…. until we grew old and got fired."

"Awful sorry to hear that. That ain't right," Junior said with his face turning pouty.

"No. It's not right," Rick chimed in. He looked at his five accomplices before head bobbing toward the two vans. "I suppose we ought to get out of your hair. I'm glad you're doing so well, Junior. I always knew you could do it. Inside that chest of yours beats a good heart."

Before they departed, Roberto returned with a fresh check. Junior signed it and doubled the amount. "Say, kids, would you all like to come inside for lunch? Roberto and I would love for you to sample our new Omaha cuisine."

Bobby Bling had the last words. "Hell, yes, we'd love to try your food," he said. "Hell, yes."

Three weeks had passed since Rick and Jessica parted company. Harvey said the *Bone Crushers* bunch moved to Chicago having secured a lucrative twelve-month contract with a "syndicate" of questionable reputation doing what they enjoyed doing—going after deadbeat accounts. The syndicate preferred the 'soft' collections approach over old-school mafia methodology. And, oh by the way, Jessica and her crew procured the job after being highly recommended by Junior Capulet.

Dr. Rick continued his door-to-door collection efforts after Jessica's departure and snagged over ninety percent of past due payments owed him. In the process, he renewed friendships and acquaintances with clients in what he termed a "win-win" situation. More importantly, Rick regained confidence in himself. He discovered newfound synergy in his special purpose as a life coach and motivator.

A few days earlier, Jessica had texted him and asked if he wanted to meet her in Las Vegas. She was attending an ACA convention but would be finished by Friday noon. They could spend the weekend hitting shows and blackjack tables if he felt comfortable escorting her. He told her that he would gladly fly out but only if she promised not to dress in her fake 'Jessica Collector' regalia. She promised to be the same seemingly normal woman who drank wine with him at the Hotel Savery and, thus, he acquiesced.

Now, the night before leaving for Vegas and lying wide-eyed in bed, it occurred to Rick how Krupa had not reared his head or drums for three weeks. This revelation pleased him. It pleased him how his sanity once again seemed intact and inner peace had been re-kindled all because of Jessica's encouragement. Staring at the ceiling, he felt like celebrating these milestones with a soothing mantra. "I will focus on gratitude. I will focus on gratitude. I will focus....," he chanted.

"That is a very good one," a voice spoke through the still of darkness. "It is one of my favorites."

"Dee. Is that you?"

"Of course. Who else speaks with you at this late hour, my friend?"

Rick thought on the question before answering. "Me.... My inner dialogue.... *God*."

"Excellent response," the voice responded. "It is the response I was hoping you would someday ultimately conclude. I knew you could do it."

And with those words exchanged, Rick fell asleep and Dee vanished forever.

...It is late at night. You cannot sleep. Krupa is still rattling incessantly inside your troubled head. The snares and claps from *Sing, Sing, Sing* and the exotic jungle rhythm beat and beat and beat until you've convinced yourself your sanity is waning. You ask yourself, *Why is this happening to me*? Why did I ever open that frigging YouTube version by Glenn Miller and listen? I should be focused on my dreams and aspirations and my many blessings. Yes, my friend. Yes, you should be doing all these things. Shame on you. After all, Krupa is dead. You are not. May I make a suggestion? Next Monday night, drive to Ankeny, Iowa and the La Quinta Inn. Plant yourself inside the glittery Hawkeyes Ballroom and listen to the motivational mantra of Dr. Rick Gaines. Listen and learn and pay the guru his paltry $50 but the key, here, is to pay him and pay him on time. For if you do not pay the man on time, woe be unto you because Dr. Rick will assuredly come knocking on your door to collect what is rightfully owed him and he will bring his sweet paramour, the young lady known by the notorious name of Jessica Collector....

Other Books by David Martin Anderson

The Cowboys of Haddington Moor

The Last Good Horse

Beaty Butte

Les Trois Papillons (The Three Butterflies)

Harry's Apology

(All books available in hardcover and eBook formats)

Made in the USA
Middletown, DE
20 January 2021